No Masters Or Kings

J E Nice

Book One

First published in Great Britain in 2019 by
Write Into The Woods Publishing.

978-1-912903-12-2

Cover design by Write into the Woods.

www.jenice.co.uk
www.writeintothewoods.com

To Bucky.

My beautiful, mischievous puppy who just so happened to be named at the same time as Captain Bucky Winters.

The Last War Series

Matter Of Time
Despite Our Enemies
In My Bones
With A Scream

Other Books By
J E Nice

The Erica Murray Mysteries:
Beginnings
Becoming

No Masters Or Kings

Find them all at **www.jenice.co.uk/books**

Grab exclusive short stories about your
favourite characters and get regular updates by
signing up at **www.jenice.co.uk/updates**

Kai

Kai stood in the middle of the landing pad, back turned to the two captains she had already dismissed. In front of her, some distance away, stood a large cargo ship, with a deep belly and stubby wings, that had been roughly painted in black, white and blue patches. It was a Reverent class, Kai would know one anywhere. Now, however, her concentration was fixed on who she presumed was the captain of said ship.

Handsome of sorts, if you liked rugged good looks and square jaws, his white skin was tanned brown. It suggested that he spent as much, if not more, time on the ground as he did in his ship. Unless he flew too close to the sun. Kai smiled. She was romanticising. It was dangerous, she had to keep a lid on her desperation. Being a woman standing in the middle of a landing pad, dressed in a torn and muddied wedding dress was all the desperation she was willing to show.

What interested Kai about the supposed captain, in his fine breeches and coat, was that he was talking to a slight, blonde woman. From the look of it, she regularly pulled up tufts of her hair and chopped it short, resulting in parts standing up in chunks. The woman wiped her nose on the back of her hand, hawked and spat onto the ground away from the captain. He barely noticed and continued talking. She nodded and moved away, up the ramp and into the ship, her stride wide and rolling, like a man's. Kai chewed the inside of her cheek. It was already raw and after flinching, she changed to prodding the flesh with her tongue. A woman on the crew was a good sign. But was it enough?

Someone brushed against her, tipping her forward. A man, rushing towards the Reverent. He looked over his shoulder to her as he mumbled an apology, hesitating as he caught her eye. She couldn't blame him. What must he think? What must any of them think? Of the woman in a wedding dress stood looking at the ships. All the more reason to find the right ship.

Anyway, she had cause to stare at him too. She watched him as he strode, not quite jogging, towards the captain. His skin was also tanned brown and he was tall with broad shoulders. He wore a coat as long as the captain's and his clothes were clean, which was an oddity on a landing pad like this. The hair on his head was dirty blonde and long, tied neatly back. His beard, also blonde, was long enough to be braided with beads. What made him stand out, however, was the number on his wrist. Although the coat did well to conceal it, his sleeve had ridden up as he had bumped into Kai.

She held her breath as she awaited the captain's reaction to the man, only exhaling as the captain greeted him warmly. The men shook hands with the captain's free hand patting the other man's shoulder. They were friends, maybe they even did business together.

That was enough for Kai. With a skip, she jumped forward, trying not to run towards them.

The captain saw her approach. With a gesture and a smile, he welcomed the other man aboard. Again, the man looked over his shoulder at Kai, and then disappeared up the ramp and into the bowels of the ship.

Kai approached with caution. A short man, grease smeared over his skin, appeared from beneath a wing, wiping his fingers on a rag. Another woman, her long brown hair pulled up and back, walked up carrying a heavy bag. She stopped beside the captain and watched Kai approach.

'Can we help you?' The captain looked her up and down. Kai cleared her throat and lifted her chin.

'I would like passage,' she told him. 'Please.'

The captain and woman stole a glance at one another.

'Passage?' A smile played on the captain's lips. 'Where to, exactly?'

Ah, that was a sticking point. Really, anywhere but here would do.

'To Northhold Port,' said Kai. Again, the captain's eyes grazed over her.

'Running away, are we?'

Kai bit painfully on her cheek to stop the retort that immediately surfaced.

'I grew up on a ship like this.' She looked behind him. He didn't take his eyes from her. 'I know my way around. I'd be no trouble.'

'Passage to Northhold Port will cost you,' said the captain. Kai relaxed a little. At least he had gotten over her appearance.

'Yes.'

He narrowed his eyes.

'How much do you have? I don't see any pockets in that thing.' He waved a hand at her dress.

'Well, no. No pockets, no bag. No money.'

The captain raised an eyebrow.

'Sorry. Can't help.' He turned to walk up the ramp.

'Wait.' Kai stepped forward and then stopped, forcing a deep breath. The captain stopped and looked back. 'Wait. I grew up on a ship like this.'

'So you said.'

'So, let me work for passage.'

The captain took a couple of steps down the ramp, rubbing at his chin.

'You any good with machinery?'

'Erm. Well, no,' Kai stumbled.

'Maps? Can you navigate?'

'Not as such, no, but—'

'That's all we need right now. Sorry, miss. If you ain't a navigator or engineer, I got no use for you. Try one of those.' He pointed towards the ships that Kai had already dismissed. 'They may need other… skills.'

The woman at his side looked sharply up at her captain.

'Bucky,' she snapped. 'Captain,' she corrected herself, eyes closed. 'Surely we can afford to take one passenger to Northhold Port. It isn't far.'

Her accent threw Kai. It was sharper than the captain's but there was a familiarity between them, and if she looked closely, a similarity too.

The captain eyed her again.

'What did you do on this ship you grew up on?'

Kai hesitated, looking from the captain to the woman and then to the short man behind them, leaning against the ship, greasy rag in hand. None of them had weapons.

'Cook,' she said to the captain. 'I can cook.'

He scoffed.

'What do we want a cook for? We've managed all these years without one.'

'Let me guess, you take it in turns?' Kai followed the captain a few steps as he turned back up the ramp. 'So for a week you all get a break from cooking.'

The captain stopped and looked back. The woman shrugged, smiling, as he glanced at her.

'Are you good?'

'Never had any complaints. And hey, if you don't like what I cook, you can drop me off wherever we stop first.' Just get me out of here, thought Kai.

After a moment, the captain nodded.

'We're leaving now. You have five minutes to get your stuff.'

Kai held out her arms.

'I'm ready when you are.'

'Great. Captain Bucky Winters.' He held out a warm hand and Kai shook it. 'That there's Jude.

And him,'—he gestured to the short man who was following them up the ramp—'that's Seph.'

'I'm Kai,' Kai told them, looking back to Seph.

They walked into the dark cool of the ship and Seph pressed the buttons to pull up the ramp and close the doors.

'Crash. We're going,' Bucky spoke into the intercom, a panel on the wall, holding down a red button.

Kai looked at Jude, alarmed.

'Don't worry. Crash is our pilot, not an omen.' Jude patted her on the arm. 'Come on, I'll show you to your cabin and we'll see if we can find something more suitable for you to wear.'

Jude began to lead Kai away, deeper into the ship.

'Check her over, Jude!' Bucky called.

Jude called back an acknowledgment.

'I'm a doctor,' she assured Kai.

'Oh.' Kai had assumed he meant check she had no weapons. Being checked over by a doctor was much worse. Still, the decision had been made.

There was a rumble as the engines started and Kai's stomach dipped as the ship rose in the air. She steadied herself against the wall.

'Thought you grew up on a ship like this?' Jude eyed her warily.

'I did. I just—' Kai's stomach rolled. 'I didn't—' She bent forward.

Recognising the signs, Jude grabbed her and rushed her forward. A left turning led them into a room and Jude hurried Kai over to a sink where she vomited a clear, stinging bile. Jude pulled her hair back and out of the way while she heaved.

Kai let Jude sit her down and took the tissue that Jude offered to wipe at her mouth. She waited, feeling her stomach turn but nothing more was coming up.

'You didn't eat anything this morning? Most brides don't, I guess.' Jude held out a cup of water which Kai took with trembling hands.

'I haven't eaten much in a few days.'

'That excited, were you?'

Kai attempted a wry smile, sipping at her water.

'Stay put and keep sipping. Sip, mind. No gulping. I'll go get you some clothes.' Jude slipped out of the room and closed the door.

The ship had steadied. There were no windows in the med bay, but Kai knew the feeling of flight. That smooth floating sensation of having nothing but miles of air between you and the ground. It felt like they weren't moving at all, despite the speed they were probably flying at.

The med bay was clean, Kai was pleased to note. She had seen plenty congealed in blood and other fluids she daren't think of, or scattered with rusty implements and left to rot by a medic or doctor who would rather drink than patch up their crew.

Kai sat on one of two high beds that worked well as dentist chairs and operating tables. It was in this position that she could see for the first time just how torn and muddied the skirts of her dress were. She traced her fingers over the ivory fabric. Such a shame. It was a beautiful dress. How crazy she must look. It was a wonder that Bucky had agreed to let her anywhere near his ship.

There was a swoosh as the med bay doors opened and Jude stuck her head through.

'How're you feeling? Ready to see your cabin? I have some clothes.' She held up the pile hanging over one arm.

Kai smiled. At least the doctor was friendly. One friendly face was all she had hoped for.

She climbed gingerly down from the table and followed Jude back out into the ship.

'Do you take passengers, or am I the first?' she asked.

'You're not the first and won't be the last. But it's a rare thing. And our passengers normally pay.'

'I'm sorry,' Kai said. 'I wish I could pay but—'

'Yeah. Runaway brides have no pockets.' Jude paused and looked back to Kai. 'Don't worry. We won't ask.'

Kai nodded in thanks. She wouldn't know where to start.

'Down there is the mess. That'll be all yours once we've sorted you out.' Jude gestured down a short corridor. 'This place is a bit of a maze. But then, you already know that. Down here are our quarters.' Jude led the way down a long corridor that ran the length of the ship. The familiarity was startling to Kai.

'It's the exact same layout that I'm used to. I'm sure I'll know my way around sooner than I'll get out of this dress.'

Jude laughed.

'Given the state of it, I'm sure that won't be long.' She stopped outside one closed door and looked at Kai. 'Tell me it was branches and brambles that did that to you.'

Kai looked down at herself.

'Not all of it. Puddles are responsible for the

mud.' Her smile faded as she looked up into Jude's serious eyes.

'I mean it. Anything bad happen to you?'

'Not today,' Kai told her. 'This is all me.' She picked up the skirts and gave them a lack lustre swoosh. 'Promise.'

Jude nodded.

'You ever want to talk about it, the med bay has no ears other than mine. I'm a good listener and can check out anything you're worried about, or anything that hurts. All strictly confidential.'

Tears brimmed in Kai's eyes. Not trusting herself to talk, she nodded and looked down.

Jude frowned and opened the door.

'This is yours. It's nothing special, but it's not for long. Get changed, take your time. I'll be in the mess. See if you can find me, and I'll introduce you to the others.'

Jude closed the door behind Kai, leaving her alone in the room. It really was nothing special. A single bed against one wall, a small desk with a chair, a rail for hanging clothes, a couple of shelves. In one corner was another door which led to a small closet with a shower, sink and toilet squeezed in.

All it was missing were the posters on the walls and the quilt her grandmother had made her. Kai sank to the floor, her back against the bed like she had done a million times on a ship just like this, and let the tears come.

Bucky

'Everything okay?'

Jude nodded at Bucky, standing in front of his crew with his arms crossed. Now that the ship was stable, Bucky had gathered them into the mess to discuss their new temporary crewmate.

'She's not in great shape,' Jude told him. 'She hasn't been eating by the looks of things. Brought up the nothing that was in her stomach on take-off.'

Bucky raised an eyebrow.

'After all that crap about having flown in a ship just like this one?'

'Well, we'll see about that. We'll see if she can find the mess on her own. But come on, Bucky. You've vomited plenty during take-off after a night of too much drink and not enough food.'

'That's different.'

'So, why exactly we takin' on passengers that ain't payin'? Remind me, oh fearless leader.'

Bucky glanced at Crash. He knew it would be her who asked that. He should have bet money on it, but no one here would have taken the bet.

'She's offered to cook for us,' he told her. Crash barked a laugh.

'How d'you know she's any good?'

'Can't be worse than you. But hey, if you don't fancy a week off from your share of the cooking, you can keep your shifts. Give our passenger a break.'

'No!' Crash held up her hands, submitting. 'You're the capt'n, Capt'n. You've already said she's doing the cookin'. Can't take that back now.'

Bucky looked at the rest of his crew. They were small. Too small. He needed a new navigator and an engineer and he needed them yesterday. His knowledge of machines would only get them so far. If the ship broke during flight, and broke bad... He'd been stupid to leave Valkwick with a passenger instead of an engineer, but it was hard to get an engineer where there were none.

Not for the first time, he was leaving their survival down to Lady Luck. But she'd been good to them so far.

'So, anyone else got an issue with this? Like I say, a week and she'll be gone. Until then, she seems harmless enough. Right?' He looked at Jude who nodded again. 'Right. We've only got this one small job to finish off—'

'Which is why it's a shame she ain't payin',' chipped in Crash.

'I know, I know. But hey, we're doing a good

deed. She was in a wedding dress, Crash. You should've seen the state of her. She's got nothing. Never know, the universe might reward us for our generous act of kindness.'

Crash tutted and leaned back in her chair.

'Anyone else?' Bucky looked around the room.

'What if she asks about what we do?' said Crash.

'We do small government jobs.'

'Which government?'

'Whichever one pays better.'

Crash grinned.

'Anyone else? No? Good. Right. Onto other things. Harley is back with us, on official business.' Bucky shot Crash a warning look. 'So best behaviours, whether we have a passenger or not. He'll be with us for a month or so, right Harley?'

The tanned, blonde man with braided beard standing at the back nodded, leaning against the wall with his arms crossed.

'Right. You're all to be your usual helpful selves. Don't suppose you've word of any talented engineers looking for a fresh start, Harley?'

Harley shook his head.

'Sorry, Captain.'

'Any untalented ones?'

Harley didn't smile. Bucky hadn't expected one but he wondered if Harley was smiling on the inside, at least. The man simply shook his head.

'Well. There you go. Class dismissed.' The crew began to move. 'Wait.'

Everyone stopped and looked back at their captain. Bucky was looking over their heads to the nearest door, where Kai stood in Jude's clothing. She had cleaned herself up pretty well, all things considered. Her face was cleaner and paler. Her red hair was loose and unbrushed, but somehow looked neater against the smart, clean and intact clothes. She was small. Had she been that small outside the ship?

'Everyone, this is our passenger and temporary cook. Kai, is it?'

Kai nodded as she glanced at each of the crew in turn.

'Welcome aboard The Magpie, Kai. You know me, Jude and Seph.' Bucky gestured to Seph, sitting at the table, head down. 'This is Crash, our pilot.' He pointed at the short blonde to his left. Crash gave a mock salute. 'And this is Harley. He's a bounty-hunter and lawman of sorts who often travels with us. Not part of the crew per se but he's become somewhat part of the family. You'll be feeding him too.'

Harley and Kai gave one another cursory nods of acknowledgment but it didn't escape Bucky's attention that Kai's gaze lingered. He'd have to have a word with her. He mentally added it to his to-do list along with keeping morale up, finding a new engineer and navigator, finding work and keeping the ship in the air.

'All right. You've all got work to do,' he said. His meagre crew left the mess, forcing Kai further in to make room for their departure. Jude stayed behind. Harley caught Bucky's eye before he walked out.

'Found us all right then?' Jude smiled warmly at Kai, offering her a seat at the table. Kai sat, eyes darting around the mess.

'Just like I remember,' she said before her gaze

landed on Bucky. They stared at one another for a moment.

'Well, I for one can't wait to taste what you're going to concoct in this place,' he told her, unblinking.

'Don't pressurise the poor girl,' Jude murmured. Something about the way she'd said it made Bucky soften, but only a little.

'There's a coffee pot over there.' He pointed to the somewhat dirty but large pot on the counter between the kitchenette and the large table. The kitchenette was lined with cupboards. Bucky paused as he looked at them, trying to remember which one had the dodgy hinges. 'Try and keep it filled. We eat at seven every evening, unless there's a job on. I like to make everyone sit down, but when we're busy some will grab and run. You'll find all our provisions in the cupboards. Careful what you use, it needs to last us.' He looked down at Kai. 'All right?'

She nodded and Bucky waited a moment to see if her calm exterior would crack at all. It didn't.

'Great.' He paused, glancing at Jude but she was busy studying Kai. 'And we don't normally like to ask questions of a personal nature,' said Bucky, avoiding looking at Kai. 'But then again people don't normally show up in torn wedding dresses.' He left that hanging for a moment. The silence in the mess became heavy. Risking a glance at Kai, he found that she was still gazing over to the kitchenette. Had she heard him?

'Bucky,' Jude chided under her breath. 'You don't have to tell anybody anything,' she told Kai. Giving Bucky a meaningful look, she left the room.

Bucky sucked at his lips.

'Will you be busy? While I'm here, I mean.'

Kai was looking up at him.

'We do have a small job. Just a drop off. So probably not.'

'So a sit down meal for all of the crew each evening at seven. What about breakfast?'

'That's a grab and run affair, usually. Some don't eat at all, they live off the coffee. Others like to start the day on a full stomach.'

Kai gave another nod.

'And lunch?'

'Same thing.'

Another nod.

'I'll leave you to it, to get acquainted. Any problems, find someone and ask. Keep us fed, keep the coffee flowing and don't get under our feet. The week will fly by.'

Kai began making her way to the kitchenette. Bucky turned to leave. 'Oh.' He turned back. 'And watch out for Crash. She eats a lot and talks a lot. There's only so many hours in the day so she's forced to eat and talk at the same time.'

'What if we're out of something?' asked Kai, opening the first cupboard. Bucky cringed in case that was the one with a bad hinges. It wasn't.

'Make a list. Nothing we can do until we hit land again. And then it depends on what we're out of.'

'Thank you, Captain,' said Kai with a small smile. Bucky gave a nod and left.

He stopped. Had he just been dismissed? On his own ship? He'd have to watch this one.

The problem of Kai filled his mind until he

reached the cockpit. Crash leaned back in the pilot's seat, her booted feet up on the console, a manual in her hand, reading as she chewed on her fingernail.

'Comfy?' asked Bucky. Instead of rushing to put her feet down, Crash leaned back to look at the captain upside down and gave him a large grin.

'Just been trying to find a fix for the broken coil.'

'Is it more broken?' Bucky sat in the co-pilot seat next to Crash.

'Not yet, but it could be any second now. And then what, Capt'n?' Crash straightened, putting her feet down and leaning closer to Bucky. 'We need an engineer to look at it.'

'Oh? Is that what we need?' Bucky busied himself looking out of the large window at the front to resist the need to smack Crash. 'I didn't realise. Why didn't you say something earlier?'

Crash leaned back.

'We don't need to hire an engineer, Capt'n, just find one in port.'

'All engineers need paying.'

'We could always offer passage to one in exchange.' Crash snorted and took control of the ship, flicking it off autopilot. The Magpie gave a shudder before returning to smooth flight.

'You think you're being funny, but if this Kai had been good with engines and she'd have fixed us for passage, you don't think I would have said yes?'

'First time I've ever known you to take on a passenger for free when the exchange is so crap,' pointed out Crash. 'Why'd you do it?'

Bucky shrugged.

'You didn't see her. Poor girl looked pathetic.'

'Wonder who she's running from.'

'Based on the evidence, I'd say a groom left at the altar.'

Crash gave Bucky a sideways glance.

'Hey, maybe he's good with engines and he'll come after her.' She barked a laugh. Bucky gave a thin smile. He wasn't sure he'd say no to that.

'We on course?' he asked.

'Nice change of subject, Capt'n. Yes, we are. We'll make landfall tomorrow, probably late afternoon. Does that suit?'

'Yup.'

'I could be more accurate but a navigator would be better with maps.'

Bucky sighed.

'Enough, Crash. I'm all too aware we're a few crew down.'

'And that a cook ain't one of them.'

'Just be glad Kai isn't a pilot.'

Crash grinned at him.

'Like you'd ever replace little me.'

Bucky looked at her.

'And yet you tempt me every day.'

Crash winked at her captain and turned back to the skies, laughing to herself. Bucky couldn't help but smile.

'In your limited engineering experience, how long do you think we've got with that coil?' he asked quietly, unsure whether he wanted to know the answer.

Crash shrugged.

'A week? Maybe two. Of course, it could blow tonight. Then what? We'll fall from the sky, but what will we care? We'll be dead.'

Bucky frowned.

'Let's hope it's two weeks. Two weeks to get paid and find an engineer.'

'Capt'n, if it were that easy, wouldn't we have fixed it two months ago when it broke?'

Had it been two months? Bucky's shoulders sagged, the weight on them growing heavier by the day.

'Maybe I'll take the manual and see if our passenger has any light bulb moments with them,' he murmured, picking up the tattered booklet Crash had been reading. It had come with the ship, back when he'd been gifted it years ago. How many years had it been? The booklet had certainly seen better days, as had quite a few things on the ship. The Magpie needed an overhaul. He was supposed to be rolling around in riches by now. Where were his riches?

With a sigh, Bucky stood and made to leave.

'I'll be in my office. Let me know if anything happens.'

'Will do, Capt'n,' said Crash, not looking at him. 'Although, if you hear a bang and get that falling sensation, you won't need me to tell you it's that coil gone.'

Bucky considered swiping her round the head with the manual, decided it was too much effort and left the cockpit.

Crash

The captain's boots on the metal floor were only just starting to fade when the alarm went off on the console. Crash sat forward, immediately finding the problem. Turning in her chair, she yelled, 'Capt'n!' as loud as she could.

She grabbed the controls and veered the ship off to the left, clinging to her seat and pushing down the wave of adrenaline.

Bucky fell back into the cockpit, bouncing against the wall as Crash righted the ship. He stumbled backwards as she accelerated.

'What the hell?' he growled, finding the co-pilot's seat and strapping himself in.

Crash didn't need to answer. There was a bang and The Magpie rocked in the air, throwing both Crash and Bucky forward.

'It would appear we're being attacked, Capt'n,'

said Crash calmly, her full concentration on the window and the vista before them as they flew in and out of clouds.

The ship rocked again as it was hit. Crash straightened it up and then dived. Bucky swore, gripping his chair. Once they'd levelled out, he stared at the controls.

'Who by?'

'Not sure, Capt'n. They're behind us.'

Bucky reached for the intercom.

'This is Bucky. Strap in if you're not already. We're under attack. Hold on tight. Crash is on it.' He flicked it off and glanced sideways at her. 'You're on it, right?'

The ship veered to the left.

'Always, Capt'n,' said Crash. 'Want me to do a loop and get behind them? Hey! I wonder if it's our passenger's wannabe husband? Maybe we should open a communication channel, see what he knows about engine coils.'

There was a long pause. Long enough that Crash looked at Bucky out of the corner of her eye. Was he taking her seriously?

'Open up a channel,' he said eventually. 'How bad are the hits?'

Crash did as she was told.

'Scuffs as far as I can tell. There's no whirring alarm sounding, so that's good. Seems like they want our attention rather than blasting us out of the sky. Probably 'cause we've got what he wants on board.'

Crash didn't look at Bucky. As they sped through another thick cloud and turned sharply, Crash allowed her mind to wander a little. She kept up the acceleration. If this was Kai's groom, Crash wasn't sure she wanted him anywhere near their passenger. Not after the little that Bucky had said about Kai's initial appearance. She hoped Bucky wouldn't take her too seriously, but then he hardly ever did.

Bucky cleared his throat and spoke into the radio microphone.

'This is Captain Bucky Winters of The Magpie. May I ask who the hell you are and why you're attacking my ship?'

Crash snorted. The captain sure had a way with words.

The radio crackled and then, just as Crash opened her mouth to suggest they weren't going to talk, a voice sounded.

'Afternoon, Captain. Just a little reminder. Keep it safe and do it right.' There was another crackle and then silence.

Crash blinked at the console and then took her foot off the accelerator.

'They've backed off.' She checked a few of the instruments. 'No damage that I can tell.' Another moment passed. 'We're alone.' She looked at Bucky. 'A reminder? What the fuck, Capt'n? Was that Kai's groom?'

Bucky was staring out of the window at nothing, his eyes unblinking. Slowly, he put the radio down.

'Maybe. Hey, they're gone now.' He returned to the intercom. 'It's over folks. Back to what you were doing. No harm done.' He switched it off and went to leave.

'That's it?' Crash screamed over her shoulder to him. They were off course. She was about to mention the need for a navigator again but managed to stop herself in time. Not now, she thought. Not this time. She'd have to pour over the maps and do the best she could to get them back on track for the scheduled drop off.

'What else is there?' Bucky asked. 'I'll go talk to our passenger, see what she says.'

Crash sighed.

'What the hell was that, Bucky?' Jude stormed into the cockpit. 'Were we just attacked out of nowhere?'

'Looks that way,' said Bucky with a touch of defiance. Crash rolled her eyes.

'Everything okay, Captain?' came Harley's voice.

Crash turned in her seat to look at Harley and spotted Seph and Kai wandering in behind him. Kai hid behind Harley, wide-eyed.

'Oh good! We're all here. Hey! While we're all here, I don't suppose anyone was keeping track of where I was flying when I was trying to get them bastards off our tail, huh? Maybe you can tell me how to get back on course—'

Bucky held up a finger to silence her.

'If this is another stab about needing a navigator, I fucking know, Crash. Shut the hell up and fly.'

Crash closed her mouth and pursed her lips, turning her back on the crew to stare between the window and the crude radar map on her console.

'Are we in trouble?' Jude asked in her quiet voice.

'No,' Bucky said immediately. Crash swallowed down a laugh.

'Did you talk to them? Who were they?' Harley

asked. 'Maybe I can help.'

'They didn't say who they were. This person you were supposed to marry. Don't suppose you can tell us who they are?'

Crash glanced over her shoulder to find the whole crew looking back to Kai. Harley moved so everyone could see her. Kai opened and closed her mouth.

'Would they have come after you?' Jude asked gently.

Kai didn't respond.

'Who else could it be?' Crash asked after Kai didn't say anything for several seconds. 'No one was attacking us before she came on board. You could have said he'd come after you with weapons. You know, given us some warning.'

'Easy, Crash,' Jude murmured.

Kai frowned and shook her head.

'Wait. If it was…he would have ordered us down. He would have wanted me back.' She looked up into Bucky's eyes. The captain shrugged.

'Well, like Crash said, who else could it be? Maybe you're not as precious to them as you thought.'

'Except that they wanted us to keep something safe, Capt'n,' Crash reminded him.

'Keep it safe? While they're shooting at us?' said Seph. Crash shrugged, turning back to the sky.

'Well, they're gone now, aren't they.' Bucky waved his hands at his crew. 'It's over. It's done. When we land, we'll take a look at the damage but right now you've all got work to do.'

'After we've tidied up. I've got instruments all over the med bay thanks to whatever that was,' said

Jude.

'One of the cupboards emptied,' murmured Kai.

'Earn your keep,' Bucky told her. 'You'll help Jude tidy up first.'

There was a pause and Crash glanced up at the captain stood by her side.

'Harsh,' she muttered.

'And then I'll help tidy the kitchen,' offered Jude.

The crew left, mumbling amongst themselves, leaving just Crash, Bucky and Harley.

'That happens again, Captain, let me know. I can find out who's responsible. You shouldn't have to foot that bill.'

'Thanks, Harley. It's fine. Whatever it was, it's fine. I doubt they'll be back.'

'Sounded like they'd be back,' Crash muttered. Bucky gave her a warning look.

'I'll be in my cabin then, unless I can help with anything?'

'No, no. You go back to your work. We'll sort it out. No problems.'

Crash bit her tongue to stop herself from responding.

She assumed Harley left, because Bucky sat back in the co-pilot's seat with a slump.

'Everything all right, Capt'n?' Crash asked in a mocking perky voice.

'Can you get us back on course?'

Crash shrugged.

'Eventually. Eventually all things are possible. I did a right and then a left, yeah?'

Bucky placed a hand on her shoulder, making her jump. He patted her, which should have been comforting but only made her tense up.

'You'll figure it out, Crash. You always do.'

'Yeah, don't I always,' she muttered under her breath. 'Capt'n?'

'Yeah?'

'Was that Kai's missing betrothed?'

'Who else could it have been, Crash?'

Crash didn't reply. She didn't like the tone of Bucky's voice. There was a silence, and when Crash glanced back she found she was alone in the cockpit once more. Although not for long.

'Did you get any damage readings?' asked Seph as he sat in the co-pilot's seat.

'Not much. Is the engine okay?'

Seph shrugged.

'Looks the same as it did before.'

'You given any more thought to retraining as an engineer?'

Seph gave Crash a rare smile.

'I'd have to leave the ship to do that. I couldn't leave you guys.'

'Oh, no, right. We'd be left unprotected and without our best bodyguard.'

Seph gave Crash's shoulder a light punch.

'Watch it.'

'Well, we're not on fire. So everything else is a bonus,' Crash said, checking the consoles again. 'We did get hit though. Be interesting to see what damage has been done. Capt'n's shipments are safe, right?'

'First thing I checked.'

''Course. Maybe this time we'll get paid enough to get everything fixed.'

'Only if we actually get paid,' said Seph, looking

out at the sky turning blue again as they rose above some cloud.

'Hmm. I like getting paid.' Crash checked her instruments again and turned the ship to the right. 'Here, make yourself useful.' Blindly, she grabbed a rolled up map and chucked it at Seph. He unrolled it carefully and stared blankly. 'Just try. You never know. Maybe you picked up the skills in your sleep.'

There was a companionable silence between the two.

'You think it was the passenger's bloke coming to get her back?' Seph asked as he studied the map.

'If your bride had run away on your wedding day and you were desperate to get her back, would you fire warning shots or would you get her the damn well back?'

Crash glanced at Seph out of the corner of her eye, expecting at least a small smile. Instead, he was staring expressionless at the map, his vision distant, not seeing anything. Crash gave a deep sigh.

'Whatever's going on, we just need to get this job finished. See what damage has been done. Get paid. See where we go from there. It was probably pirates, trying to see what they could get, anyway. It's probably nothing.' She didn't believe a word of that so she wouldn't have blamed Seph for not believing her either. If it had been pirates, they would have forced them down. If it had been a stubborn groom, he would have forced them down. No, this had been something else, something just a little bit too out of the ordinary, and the words their attackers had given to Bucky went round and round Crash's head.

Harley

Rubbing at his eyes, Harley tried to focus on the sheets in front of him. His cabin on The Magpie was small, but so was everyone's. It was a luxury to have a desk, such as it was, but he wished it was bigger. He wished that every time he flew on The Magpie. He needed an office, on the ground, with other lawmen and an official badge. But until then, he enjoyed being out in the field, a free man to go wherever the work sent him. He just needed something bigger to lay all of these sheets on. He needed to see the bigger picture. When he lay each sheet out, they overlapped. Soon, he couldn't see the face of the man he was chasing, let alone the pieces of evidence that would tell him if he was chasing the right man.

It was a small case. Insignificant, even. But he'd

spent one long month on the ground, in and out of volunteering with the local police, and it had been one month too long. He needed to be back in the world, working a case and—although he hated to admit it—around different people. These people. This crew. They weren't the most law-abiding, although they did their best to hide the worst of their crimes from him and he did his best to ignore it. They didn't murder or rape, they were good people deep down. For the most part. Sort of.

Harley rubbed at his eyes again. His vision was blurring. It was hard to focus on the writing on a good day on this tiny desk but when he was tired it was near impossible. Especially after they'd been shot at, with the captain being cagey and a newcomer on board.

He had a good deal going here. Passage to wherever he wanted for a fraction of the price of other ships. Law-abiding ships charged a premium for a good-sized cabin with a proper desk, and Harley had just never had those kind of expenses. Maybe if he ever joined the police service officially. Maybe if they ever allowed him in, if he could pass the tests and receive a regular salary, but that hadn't been a fight he'd been able to win yet. So he'd had to go searching for other means. He'd found Captain Bucky Winters, desperate for some help. Free passage had been too good to pass up, and now Bucky only asked for a tiny amount each time Harley travelled with them. In return, Harley looked the other way and showed his private detective badge when asked. One flash of the badge and people gave Bucky and his crew the space they needed. And no one asked him questions. Not one crew member had asked him why he wanted to be a lawman, why he'd become a private detective, not one of them had asked how he came to be here. All of which he was glad of.

He knew their secrets, more than they thought, but that was only because he was good at his job. He would keep their secrets. He owed them that.

This new crew member wouldn't change that, but she could cause upset. Finally, Harley allowed himself to think about Kai. She'd been there, on the periphery of his thoughts, since he'd left the meeting in the mess. It was almost as if he'd been waiting for a reasonable and logical excuse to bring her to the forefront. The attack was the excuse he needed. He thought he'd hardly see her. The captain said she'd be gone soon. He'd spend that time in his cabin, working on this case. That attack had immediately changed things. If she was being chased, hunted even, then he had cause to get involved. It was his duty to protect her.

Harley sighed.

And he couldn't work on this case on this tiny desk. His chair creaked under his weight as he leaned back.

Kai was a strange occurrence, that much was true. Turning up in a torn and muddied wedding dress. Of course, it was most of the crew's way not to ask questions, although Harley wondered if even Bucky could resist temptation that strong.

She was obviously running away, and the logical mind said she was running away from a jilted groom. Was Bucky right, is that who had attacked them?

Poor fella, Harley thought. When had he realised

she was gone? Had he been there, in front of their guests, waiting for her? Or had someone told him before he'd had to face them. Why had she taken so long to change her mind?

Thinking like that, it seemed obvious that there was nothing exciting about the passenger. Nothing of note. Just another runaway bride. A woman who had changed her mind at the last minute.

Or had only had a chance to escape at the last minute.

Harley blinked.

Why else would the groom chase after her and threaten them? Men like that, who trapped a woman in such a way, would see her as property. He'd want her back.

She was a pretty thing, too.

Harley's back stiffened. He hadn't meant to allow that thought out. Attractiveness wasn't a factor in controlling relationships and men who thought they could own another human being. He knew that. Appearance had nothing to do with it.

Yet, he had been unable to look away from her red hair, her eyes, her turned down mouth.

Harley ran a hand over his own long hair, pulled back over his head.

It would be wrong of him to overlook the fact that she could be in trouble. He couldn't in his right mind allow her to leave the ship if she was worried for her life.

He stood and gathered his papers. The table in the mess was larger, and there was coffee in there. A good hit of caffeine would help his aching eyes.

There was a crash as Harley entered the mess

and then Kai's head appeared above the counter separating the kitchenette from the large dining table. He froze as their eyes met. Slowly, he placed his papers on the table and glanced at the large coffee pot. She followed his gaze.

'Oh, the coffee. I'll make a fresh pot.'

She leaned over and picked up the heavy pot with more ease than he'd thought possible, turning her back on him.

Harley began to meticulously lay out the pieces of paper. This was better. He could see each piece, he could see the man's face, he could see specific words and images and interview transcripts.

'Milk?'

Harley looked up into Kai's inquisitive eyes and he caught himself wondering what colour they were.

'No.'

Kai poured him a cup and brought it over, her eyes flickering over the papers.

'Harley? Wasn't it?'

He nodded and she cocked her head at him curiously. For a moment they stared at one another.

'What's all this?' She gestured to the papers.

'My desk isn't big enough,' he said, as if that answered her question. She frowned, her eyebrows knitting together. Harley looked away. 'I'm a lawman. A private detective,' he said, trying to put his attention back on the papers. 'I'm looking for someone.'

'That someone?' Kai pointed to the image of a man's face. Again, Harley nodded. 'What did he do?'

Harley gave Kai a sideways look. It was the

exact same question he wanted to ask her.

'Petty theft. Except for the expensive antique painting he stole from a rich man.'

'Ah. So, suddenly he needs to be caught.' The corners of Harley's lips lifted in a twitch. 'Just trying to feed his family,' Kai murmured, fingers tracing over the image of the man. Harley studied her, trying to make sense of what was lying between her words.

'Why'd you say that?' he asked, his eyes narrowing. It was true that the man had a young family. His wife had no job and she had three small children hanging from her. The man in question had applied for every job going in their town before he started turning up in neighbouring towns, and then the city. That was when the thefts had started. 'You know him?' Harley asked.

'No.' Kai turned her back on him again and returned to the kitchenette. She picked up a cloth and started cleaning the worktops, although given the wet glint already on them, she'd only just cleaned them.

'If you know him, you need to tell me.'

Kai looked up at him and it occurred to him then that her eyes weren't sad, as he'd assumed and expected. Her eyes were clever.

'I don't know him. Sorry. I've never met him before. Never seen him until just then. I just assumed. Most people steal out of desperation, don't they? From what I've seen of the world, most people get real desperate when it comes to their family and trying to keep them alive.' She shrugged and went back to her work.

Harley looked back down to the papers. He couldn't

argue with that. Placing his palms on the table, he leaned over the words. The steam from his coffee drifted up to his nostrils, the strong scent alone was enough to wake him. Or maybe it was talking to another human. He risked another glance at Kai. She looked away, startled.

'What about you?' he asked. She still didn't look at him, but she stopped cleaning.

'What about me?'

'Are you running from a bad decision? Or something more?'

Kai turned to look at him, mirroring his position, her palms on the worktop as she leaned forward.

'I was told when I boarded this ship that no one would ask questions. So far, that's all people have done.'

Harley didn't smile.

'I'm a lawman. It's my job to ask questions. And,' he continued as she opened her mouth to reply, 'it's my job to ensure your safety.'

Kai smiled, a slow and sweet smile that didn't show her teeth.

'Where I'm from is not in your jurisdiction, lawman. I'm not your responsibility. And I can take care of myself.'

'That why you turned up in a torn wedding dress?'

Kai gave a soft growl of exasperation.

'I wish people would stop focussing on that. Ain't it proof? I'm not married, am I? I can take care of myself.'

'Was that him coming after you?'

Kai hesitated and looked up, her eyes distant, looking at nothing.

'I don't know.' She focussed on Harley. 'If it was, why didn't he take us down? Why didn't he do more to get me?'

Harley didn't respond. He watched her a moment longer and then sipped at his coffee.

'What about you?' Kai asked.

Harley turned back to his papers, pretending to ignore her. Don't ask, he thought. No one ever asks.

'What's your story?'

He looked back up at her and saw the determination in her eyes.

'You don't tell me yours, I don't tell you mine.'

Kai grinned and the sight of her lips parting and eyes lighting up was a shock to Harley. He paused, taking her in.

'Fair enough,' she told him. 'Maybe another time.' And just like that, her grin was gone. 'You're from Aegirheim? I hope that isn't presumptuous of me.'

Harley's breath caught in his throat.

'I am. It's not.'

It was obvious, was what it was. It had always been obvious where he was from. His pale skin and style of hair gave it away sometimes, the number burned into his wrist gave it away every time.

Perhaps the mess had been the wrong decision. He was getting no further in his work. There was nowhere else to lay all of his papers out to see all of them at once, apart from the loading bay. Harley straightened and began gathering his papers.

'Going so soon?' Kai asked in a small voice.

'I need somewhere bigger,' he muttered, leaving the mess without a glance back at her. He regretted that as he headed towards the loading bay. He should have looked back to her. He should have thanked her for the coffee. No one on the crew really spoke to him, apart from Bucky and Jude, and even then the conversations were stilted. He'd always assumed it was him. All of his conversations were stilted. But Kai had talked easily, she had asked questions. It wasn't the done thing. He slowed, his heart pounding, but that was probably the caffeine.

Kai

Kai considered going after Harley, having instantly regretted asking him where he was from. It was obvious what his past was. She'd seen the number on his wrist, she knew her history, she heard the news. But he hadn't answered her questions and it turned out that this was a man she needed to know the answers to. Not only because she was curious, but because of what it would tell her about the crew she was flying with.

It hadn't mattered much before. They'd seemed nice enough people, enough for her to feel safe to fly with for a week. But that attack had changed things. If that was her groom coming to get her, how far could she trust Captain Winters to not simply hand her over? Would Harley really protect her?

And why hadn't her groom finished the job, taken the ship down and gotten her back? That was the part she was really struggling with.

Kai threw her cloth down and sighed hard.

'Fed up already? You ain't even cooked anything yet. We can drop you off sooner rather than later if you prefer.'

Kai, mouth dry, looked up as Crash wandered lazily into the mess and perched herself on a stool on the other side of the counter.

'No, no. I'm not fed up,' Kai said, the words coming in a rush. Crash grinned at her. Her two front teeth crossed a little at the bottom.

'No worries, New Girl. I'm winding you up.'

Kai stared for a moment before smiling.

'You do that a lot?'

'You betcha.' Crash winked at her. 'So get used to it. Some would say you'll be glad to get off this ship in a week.'

Kai felt her features drop but she didn't think it had been so noticeable to Crash. The petite woman cocked her head, narrowed her eyes and then barked a laugh, making Kai jump.

'You want to stay? Already? You've hardly been here. Just 'cause the Capt'n didn't hand you over straight away to whoever was shooting at us.'

'Yeah. I'm sorry about that,' Kai said awkwardly. 'I grew up on a ship like this,' she murmured. The longing to go back there ached in her, threatening to come out in an explosion of emotion. Crash poured herself a coffee and sipped it. Kai cringed. She must have burned her mouth although she gave no indication.

'What did the crew do? Take on passengers?'

'No.'

Crash grinned again and made a continue motion with her hand. Kai leaned her elbows on the worktop.

'You don't take on passengers either. So what do you do?'

Crash waggled a finger at her.

'Good question. Well played. We do what we can. Officially, it's governmental jobs. We take things from here to there. A delivery service, if you will. We're the middle people between countries sometimes. You know, odd jobs. Odd, official jobs.'

Kai maintained eye contact, a smile slowly spreading on her face.

'Yeah. That's what we did too.'

Crash laughed loud.

'No wonder this place makes you homesick. Why'd you leave?'

'I was forced.'

Kai shut her mouth. She hadn't meant to say that. The humour went from Crash's face.

'By who? The person who stuck you in a wedding dress?'

Kai paused a moment.

'Everyone knows about the wedding dress, huh?'

The smile was back on Crash's lips.

'Oh yeah. That's not something you can keep quiet. Sounds like the Capt'n took pity on ya. He's a softie sometimes. Infuriating and an idiot, but a softie deep down. Is he why you're chucking dishcloths around already?'

'Oh, no. I just managed to scare Harley away. I was just angry with myself, that's all.'

'Oh, Harley. That all? Don't mind him. He

doesn't talk to anyone. Only reason he's here is because the other lawmen won't let him into their gang, on account of who he is. What he was. He doesn't quite fit into his own world, you know? The world he chose. Difficult that. Can't say I understand it fully. Just feel sorry for him. So, don't you mind him. Stay out of his way, don't talk to him and you'll get on fine. That's what the Capt'n always says to me, anyway. Stay out of the lawman's way. Him and the Capt'n have an agreement. We don't want to get in the way of that. Well, I don't. I have my job to think of. And if you know what's best for you, you'll stay out of his way too. It's only for a week, it's not hard. Don't take offence so easily.'

Kai stared at Crash, waiting for her to take a breath. When she did finally stop to take a gulp of her coffee, the silence pulsed around them.

'So…no one talks to him?' Kai asked finally.

Crash shook her head.

'Except the Capt'n and the Doc.'

'But don't you want to know who he is? What he's been through?'

'No. Why? He doesn't care what I've been through.'

Kai looked Crash up and down.

'What have you been through?'

'Not much.' Crash shrugged.

'But he has. He…He's a…I mean…' Kai sighed. She wasn't sure how to finish that sentence in a politically correct manner.

'He's an ex-slave,' Crash said matter-of-factly. Kai stared wide-eyed. 'That's what that number is on his arm. Didn't you see it? They burned it into him. I got him drinking once. He still didn't talk much, but he told me about that. They burned the number into his skin. Can you imagine? Said he could smell his own skin cooking.' Crash gave a shudder. 'The number shows who owns him. There's a big database somewhere, has his whole history on it. He says it's still there, even though he's free now.'

'Most of the slaves are free now. You'd have thought they'd get rid of the database,' Kai said quietly, wondering how far away from the mess Harley had gone. Could he hear them?

'You'd think, but rich people find change hard.' Crash shrugged again and took another gulp of coffee.

'Not just rich people,' Kai murmured to herself. The pause that followed went on too long and Kai looked up to find Crash staring thoughtfully at her.

'You gonna tell me your story then?'

'You know, when I came on board I was told no one here asked questions,' Kai said.

'Oh yeah? Who said that?'

'The Doctor. Jude, isn't it?'

'Yeah. She's the Capt'n's sister, you know.'

Kai gave a small nod. That explained the familiar features between them.

'They're from money,' Crash continued. 'Not that you'd know it.' She looked around the mess, crinkling her nose. 'Stupidly wished it all away and now we're stuck on a boat that's gonna drop from the sky at any minute.'

'What?' Kai snapped.

'Nothing. Nothing to worry your pretty head about, New Girl. This coffee's good though, better than what the others make.' Crash gulped down the dregs in her cup and poured herself another. 'Could do with being a bit stronger, but I ain't complainin'.'

'You like it stronger than the others?'

Crash nodded as she sipped, somehow managing to not spill hot liquid everywhere.

'So.' Kai left a pause as she began wiping clean plates and putting them carefully away. 'We're about to drop out of the sky?'

Crash laughed.

'Nah. We'll be fine. Just need an engineer, is all.'

'How long have you been flying without one?'

'Too long. Last one left about five months ago, haven't been able to replace him.'

'Why'd he leave?'

'Ask a lot of questions, don't ya.' Crash narrowed her eyes at Kai and then barked her laugh. 'Someone offered him more money. Like I say, the Capt'n and Doc are from money but they ain't got any.'

'Doesn't the work you do pay well? My...the ship I was on before, we always seemed to have enough. Maybe we're not in the same line of work, after all.' Kai went back to leaning on the counter. Crash mirrored her, placing her coffee cup on the counter between her hands, fingers stroking the hot ceramic.

'We're pretty much common thieves,' said Crash, looking Kai right in the eye, daring her to say something. Kai frowned.

'So were we. My...the Capt'n preferred the term pirate though.'

Crash grinned, her eyes sparkling.

'Pirate. I like that. But I prefer outlaw. Has a certain irony when you consider Harley being on board. So, what was this capt'n to you? You keep saying my and then changing your story.'

'She was my aunt.' Kai straightened, wondering if she'd said too much again. She thought frantically for another question to ask but Crash got there first.

'Your aunt forced you off her ship?'

'What? Oh, no. No, she wouldn't do that. She's…I'm…I think I'm trying to find her. I think.'

Crash raised an eyebrow.

'Might want to make a decision on that one.'

'Yeah. I know.'

'Who is she? Maybe we know her.'

Kai looked Crash up and down. For that information, Kai needed to know she could trust this crew. The rate that Crash talked didn't mean she wasn't trustworthy, but Kai had learned nothing to suggest that she, or the rest of the crew, could be trusted with that information.

Crash leaned back.

'If we were gonna kill you, we would have done it by now. Or we would've handed you over to whoever was shootin' at us.' She sipped at her coffee.

'I didn't think you were gonna kill me.'

'No?'

'No. But others might see Harley and wonder at whether he was being kept here against his will.'

Crash didn't laugh. Her features darkened for just a moment and then she shrugged, looking down into her cup.

'You think we'd keep you here to do our

biddin'?'

This time Kai shrugged, inwardly cursing herself for saying something so ridiculous.

'I'm sorry,' she said before she had time to think about it. 'I didn't mean to insinuate anything about you or the crew.'

'Woah. You're gonna need to speak English, New Girl,' said Crash, still not smiling.

'I'm sorry,' Kai repeated. 'It was a stupid thing to say. Actually, Harley being on board is the reason I thought I could trust this crew. That and the fact that the Capt'n didn't leer at me when he caught sight of me. That helped a lot too.'

The tension in the room lifted as Crash broke into a grin.

'He didn't leer? At a pretty girl in a torn wedding dress? Must be our financials are worse than I thought. Saying that, Capt'n's a good man, even if he does like his women. Many Capt'ns ain't good. Guess they're the ones you were asking before us.'

Kai smiled.

'Many would say it comes with the line of work, but we both know that ain't true,' she told Crash, relaxing. 'In my experience, limited though it is, it's the law-abiding, rich men who are the problem.'

'They have no code,' Crash agreed. 'Us crooks, we have a code.'

The women smiled at one another.

'So people on this ship do ask questions, then?'

'Yup. Just Jude who don't, she thinks everyone's entitled to their privacy. And Harley don't answer, so he's no fun. Seph don't talk much either, come to think of it. And they wonder why I talk so much. They leave so much silence to fill between them.

And don't believe that they're not nosey. They want to know about you and your wedding dress. They're just scared that if they ask, you'll ask about them. Harley's a lawman. It's his nature to ask some questions, but he'll get grumpy if you ask them back.' Crash snorted and took a gulp of coffee.

'And what about you?' Kai asked quietly. 'Are you scared I'll ask about you?'

Crash opened her arms, sloshing a bit of coffee over the side of her cup. Kai watched it go and made a mental note to clean it up when Crash had gone.

'Ask away!' Crash declared.

'Okay, okay.' Kai leaned forward on the counter again. 'Why'd they call you Crash?'

A slow mischievous grin spread on Crash's lips.

'Ah. Well. Now, I think that story deserves payment.'

'Payment? The coffee isn't enough?'

'This?' Crash held up her cup. 'This is you doing your job. No. Like for like. A story for a story. I'll tell you why they call me Crash, but you gotta tell me something in return.'

'Like what?'

Crash pursed her lips as she considered this, giving it enough thought to push Kai from nervous into full blown anxious.

'So many questions,' Crash murmured. 'Let's start with the obvious, though. Why were you in a wedding dress and who were you supposed to marry?'

'That's two questions,' Kai pointed out, cringing inwardly.

'Okay. Just answer the first.'

46

Kai chewed on the inside of her cheek.

'You first,' she said.

Crash

'Okay, first you need to understand that I've been pilotin' since I was a kid and I'm damn good at it,' said Crash, getting comfortable on the stool and refilling her coffee cup. Kai leaned across the bar and waited. 'But, you know, I'm human. I make mistakes. Everyone does.'

'Of course.'

'Some mistakes stay with you. That's why they call me Crash.'

'So…you crashed once?'

'Boy, did I crash once.' Crash's eyes became distant as she stared down at the counter between them, her mind filling with the memories of the noise, the rush, her own breathing.

'Was anyone hurt?' Kai murmured. Something inside Crash winced.

'Yeah.' Crash left a long silence. 'A boy. A little

younger than me. We were racin'. That's what I was gonna do, back then. Be a racer. My boat was a beauty. She was so fast and I was the only one who could get her round those tight corners. We were unbeatable for a whole season. Then this boy turns up with his modified boat. Modified to look like mine. Shit, that boy copied everything he could about my boat. Impressive. Really impressive.' Crash sniffed, still not looking up from the counter. 'Can't blame him. I made a good livin' from winning races with that boat. 'Course he wanted some of that.'

'How did you get the boat?' Kai asked.

'I won it.' Crash looked up into Kai's eyes and grinned. Despite everything, she missed that boat. 'Told you, I was a good pilot even back then. I won that baby in one of the big races. My first big win. Best prize I ever won, too. She certainly earned her keep. Boat like that can be expensive to run but the winnings I got the followin' season—and we won every single race—kept her in the air and runnin' smooth.

'Anyway, so this one race, this boy turns up with the clone of my boat. Only he made it, modified his old boat. So, it ain't pretty but boy does it pack a punch. That first race, we were neck and neck. I beat him by a hair. It was too close. I admit, I might have had a little panic after that race. I thought I'd be okay when my winnin' streak was over. That's the whole point, you know? The thrill of the chase, the unpredictability. 'Cept I'd gotten used to the prize money. Plus, like I said, the boat cost money to run. So the next race, I got a bit desperate.'

'What did you do?'

'Now, I ain't proud of this,' said Crash, raising an eyebrow to emphasise how serious she was. Kai waited a beat.

'You didn't do anything to his boat?'

'Oh no. I'm not an idiot!' Crash took a long swig of her coffee. 'I may have just…pushed too hard. I pushed my little boat as hard as she would go. And then I got a tad…careless.'

'Oh.' Kai bit her lower lip.

'Yeah. We were neck and neck again and the finish line was fast approachin'. And I mean, fast. He was edging out in front. He was gonna win. We had one more corner. Remember, I told you, I could do those tight corners without hardly slowin' in that boat. That's how good she was and how good I was. 'Cept, on that race I lost a little concentration. I took the corner hard, pushing all the way, and scraped up against the cliff we were navigatin' around. The boat wobbled, must have clipped off a rock and spun, straight into that boy. And down we came. Me, the boy and our boats.'

'Was he okay?' Kai poured herself a coffee.

'He survived, if that's what you're askin'. But no. Broke both his arms. His head got pretty bashed in. He couldn't talk well after, and he could talk fine before. Damaged his brain.' Crash's chin trembled and she bit her lip to steady it, then shook it off and downed her coffee in one. She poured another. Time hadn't made telling this story any easier.

'I'm sorry,' said Kai, watching her closely. Crash shrugged.

'Was a long time ago. The others started callin' me names, you know, in whispers. I weren't supposed to hear but I did. Thought if I took ownership of it, they'd stop. The name Crash stuck. Took a bit of explainin' the first time I got a piloting job, and the Capt'n weren't sure of me at first. But I prove my worth every time, and I'm always worth it.'

Kai nodded.

'Were you hurt?'

'Broken arm, dislocated shoulder, concussion, six fractured ribs, fractures in my fingers and one leg, and one hell of a black eye. And my pride, of course. And reputation. I didn't race again. That was my last.'

'But you still fly.'

Crash grinned.

'Ain't nothing gonna take me out of the sky. Not for long, anyway. So.' Crash leaned forward across the counter and refilled Kai's coffee cup which wasn't close to empty yet. 'Explain the wedding dress.'

Kai swallowed and Crash narrowed her eyes. Was the new girl going to tell her the truth? If not, she wondered how good she was at lying. From the look of her, Kai was wondering the same thing. How much of the truth to tell.

'Today was my wedding day,' she started. 'And I ran away.'

There was a pause.

'Nah. You can't just leave it at that, New Girl. C'mon, I gave you a full story. There was a build-up, characterisation, drama and tragedy. Tell me the full wedding dress story.'

Kai smiled.

'That's a long one.'

'Give me the short version, then.'

'Okay.' Kai gave this some thought. 'Before I was born, when my mother was pregnant with me, I was promised to a boy. The son of…someone my parents knew. About a week ago, he found me, forced me off my ship and back home to go through with the agreement.'

Crash's eyes widened. She'd been expecting a wealthy groom, a change of heart, marriage for all the wrong reasons but not with force involved.

'That's shit! Go through with the agreement, indeed. You mean the agreement you never agreed to on account of not being born yet.'

'Well, yeah.'

'And I bet the boy didn't agree either?'

'He was a baby at the time.'

'It wasn't love at first sight then?'

'Can it be love at first sight, when you're forced from your home and into his arms?'

Crash shook her head.

'Disgustin'.' Her eyes grew distant again as she thought it through, then she focussed on Kai. 'You should tell the Capt'n. He, I mean, we can help. Ain't no woman should go through that shit.'

'Well, it's okay now, isn't it. I got away. I'm not married.'

'Except he just came after you.'

Kai frowned.

'Did he?' she murmured. 'If he was just after me, why didn't he shoot us down? Or tell the Capt'n to hand me over? He just stopped shooting, said something strange and left.'

Crash stared into the distance. If two people had the same doubts, that gave them more weight, didn't it?

'He told the Capt'n to take care of…something. Why would he ask him to take care of you? Maybe he's planning on gettin' you when we land.'

Kai shifted.

'I need to find my aunt's ship. Back where I belong. She'll know what to do.'

'Ah, so that's the plan? Go back to the ship where he found you in the first place.'

Kai sighed and returned to leaning on the counter.

'Will he give up?' Crash asked. 'Surely it ain't that important that you marry this guy?'

Kai bit her lip.

'It kinda is. But I don't know how long he'll chase me for. If I can get back to my aunt's ship, they'll help me.'

Crash gave Kai an appraising look.

'They're family. Not just your aunt, but the crew.'

Kai nodded.

'I get that,' Crash continued. 'We're family here too. You stay with us, you could join this family. Like I said, talk to the Capt'n.'

'To be honest, I'm worried about getting my old crew in trouble. I don't want anything to happen to them because of me.' The words tumbled out of Kai and she avoided eye contact with Crash, turning to restack some plates that were close to falling down.

A grin grew on Crash's face as her caffeine fueled mind whirred. Aware of the silence, Kai looked back at her.

'It's been a while since we had trouble. I reckon we're due. I can talk to the Capt'n if you like?'

'No! No. Thank you.'

'You sure? His office is just down the way. It won't take a moment.'

Kai stared at Crash.

'Who's piloting the ship right now?'

Crash laughed. She refilled her coffee cup and stood up from her stool.

'I get it. It's your story to tell. Thanks for the coffee, New Girl.'

Crash left the mess with a swagger, heading back to the cockpit. She wouldn't tell anyone. She would wait.

Jude

Knocking on the captain's office door, Jude stepped back and fretted, putting her thumb nail between her lips and nibbling.

'What?' came Bucky's voice. Jude pushed open the door and walked in, taking only a second to glance at Bucky.

The captain sat behind his large desk. Two large leather-bound ledgers sat between him and Jude as she walked over to a small bookcase and ran her fingertips over the spines. It was what she did when she wanted to talk to him about something serious. He leaned back and sighed.

'What, Jude? What is it? I'm busy.'

'Doing what? You can't find us more money stuck in here. Or a new navigator or engineer. What are you doing?'

'I'm thinking.'

Jude turned to look at her brother.

'No. Seriously.'

Bucky didn't smile. His eyes didn't soften. He looked down at the desk and heaved another sigh.

Jude sat in the small chair opposite him and moved the ledgers so she could see him clearly.

'We're gonna fall out of the sky, Jude,' he murmured, not looking at her.

'Crash tell you that?' Bucky nodded. 'How long do we have?'

'She doesn't know. Could be in a week or so, could be today. She's not an engineer.'

'How much money do we have?' Jude glanced down at the ledgers, resisting the urge to pick them up and leaf through them. She'd done that often enough. There was nothing new in there. Just lists and lists of figures showing them falling further into debt.

'Barely enough to feed the crew. Maybe…'

The meaning behind that one word filled the room.

'No,' Jude whispered. 'We're not going to disband. Not yet.'

Bucky attempted and failed at a smile. He turned to peer out of the window, at the clouds parting as the ship swam through them.

'You're good at this, Buck. You can get us through this. You've done it before.'

Her brother didn't move. 'Bucky,' Jude hissed, pausing until he met her eyes. 'We've been here before. We've gotten out before. We can do this. I'm not going back. And I know sure as hell you're not.'

Bucky's gaze hardened.

'Right.'

'You're Captain Bucky Winters.'

'I am.'

'Of The Magpie.'

'Yes.'

'And you're gonna keep us in the sky.'

Bucky gave his sister a genuine small smile and she relaxed a little, leaning back. 'I'll help,' she offered. 'We need more money so we need more jobs, right?'

'Right. Or…'

'Or?'

'Or one job. One really big job that pays enough. Getting one job is easier than getting many jobs.'

'That's true.' Although Jude pulled a face. 'You have something in mind?'

'Yeah. But you won't like it.'

Jude stared at him, waiting. Bucky looked back at his desk, picked up his pen and played with it, twirling it around his fingers.

'I've had a job offer from Castell.'

The silence that followed was palpable. Jude didn't know what to say. She wanted to scream at him, to hit him, tell him what an idiot he was. But, and this pained her to admit, he was right. They needed the money badly and a job from Castell would set them right for months to come.

'How much?' she asked quietly.

'Ten thousand.'

Jude bit her lip. That was more than she'd hoped. That would pay for a new navigator, engineer and fix whatever was broken while keeping them in food for at least six months.

'What would we have to do?'

Bucky opened and closed his mouth, then said, 'I don't want to tell you.'

Jude gave her brother a withering look.

'We're not kids anymore, Buck. You're a captain, you can't keep these secrets.'

'If I tell you, you'll say no.'

Jude sat back and crossed her arms. Of course she would say no. This was a job from Castell, it was hardly going to involve anything legal.

'How unethical is it? Will people die?'

'Maybe. But ours shouldn't die.'

Jude sighed.

'We're four people, Bucky. We don't matter in the grand scheme of things.'

'Six including Harley and our new passenger.'

Jude frowned.

'And what about Harley? How will you keep this from him? He's on the ship, Buck. He's right here with us. When are you planning on doing this job?'

Bucky shifted in his chair.

'That's a problem, yes. But we'll figure it out. And that's why I don't want to tell the rest of the crew. They don't need to know. Crash's mouth is too big. I'll tell Seph when I have to. Kai and Harley have no need to know. So, that's that.'

'So, it'll be just you and Seph doing this job, huh?'

Bucky rubbed at his face.

'He won't mind. He knew what he could be getting into.'

'You don't know that, do you? The man doesn't talk.'

Bucky shrugged.

'I never said this thing would be straight forward

or risk free, I'm just saying it's an option. A quick fix, and a big fix at that. But if you think we should keep scrabbling around in the dirt looking for little law-abiding jobs and paying our dues, then fine. We can do that. I'll go through some contacts when we land, see what's going on. Maybe we'll get lucky.'

Jude and Bucky stared at one another. He wanted her permission. He'd been like this as long as she could remember. He never asked for permission from their parents or teachers. No, for some reason it was always Jude he looked to.

What could she do? If she allowed him to do this, she could be putting the whole crew and their ship at risk of death, or worse. But if she didn't, there was a good chance the crew would disband and this would all be over. Then what? What would she do? Bucky would go and find work on another ship but there was no guarantee he could take her with him. She wasn't sure she wanted to branch out on her own, the thought brought on a cold sweat. She wouldn't go back, but she could set up her own practice. Get out of the sky, back on land and set up on her own.

No. Jude looked past Bucky to the clouds outside. She didn't want any of that. She wanted to stay here, with him, where it was safe and comfortable and known.

'Don't tell me,' she told him without breaking her stare out of the window. 'Don't tell me what the job is. And you're right, don't tell Crash. If you feel that that's right and what we need to do, then that's what we do.' She looked at Bucky. For a moment, she expected the big six-year-old eyes of her baby brother staring back at her, but the eyes of a grown man gazed back with intent. 'You know what the right thing is for the crew and the ship,' she told him. 'Your gut knows. Listen to it.'

Bucky gave a nod and a small smirk.

'So, not the Judy voice in my head then?'

Jude hesitated.

'What's she telling you to do?'

Bucky shrugged.

'She's being annoyingly quiet on the subject but I reckon if I stopped holding her back she'd tell me not to do it and to look for those small jobs.'

'Those words are good in theory,' Jude said carefully. 'But in reality…'

Bucky agreed.

'The passenger won't be a problem, anyway,' he said. 'She's getting off soon. We'll finish off this job, deliver the package, get this other job and be on our way. Nice and quick. Just like that, we'll be back to four plus Harley. Then it's just the lawman that's the problem. But we can keep him at bay. Keep it quiet. We've done it before.' Bucky cocked his head at Jude. 'And I can trust you to keep it quiet?'

Jude blinked.

'Of course you can. I won't say a word.' No, she thought, I'll just worry myself to sleep every night. She bit her lip again. 'What if it backfires?' she murmured. 'What if they come looking for us. Hunt us down.'

To her great alarm, Bucky grinned.

'Then we fight.'

Another pause stretched out.

'And you think that'll end well for us?' said Jude eventually.

Bucky shrugged.

'I'd rather go down with my ship than die of old age somewhere on the ground, bored out of my mind.' He hesitated. 'Unless it was in bed, of course, with a young pretty woman or two.'

Jude rolled her eyes and moved to stand.

'You did a good thing, by the way,' she murmured.

'I did? When? Doesn't sound like me.'

Jude smiled.

'With Kai. Taking Kai on board. You did a good thing. She's grateful, and so am I.'

Bucky waved her away.

'Yeah, yeah, I'm a great man and all that. I know.'

'Greater than you think. Greater than you give yourself credit for. Don't forget that.'

Bucky's smile twitched away.

'What if I get the crew killed?' His voice was barely audible and Jude gripped herself in a hug.

'What if you save us all?' she asked.

His smile was back and he looked down at his desk. Jude moved away and left the office, closing the door with a click behind her.

She stopped and breathed.

After a moment, she walked back to the med bay and sat at her own small desk, tapping her fingernails against the table. She should prepare. There was a chance this med bay would be needed soon. She only had two beds, would that be enough?

She glanced at where her instruments were kept. She'd need more supplies too. She should have mentioned that to Bucky. Not that they could afford them. She would add them to the list. Not that there would be much point. If Bucky got this job from Castell and it turned sour, there was a chance they wouldn't get any of the supplies they needed in time.

Jude closed her eyes. When she opened them, she found her hip flask hidden beneath a sheaf of paper and took a swig of the sweet, strong brandy inside. Then she opened up a thin drawer hidden from view in her desk and pulled out a bar of chocolate, slowly opening the wrapper.

Seph

Bucky and Seph were going through a large crate in the loading bay when Kai found them. Silently, she walked over and stood close by, watching. Seph caught her eye and then looked away. Bucky turned and jumped.

'What do you want?' he barked, attempting to hide the sudden shock of finding her there. Kai gave an apologetic smile.

'Sorry, Capt'n. I didn't mean to creep up. It's just—'

'We're busy. Shouldn't you be in the mess? Or in your cabin? That's generally where we find passengers. The mess or your cabin. So what're you doing here?'

'I was wondering if I could help?'

Both Seph and Bucky stopped, straightened and

stared at her. The poor woman appeared to instantly regret her offer, although as the shock wore off, Seph raised an eyebrow and looked around, wondering briefly what job to give her. Bucky shook his head.

'No. You can help by either going to the mess or your cabin. Don't you have coffee to make? Meals to prepare?'

Kai straightened, her cheeks straining as she gritted her teeth.

'When will you be back, Capt'n? So I can prepare something for the crew to eat.'

Bucky waved a hand at her dismissively.

'I don't know. A few hours.'

'If I'm going to prepare something for the crew to eat on your return, I'll need more ingredients.'

'You leave the ship, you're off. And you're welcome to leave us here.'

Kai visibly swallowed. Seph frowned to himself. The captain could be rough, but he was being particularly short with Kai. Seph could understand some of the pressure the man was under and while he wasn't sure if Bucky's bluntness was justified, he knew it didn't concern him. He silently urged Kai to leave. The sooner the captain relaxed, the easier it would be for everyone. Not that Seph cared, he reminded himself. The captain was always good to him and that was all Seph ever asked for.

Without another word, Kai left Seph alone with the captain again. Bucky caught his eye and shrugged.

'She's not paying,' he grumbled. 'If she was paying, I'd be nicer.'

Seph raised an eyebrow. There was no need to

point out that he hadn't asked. Seph continued loading the old four-wheeled vehicle with the crates while Bucky hesitated, a hand on his hip, glancing back to where Kai had gone.

'Was I too harsh?'

'Your ship, Capt'n,' Seph grunted. Bucky gave a single nod but he didn't seem satisfied.

They worked on in silence.

Seph drove their small quad vehicle off the ship. It was spacious considering its size, with four seats and space at the back for a couple of crates piled on top of each other and strapped on. It was an older model and known as the Bumblebee, thanks to the sound it made whether it was trundling along or being pushed to its limits. Seph stopped on the landing pad with a bump. He always came on these jobs with the captain, this was half of what Bucky paid him for. While Seph enjoyed getting off the ship and couldn't help but get a little thrill from the work itself, these times were always tinged with anxiety.

What if someone recognised him?

Not that anyone ever had. Not yet, anyway. But there was always today.

Seph parked the Bumblebee and gave the steering wheel an affectionate pat. He'd never been good with machines but it didn't take an expert to know that this one was nearing the end of the road. So to speak. He doubted there were any funds to repair it, let alone buy a new one.

Jude appeared by his side, fretting, rubbing at her fingers and chewing on her lower lip. She gave him a weak smile.

'Everything okay, Doc?' he asked. She nodded, looking back into the ship, presumably for Bucky. Seph stared at her worrying fingers. 'You sure?'

'Yeah, yeah. Look, Seph.' Jude paused, considering her words. Seph cocked his head at her. 'Watch out for Bucky, okay? Keep him safe.'

'Always do, Doc.'

Jude nodded again.

'I know, I know. Thank you. You always do.'

Seph narrowed his eyes at her.

'Something special about this job he hasn't told me, is there?'

Jude's eyes widened.

'Oh, no. No, no, no. Nothing special. Run of the mill and all that. Just a normal job.' She bit her lip. 'Just, you know, watch out for him.'

'That's my job.'

'Yes. Thank you.' Jude turned to leave and then hesitated. 'How are you, Seph? We haven't spoken much recently.'

Seph kept a straight face but inside he gave a snort of a laugh. They hardly ever spoke, unless the Doc was patching him up or telling him to watch out for her brother, like he didn't know his own job. Like that wasn't why she was always having to patch him up.

'I'm fine,' he said.

'Spoken to our passenger much?'

'Nope.'

Jude bit her lip again, nodded and walked back onto the ship. Seph watched her go, his shoulders relaxing a little. Bucky trotted down the ramp, catching his sister's eye as he passed her.

'You coming?' he called over his shoulder to her

as he reached the Bumblebee. Jude gave him a withering look and disappeared into the ship.

'Just us, Capt'n?' Seph asked, preparing to leave.

''Fraid not.' Bucky pulled a genuinely apologetic face as Crash skipped down the ramp and jumped into the back of the vehicle.

'I'm here!' she announced. 'We can go now.' She pulled out her gun, checked it was loaded and then placed it back into her holster. 'Okay. Now I'm ready.'

'You're not gonna need that, Crash. No guns. This is a simple drop off. Drop off the goods, get paid, get back to the ship. That's it. I told you, it'll be boring,' the captain said, climbing in beside her.

Crash shrugged and grinned at Seph.

'You never know, right Seph?'

Seph remained expressionless, but as he turned his back on his crewmates, moving the Bumblebee off the landing pad and onto the road, his stomach turned.

You never know, he thought.

The drop off wasn't far from the landing pad, although by most laws, landing pads had to be built a certain distance from the town or city they served. No one wanted to live near the exhaust fumes of all those ships coming and going, and pretty much no one wanted to work near them either, unless they were getting paid to. As with most landing pads, this one was surrounded by warehouses and storage units. The road wove between them, leading into the large town with its tall, wide buildings built too close to one another.

Although it wasn't raining, thankfully, as the

Bumblebee had no roof, the sky was thick with dark clouds and the wind rushed at them as they picked up speed. Seph kept his head down, eyes on the road as he drove. Crash was eerily quiet behind him, although he imagined she was grinning inanely at everyone they passed. Just enough to draw attention to them, even though the captain always berated her for doing it. Especially when Seph was present. He should probably tell Crash why they needed to be careful, but Bucky said her mouth was too big. Telling her would only put Seph in danger.

Thankfully, they didn't need to go into the town. The drop off was at a warehouse on the edge. Seph pulled up outside and turned back to Bucky to make sure they were in the right place. Bucky gave a subtle nod.

'Stay here. Don't touch anything and don't say anything to whoever comes to collect the goods. We'll be right back,' he told Crash who gave a shoddy salute.

Seph gave Crash a warning look but she only grinned in response. With a sigh, he followed Bucky into the warehouse.

There was no one to meet them inside, which only meant that this job wasn't as illegal as some. It meant that Seph would probably make it back to The Magpie in one piece, which would be nice.

They reached what looked like an innocent reception desk, albeit a cheap and run down version of one. A man sat behind the desk looked up at them.

'Yes?'

'Drop off for Mr Kline,' said Bucky. The man nodded, stood and left without a word.

'Looks like this'll be nice and easy.' Bucky caught Seph's eye. 'I've just jinxed us, haven't I?'

Seph gave a small smile.

The man reappeared and led them up a flight of stairs, to the top of the warehouse where there was a large office space. At one end was the biggest oil painting Seph had ever seen, although admittedly he hadn't seen many. It took up most of the wall, though. The thick strokes depicted a bare-breasted slender woman with a flowing skirt tangled around her legs. Seph ripped his eyes from the breasts to look at the tall man stood between the painting and a large, dark desk that was strangely clear of anything.

'Captain Winters,' said the man, giving Bucky a nod. Bucky greeted Mr Kline and stopped in the centre of the room, looking around with appreciation. Along the left side, there were windows, filling the room with light. The right side looked down onto the warehouse floor from where the muffled voices of men at work could be heard.

'Nice painting,' said Bucky. He tilted his head, narrowing his eyes. 'I think I know her.'

Mr Kline gave a thin smile. 'Your shipment is downstairs with my colleague. All present and correct,' Bucky told him, getting straight to business.

Mr Kline walked slowly around the desk and stopped at the filing cabinet. Carefully, he unlocked it, his back to Bucky and Seph, and pulled out a box.

'That the payment?' Bucky asked. 'Or you gonna offer me a cigar? Wouldn't say no to either.'

Mr Kline laughed.

'First, we wait to see if the shipment you have brought me is indeed present and correct, Captain Winters. Then, you may have the contents of this box.'

'Fair enough.'

A long silence followed. Seph did his duty, checking the room with a practiced eye for any weapons. Finding none, he allowed himself to find those bare breasts again behind Mr Kline's head. Mr Kline followed his gaze.

'They do attract the eye, don't they?' he murmured. 'I find them useful.'

'I bet,' said Bucky.

'In making business deals,' Mr Kline finished.

Seph ripped his eyes from the painting. It was a distraction. He put his focus onto Mr Kline who smiled appreciatively at him. Bucky, however, continued to study the painting.

Two men entered the room behind Seph and Bucky. Seph turned to meet them. Bucky glanced over his shoulder.

'Gentlemen,' he said by way of greeting. Neither men appeared to have weapons and one nodded to Mr Kline.

'Very good. It appears all is well. Here, Captain Winters, is your payment. Thank you for your service. Perhaps I may be able to use you again.' Mr Kline opened the box and pulled out four bundles of money.

'Marvellous,' said Bucky, taking the wads of cash. 'Yes. If you ever need a delivery again, I hope you'll think of us. You know how to reach me.'

'Indeed.' Mr Kline gave a nod, which appeared to end the conversation.

'So…we'll be leaving then.' Bucky stepped backwards.

The two men by the door parted, allowing Seph and Bucky to walk between them.

Bucky jogged down the stairs, Seph rushing to keep up.

'Everything okay, Capt'n?'

'Hmm. I just think it'll be best to get away as fast as possible, that's all.'

Seph slowed.

'Why?' He cringed, already dreading the answer.

'Because the shipment may not actually, entirely be all present and correct,' Bucky whispered as they left the warehouse and marched to the Bumblebee. Crash moved out of the driver's seat and into the back.

'That went well then?' she asked.

Bucky flashed Seph a look. Seph took the wheel, started the engine, which coughed and shuddered into life, and immediately began to drive away.

'It didn't go well?' Crash looked between the men.

'It went very well. Now be quiet and keep an eye out. Oh, Seph, we're not done yet. We need to pop into town quickly.'

A ball of fear smashed into Seph's belly, his throat constricting. He coughed and inhaled with difficulty.

'Another job, Capt'n?'

'Hopefully.' Bucky leaned back in his seat, glancing over his shoulder back to the warehouse they were driving away from. The steering wheel soon became wet with sweat from Seph's palms. He wiped them one at a time on his trousers.

Bucky

'Left here,' said Bucky, as they drove into the town. The crowds and noise thickened, the warehouses giving way to small buildings, shops and a couple of houses. Seph took the left, having to slow down as he joined the rest of the traffic on the roads. Some people crossed in front of them, slowing them down more. Seph kept his head down, as well he should. Bucky always felt bad, dragging Seph into busy places, but it had to be done. It was a part of life, and a part of the job.

'Look!'

Crash's outburst made Seph jump. His knuckles turned white as he gripped the steering wheel tighter.

'What?' asked Bucky.

'There's a market down the road we just passed.

They might have a replacement coil. Or know where we can find a good engineer.'

'No.'

'An okay engineer?'

'No.'

'Any engineer, then.'

'Crash, we're not stopping. Only for this job, but nothing else. Then we're back to The Magpie and off again. I'm not staying longer than we have to.'

'Why not?'

Bucky didn't reply. He was calculating how long it would take Mr Kline to realise that something wasn't quite right with his shipment. It had been a risk to tamper with the client's merchandise, but necessary. Although he couldn't tell his crew that.

'Capt'n, we don't fix that coil, we could fall outta the sky,' said Crash.

Seph blew out his cheeks.

'Crash, I promise you, hand on heart, that once we've done this, at the next stop we'll get a coil. Or an engineer, if we can find one.'

'Really?' said Crash. 'Promise?'

'Look, I don't want us falling out of the sky either. Right here, Seph.'

Seph turned the Bumblebee off to the right.

'Who's this job with?' asked Crash.

Bucky pursed his lips.

'Tell you what, Crash. Why don't we drop you off at the market? Go get some odds and ends with what cash we've got.'

'Why bother with the odds and ends if we're gonna fall outta the sky without that coil?'

Bucky rolled his eyes and gestured to Seph to stop. The Bumblebee slowed to a halt. Bucky turned to face Crash and shoved his hand into his pocket. He pulled out some coins and thrust them at Crash. She eyed them warily.

'Take these, go to the market, buy whatever and we'll pick you up on the way back. Okay? Buy whatever you want.'

Crash narrowed her eyes at her captain. She climbed out of the vehicle, turned back to Bucky and pointed a finger at him.

'You better come back for me, Capt'n.'

''Course we will. We can't fly without you.' Bucky attempted a warm smile which seemed to work. Crash returned the smile but she still looked worried. Damn that girl. Bucky often forgot how bright she was, he constantly underestimated her. He turned back to Seph.

'Drive. Just down here and to the left.'

'This a bad job, Capt'n?' Seph murmured as the Bumblebee pulled away.

'Why'd you ask that?'

'You sent Crash away.'

Bucky sighed.

'Yeah. It's bad. But not doing it is worse.'

Seph took his eyes off the road long enough to give Bucky a raised eyebrow.

'You sure about that?'

Bucky shrugged.

'Depends how much you like us all being part of the same crew, I guess.'

Seph put his attention back on the road and said no more.

Bucky stopped them outside a warehouse that looked like all the others. He looked glumly up at the dirty windows and heaved a sigh.

He could still turn back. He could just tell Seph to turn the vehicle around. They could pick up Crash and be on their way.

But then what? Castell's right hand man, Crocodile Crick, was expecting them. There would be a high price to pay if they simply didn't show up. Castell had sent too many warnings. It was almost as if he knew Bucky might have a change of heart.

Mr Kline would know something was up by now. He'd be looking for them. Bucky had to get his crew back to the ship, and the only way to do that was to get this meeting over and done with.

Bucky wetted his lips, cleared his throat and jumped down from the Bumblebee. Seph followed closely and silently. That was why Bucky had hired him. The man never asked too many questions, he just got on with the job at hand. Sure, he was small and yes, they needed to keep him hidden for the most part, but he was damn good at his job.

A man met them at the door and showed them through to the main part of the warehouse. There was no office welcome this time. Instead, they were left in a large hangar, the remains of engines and ship wings piled up in the corners.

'Wonder if there's a working coil around here,' Bucky murmured through gritted teeth. Seph glanced at him. He didn't offer an answer so the two stood in silence, waiting for the doors ahead of them to open.

When they did finally swing open, they did so with a creak and bang, making both Bucky and Seph jump. Five men walked in and in the centre stood Crocodile Crick. When his four companions —were they henchmen or lackies? Bucky wondered, was there a difference?—stopped walking, Crick continued until he stood opposite Bucky.

'Captain Winters,' he said with a sickening smile. It wasn't obvious at first glance why this man had been nicknamed Crocodile. He was only a little taller than Seph, which was hardly impressive, and his dark hair was oiled back giving the appearance of a slimy little con man. But looks were deceiving. This was no con man. This man was an artist. His art was known throughout the city, and neighbouring cities, to the extent that the stories were almost as good as myths. Bucky wasn't sure which details were true and which were lies, neither did he wish to find out.

Crick's eyes, however, suggested that all the stories were true. They were small and hard, focussed on Bucky with a dedication that brought Bucky out in a cold sweat.

'I understand you have some packages that need to be delivered,' said Bucky. His voice didn't sound like him. It was as if he was floating above them all, watching this strange man who looked like him making a deal with a demon.

Crick smiled again.

'Indeed, I do. I'll have my men move said packages into your vehicle.' He gave a gesture and one man peeled away from the group, disappearing behind Seph and Bucky. 'A quarter payment now, as agreed with Castell. The rest upon delivery.' Crick clicked his fingers and another of his men stepped forward. He was holding a black bag that Bucky hadn't noticed. He opened the bag and showed Bucky and Seph the coins inside. The bag was closed and thrown onto the ground. 'If there is any problem with the shipment, Captain Winters, it won't just be the payment that is, how should I say this, slashed.'

A silence grew between them.

Bucky gritted his teeth, feeling Seph shift beside him.

'Of course. There won't be any problems. You can trust us.'

'So I've heard,' said Crick. 'Then again, I've also heard that some of your shipments can go missing. Perhaps be a little damaged. Especially when you seem to be falling on hard times, and you are on hard times, are you not, Captain?'

How did he know? And if he knew, then Castell knew.

Bucky kept his mouth shut, but this was enough of an answer for Crick.

'I understand you are in need of an engineer. You've been searching for quite some time. Perhaps, Mr Castell can be of assistance.'

Of course, Bucky thought. He'd been putting out messages for months at every port where he thought he stood a chance of finding a good engineer. Why did these things always come back to bite him?

'Assistance?' Bucky asked. He managed to not squeak the word but his voice was too quiet for his liking.

Crick nodded.

'We have an engineer. He can be loaned to you, for a reasonable fee. While he's on your ship, he can fix it, keep you in the sky and make sure Mr Castell's shipment gets to where it needs to be on time. Oh.' His smile fell, replaced with a frown that darkened his features. 'That is unless that foul lawman is with you, still?'

Bucky stopped himself from grinning.

'I'm afraid he is.'

Crick narrowed his eyes.

'That won't be a problem for the shipment?'

'The lawman travels with us regularly, it's never been a problem before. We're good at what we do, sir, isn't that why Mr Castell hired us?'

A smile crept back onto Crick's lips and he stroked his hairless chin.

'Indeed. Indeed.' He looked behind Bucky and Seph and nodded. Bucky glanced over his shoulder to see the man who had left returning. 'The shipment is loaded onto your vehicle. Tell me, Captain, how close are you to falling from the sky?'

'Nowhere near. In fact, we just picked up a new engineer. There won't be any problems.'

'Is that right? Well, excellent. Excellent. Take your payment. The rest on delivery.'

Bucky bent to pick up the bag. When he straightened, he found that Crick had taken a couple of steps forward, leaving their faces awkwardly close together. 'And don't fuck this up, boy,' he hissed.

Bucky stepped back. Not trusting himself to reply, he gestured to Seph for them to leave.

Bucky practically jogged out of the warehouse, glancing over his shoulder a few times as he went. Seph stayed close and for the first time, Bucky noticed the man had his fingertips ready on the handle of his gun, hidden in its holster under his coat.

The Bumblebee was laden with crates. The men

climbed in, Bucky tucking the bag of coins safely into the footwell, and in silence, they pulled away.

'Well. That was… We should go pick up Crash,' said Bucky, checking over his shoulder to make sure they weren't being followed.

'Yes, Capt'n,' said Seph.

'I wonder why they didn't check us for weapons,' Bucky mused. 'You'd have thought that would be part of their security.'

'Maybe they didn't need to,' Seph offered.

That was a chilling thought. Bucky chewed on his tongue as he considered it.

'Capt'n?'

'Hmm?'

'We don't have a new engineer.'

'If anyone asks, our passenger is an engineer.'

'She's getting off at the next stop, Capt'n.'

'The delivery point isn't far from there. It'll be fine. The money we'll get from this job will sort us out, Seph. We can figure out the finer details as we go. Then we'll have the ship fixed, and our new engineer. And maybe a navigator, too. And we can all have a couple of days leave. How does that sound?'

Seph didn't seem thrilled, but then he never did.

'Shit.' Bucky gripped at the door handle of the Bumblebee as the market came into view and, right by the road, Mr Kline stood with his hand gripped around Crash's arm. Behind him was a small group of his men.

'What should I do, Capt'n?' Seph asked.

'We get Crash and we run.' Bucky fished around the glove compartment of the Bumblebee and pulled out his revolver, checking quickly that it was loaded. Seph, without missing a beat, pulled out his own gun and continued forward at the same pace.

Both men hid their weapons as they slowed and stopped in front of Mr Kline. Crash glared at Bucky. He did his best to avoid eye contact with her.

'Mr Kline. What's the meaning of this?' he bellowed.

Mr Kline narrowed his eyes at Bucky.

'You, Captain Winters, have taken your last chance. Part of my shipment is missing. What do you know about this?'

'What? I suggest that if part of it is missing, then you take it up with the supplier. I delivered everything that I was given.'

Mr Kline smiled and raised his free hand, which happened to have a pistol in it, aiming it at Bucky's head. His men followed suit, aiming their weapons.

'Liar!'

Bucky ducked instinctively, despite there being no gun shot. Seph aimed his own gun at Mr Kline and after a moment, Bucky collected himself and did the same.

'What do you want, Mr Kline?'

'What is rightfully and legally mine, Captain. But unless you have my missing piece of shipment about your person, I'll be taking your pilot instead. I'm always on the lookout for good pilots. I can pay you more than he does,' Mr Kline whispered to Crash.

'Not difficult,' Crash said.

Bucky raised an eyebrow at her. Did she want to stay with Mr Kline? Crash pulled a face. No. No, she definitely didn't.

'Sorry, sir, I can't allow it. You'll have to take the matter up with the supplier.' Bucky noticed belatedly and with horror that Mr Kline had started to eye up the crates on the back of the vehicle.

'Or I could take some of these to make up for my loss.'

Before Bucky could reply, Crash drove her elbow into Mr Kline's side and twisted her arm free. She leapt onto the Bumblebee and into Bucky's lap with a screech. Seph fired a shot towards Mr Kline and his men as he pushed his foot down on the accelerator. The Bumblebee pulled away, although not quick enough. Bucky leaned down over Crash, covering his head with his hands, as bullets flew over them.

'Faster, Seph.'

'Going as fast as we can, Capt'n. Crates are weighing us down.'

The Bumblebee built up speed. Crash wiggled her way further onto the vehicle and took over the wheel from Seph, who turned and began firing his gun behind them. Bucky glanced back to see Mr Kline in his own transport, racing after them and firing shots that were wildly off target. Bucky picked up the Bumblebee's radio and shouted into it, 'Jude! Start the engine. We're leaving as soon as we hit the ramp. Now!'

Then he turned to join Seph in firing at the vehicle full of men chasing them.

Kai

Tapping her fingers against the large dining table in the mess, Kai sat back in her seat and sighed.

Shouldn't everyone be back by now?

'What's this?'

Kai snapped her head up to look at Harley standing in the main doorway.

'What? What is it?' She jumped up.

'That smell.' Harley paused and breathed in deeply before his eyes met hers. 'What are you cooking?'

'Oh.' Kai made her way back into the kitchenette and gave the pots on the hob a stir. Harley followed her slowly. 'I thought, seeing as how we're all from different places, it might be fun to try and make food from each of our homelands.' Kai grimaced, realising what she'd just said. She glanced over her shoulder at Harley. 'I'm sorry. I didn't think that one through. I just—'

'I haven't smelt anything that good since I was a boy,' said Harley. He waited for her to look at him properly and then smiled gently. 'It's a nice idea.'

'Well, it probably won't be as good as you remember.' Kai turned back to the pots, her stomach twisting. She should have given this more thought. It was just that standing in the kitchen all day, wondering when the crew might kick her off or her groom would shoot them out of the sky, was so boring.

'Where did you learn the recipes?' Harley walked around and into the kitchenette, taking the stirring spoon from Kai. He lifted the lid from one pot and stuck the spoon in, breathing in the steam that was released.

'I served as a cook for a while on my last ship,' said Kai. 'We once had a passenger from Helayaia, or rather from Aegirheim. She taught me some of the recipes. She was on her way back to where she'd been a…'

'Slave,' finished Harley. Kai nodded.

'The man she loved lived there. That's why she went back after she was freed.' Kai looked down at the pots. 'I think about her sometimes. I wonder what happened to her.'

Harley handed her back the spoon.

'And you assume because I have a number on my wrist that I too was a slave?'

The heat in the kitchenette became unbearable for a moment.

'Well, no… Crash told me, though. That you were a…'

'Slave.'

'Yes.'

Harley smiled.

'It's okay. You can say that word.'

Kai looked away and swallowed against her dry mouth. Grabbing a glass, she filled it with water from the tap and took a sip.

'Did you want a drink?' she asked.

Harley was watching her, the smile still on his lips. He shook his head.

'No. Thank you. The smell of the food drew me in, that's all. Have you been here all day?'

'I don't know where else to go. I don't want to be in the way. Did you find somewhere to look at your papers? I'm sorry, I didn't mean to…scare you off.'

'You didn't.' Harley walked out of the kitchenette and put his hands on his hips, surveying the empty dining table. 'And yes, the loading bay worked well. I can get some good height in there.'

Kai relaxed a little.

'Are you chasing someone?' she asked, following him out and towards the dining table.

Harley looked at her and raised an eyebrow. 'Right. You can't say. 'Course you can't.' She held up her hands in surrender. There was a pause. 'Are they usually gone this long?'

Harley turned back to the empty mess and sighed.

'Sometimes. It's not really my business.'

'It sort of is if the pilot is out with them. I flew on a ship like this but I can't fly a ship like this.'

Harley gave a small smile that Kai was beginning to feel familiar with.

'Can you fly any ship?' he asked her.

She grinned.

'Well. No. All the more reason why we need Crash back.'

'It's a good point,' Harley murmured. 'They'll be back,' he told her. 'They always are.'

Kai nodded but her smile faded. Crew always came back from a job, until they didn't. She'd experienced that enough times.

'How long have you flown with them?' She leaned back against the breakfast bar, hugging herself.

'Long enough to know them,' Harley said, his back to her. 'They've never not come back, if that's what you're asking. They always come back. Captain Winters doesn't leave anyone behind on a job. Not unless they want to be left behind.' He glanced back at her. 'You're getting off at the next stop, right?'

Kai nodded, stopped and then shrugged.

'Maybe. Yes. I think. Probably.'

Harley stared at her.

'Capt'n said you were getting off at the next stop.'

'Then I guess I have to, don't I.' Kai looked down at the worn wooden worktop behind her, wondering briefly who had driven a groove through one of the grains.

'You've nowhere to go?'

'I've somewhere. I just don't know if I should.' Kai met Harley's gaze. 'The man I was supposed to marry knows about my aunt's ship. That's where I'd be heading. That's where he found me in the first place. I don't want to get her in trouble. And I'm not going back with him.' Her eyes stung but she held back the tears she hadn't been expecting. It was the memories that had caused them. The memories of fear, of having the control over her life taken from her so easily. She would rather have died. At least then she and her aunt's crew could be safe. Better yet, she'd rather live, free, doing what she wanted to, even away from her aunt if she had to.

Harley's gaze hardened.

'He can't take you anywhere without your consent. Maybe you should stay here until we can get this sorted.'

Kai cocked her head at Harley.

'I'm not sure the Capt'n would appreciate that.'

Harley shrugged.

'You prove you're useful and free, he'll keep you on.'

Kai narrowed her eyes. Could she work for free in exchange for safety?

'And what? You'd protect me? Thought you weren't always here?'

Harley looked past her.

'That's true. I go where there's work, though. I can find this man of yours, make sure he leaves you alone.'

Kai stiffened, that familiar ball of anger dropping into her gut. She caught his eye.

'He's not my man,' she told him.

'And you're not his property,' Harley pointed out.

Kai looked down at the floor and gave a singular nod.

'Maybe you're right,' she murmured. 'Maybe it

would be better to stay here, work for free and be safe rather than tempt fate.'

'I'll talk to the captain,' Harley said. There was a pause as it looked like he might reach out to her, perhaps to give her arm a comforting squeeze, but he quickly thought better of it and moved away.

Kai watched him, softening.

A loud crackle made them both jump and Kai snapped round to face the ship's intercom.

'Kai, Harley. Company's coming. I need you both in the loading bay. Open the doors. Let Bucky in while I get us ready to fly,' came Jude's voice.

In response, the engines shuddered to life. Kai steadied herself and turned to Harley, her eyes wide.

'That doesn't sound good,' she murmured.

'It happens,' Harley mumbled as he left the mess. Kai turned off the hobs, giving the food one last stir and followed Harley out.

They ran through the corridors, down the stairs, around corners and finally arrived in the loading bay. Harley was already opening the doors, and Kai stood beside him, her fingers itching.

A gunshot sounded.

'I don't have a weapon,' Kai murmured. 'What do they want me to do?'

Harley lifted his coat to reveal a holster with two revolvers. He handed one to Kai.

'Only shoot if you're shot at. We don't know what's coming. It's loaded. You know how to take the safety off?'

Kai stared at him a moment and then said, 'Yes.'

'Good.' Harley gave her a nod. 'Go stand over there, use the crates as cover. I'll be on this side. Hopefully the captain, Seph and Crash will come through first.'

Kai watched Harley walk away. She made her way to her position, feeling the warm weight of the gun in her grip. It felt like it had been an age, in reality it had barely been a week. A smile played on her lips as she lowered herself behind the crate and kept her eyes on the door.

Whatever was coming for them, let it come.

There was a roar and then the Bumblebee burst into the loading bay with a screech as Seph slammed on the brakes. Kai aimed at the door behind them, her finger flicking off the safety. Crash was lying in the back of the vehicle, reloading her gun. Bucky jumped down and stood squarely facing the doorway, firing his own weapon. Seph was on his feet and out of the Bumblebee within seconds, shooting at their attackers. Kai frowned. Who were they firing at?

She didn't lower her weapon, keeping it fixed on the door.

Bucky swore loudly, grasping at his arm and dropping to his knees, his back against the Bumblebee in an attempt to use it as a shield.

This was stupid.

Kai stood up, left the cover of the crate and walked towards the open door.

'Hey, New Girl! What do ya think ya doin'?' Crash screeched as she pulled the trigger of her gun over and over. The last time rang hollow. She was out of bullets again. 'I'm out! Properly this time.'

As Kai neared the Bumblebee and doorway, she could see their attackers. Five men, maybe six, hiding behind their own vehicle, popping around or up in synchronised patterns to fire at them. Kai was surprised they'd only hit the captain so far, and given how he was moving, they'd probably only grazed him.

Kai aimed her gun and fired.

One man toppled forward, dead.

Again, she aimed and fired.

Another man gave a cry and fell behind the vehicle. He didn't reappear.

Harley had moved and joined Kai's side, firing when the attackers showed themselves. They moved to press themselves behind the door, giving them some protection. Behind them, Kai could hear Crash talking to the captain.

Seph joined Kai and Harley, repeatedly firing his weapon. One more man went down.

Kai didn't pull her trigger. She knew how many bullets she had and she wasn't going to waste them. Instead, she waited.

Then, the gunfire stopped. Kai held her breath, listening.

'Is it clear?' came Bucky's voice behind them. Without replying or even a glance at Kai and Harley, Seph wandered down the ramp towards the vehicle. No one shot at him.

Harley joined him and Kai reluctantly followed.

'Dead,' said Seph, moving one corpse with the toe of his boot. 'Looks like they're dead.'

'Well, good,' murmured Bucky, watching from the doorway.

Harley looked at Bucky over his shoulder.

'Should I ask?'

They all ducked as a loud gunshot rang out. Harley and Seph both aimed their weapons at the source and found themselves aiming at Kai. She lowered her gun as the man behind Harley, his hand carrying his aimed gun still outstretched, crumpled to the ground.

Harley stared wide-eyed for a moment and then looked at Kai. She ignored him.

'Now they're all dead,' she murmured before turning and walking back up the ramp and back to her kitchen.

Bucky

They were in the air before Bucky had a chance to clean himself up and get to the med bay. Jude clucked her tongue at him as he sat down and gingerly took off his shirt to reveal his wound. She went straight to his shoulder, poking and prodding gently at the skin. Bucky winced.

'Did it go well?' she asked.

'I got shot.'

'Did we get paid?'

Bucky looked away.

'We did.'

Jude reached for a silver instrument that Bucky was all too familiar with. He gritted his teeth and took a deep breath.

'But?'

'But what?' mumbled Bucky. He let out a growl

as Jude inserted the silver tongs and carefully pulled out the bullet. It clattered into a nearby dish.

'You don't look happy. Something about the job didn't go well.' Jude straightened and looked her brother in the eye. 'Or the job went fine but the meeting after didn't?'

Bucky leaned his head back and closed his eyes. Couldn't this wait? Couldn't he have a moment of peace before the questions started?

'I really need to go talk to our passenger,' he said without opening his eyes. 'You should have seen her shooting. No way she was just a cook on her last ship.'

'You're changing the subject. This is serious, Bucky.'

Bucky opened his eyes and stared up at the ceiling. There was a damp stain in one corner that had been there since he'd got the ship. He narrowed his eyes, trying to judge if it had grown.

'I know it's serious. It's always serious. But damn that girl can shoot. If I'd have known, I could have taken her with me.' He looked down to Jude.

'We can't afford another merc,' she told him, wiping her surgical instruments.

'Might be we can't afford not to afford her,' he murmured. He grinned as Jude gave him a worried look. 'It's fine, sis. Don't you go worrying.'

'So? What happened?'

'We got full payment on the job and we have another job. It all went well.'

'Except they chased you and shot at you.'

'Ah, well. The shipment we delivered may have been damaged en route. They probably wanted a re-fund but our passenger decided to show us her true colours. Like I say, I need to chat with her.' He went to slide off the chair but Jude stopped him.

'Damaged en route? Bucky.'

He held up his hands.

'My fault. Purely my fault. I got desperate. We needed some money so I may have opened a crate and sold something inside.'

'Bucky!'

'We needed food, Jude. I wasn't drinking it away, or fucking it away, for that matter. I needed to feed the crew. And then we were running low on fuel, so…'

Jude stared at her brother.

'You need to tell them, Buck.'

'If I tell the crew, they'll leave. There are captains out there who can offer them better. And if they leave, we're dead. We won't fly again. You want that?'

'Who's going to leave, Bucky? I'm not going anywhere and neither is Seph. Crash will shout about it but she's all talk. Even if she does leave, you can fly us. Kai's leaving us anyway and Harley likes using us. You should ask him to pay us more for the trouble.'

'He pays us enough. He pays us in protection.'

Jude rolled her eyes.

'Protection doesn't keep us flying, Bucky.'

'Yes. It does.' Bucky hopped off the chair and winced as his shoulder throbbed. He gave his sister a fleeting kiss on the cheek and went for the door. 'Grub time. You coming?'

'We need to talk,' said Bucky as he walked into the mess. He stopped and snapped his mouth shut.

Crash and Seph were already seated around the table, Crash falling silent as the captain entered. Kai was placing steaming bowls of food around the empty plates. She looked at him, startled.

'Who you talkin' to there, Capt'n?' asked Crash.

'What's all this?' Bucky asked, opening his arms to encompass all the food on the table. Kai visibly squirmed.

'Dinner,' said Crash with a grin. 'The new girl came through.'

Kai wilted a little under Bucky's gaze and moved back into the kitchenette, only to reappear with yet more food.

Bucky took a deep breath in through his nose and felt the weight lift from his shoulders. Damn, but it smelled good. He tried to remember what he'd been saying when he walked in, but it was gone. He sat at the head of the table and watched Kai place more bowls in the centre.

'It's food from Aegirheim, Harley's homeland,' explained Kai in a quiet voice. 'I want to do the same for all of you, if that's okay. I thought it was a good way of getting to know you all. Even though I'm not staying.' Kai shrugged and went to move away.

Something clawed at Bucky's thoughts. Harley and Jude joined them, taking their seats. Harley didn't seem as shocked as Bucky had expected, but there was a hint of a smile that was rarely seen.

'What'd you need to talk about, Capt'n? Is it about why we got shot at today?' Crash was already helping herself, piling the food high onto her plate. Bucky watched her.

'Hmm? Oh. Oh, yes.' He looked up at Kai. 'You

never said you could shoot.'

Kai didn't make eye contact.

'Anyone can shoot a gun,' she said.

'Not like that. Someone taught you to shoot like that and then you must have had a lot of practise. You didn't say.'

Kai looked him in the eye and there was a pause.

'You didn't ask,' she said finally, moving away to sit at her place. 'Help yourself.' She gave Harley a smile before reaching to scoop potatoes onto her plate. The rest of the crew followed suit.

Bucky didn't move.

'Where did you learn to shoot like that?' he asked.

The others looked between their captain and the passenger.

'On my old ship,' said Kai in a soft voice.

'Your aunt's ship?' Crash piped up, her mouth full of food.

Kai nodded.

'The Reverent?' asked Bucky. Again, Kai nodded. 'Why'd you leave?'

A heavy silence fell over the table. Jude and Harley stopped eating.

Kai stared at her plate of food, her eyes flickering as she thought. She shot Crash a glance and the pilot closed her mouth.

'You don't have to tell us,' Jude said gently. She gave Bucky a meaningful look.

'No,' he said, piling his plate high with food. 'Might be good to have another merc around here, though. The pay's better than cook. Although.' He chewed a forkful of food and swallowed. 'You're a damn good cook. You know, if you wanted to stay.'

Crash raised an eyebrow and Bucky realised what he'd said.

'So, we can afford another merc but not a coil to keep us in the sky?'

Bucky waved a hand at her while he battled with a mouthful of food.

'The extra merc will help us get the coil.'

'So, we have another job?' she asked.

Without thinking, Bucky glanced at Harley. His eyes were down on his food.

'We have another job,' Bucky said carefully. 'And we'll get it done faster with more manpower.'

'Womanpower,' Crash corrected with a grin before opening her mouth wide to shovel in another forkful of food.

'Whatever. We finish this new job, we'll get the new coil.'

'Where's the new job, Capt'n?'

The crew turned to him expectantly. This time, Bucky glanced at Jude. Unlike Harley, she was watching him. She gave him a subtle, slight encouraging nod of the head.

'Another delivery job,' said Bucky. 'But don't you worry. We'll have that coil soon enough' He turned back to Kai. 'So, your last ship was your aunt's? That's where you're headed?'

'I told her we wouldn't ask questions,' said Jude.

'Well, that was stupid of you,' Crash mumbled loud enough for everyone to hear. Bucky smiled to himself but avoided looking at his sister. Instead, he glanced at Kai out of the corner of his eye. She was too good a shot to miss out on.

'All right. I won't ask,' he said. 'Except, would you want to stay on, as a merc?'

Kai pushed her food around.

'You don't have to answer that now,' Jude told her. Bucky gritted his teeth. Sometimes Jude's bedside manner forgot who was captain on this ship.

'I do need an answer,' he told Kai. 'Before we start this next job.'

'What is the job?' asked Crash.

'Only the mercs need to know for now. Don't you worry yourself with that. Just concentrate on keeping us in the sky.' Crash went to answer but Bucky held up one finger to silence her. 'I swear to all the gods, Crash, you mention that damn coil one more time.'

Crash went back to the food. It was damn good food.

'If you stay on, we might need you to stay on as cook too,' Bucky murmured. He was pretty sure he caught sight of a smile touching Kai's lips. Still, she said nothing.

The crew ate in silence for a while, until Crash could bear it no longer and began telling the others about how they'd come to be chased back onto the ship, guns blazing.

'Does that happen often?' Kai asked, pushing her empty plate away from her and sitting back.

'More often than I'd like. There's no pleasing some people,' said Bucky, helping himself to the last of the chicken chunks.

'We got paid though,' said Jude. 'That's what's important.'

Bucky pulled a face.

'Nice to get paid,' said Crash, saluting the captain with her drink before downing it.

'Always.' Bucky mirrored her, swallowing the last of the chicken and emptying his own cup. 'Now.' He slammed his hands down on the table. 'If you've work to do, then back to work. I almost feel bad leaving our temporary cook here to clean up this mess, but that's what she signed up for. Passage to Northhold, still? Or have we changed our mind?'

Kai didn't nod but nor did she shake her head. She glanced at him and seemed to drift off into her own world. Bucky decided to take that as a good sign.

'I'll be in my cabin,' he told the crew as Seph and Crash left the mess. Harley and Jude seemed to hover, as if they would help Kai tidy up. Bucky left them to it, taking his full belly to his bed where he could sit and ponder the decisions he'd made that day.

Jude

Harley stayed behind to help Kai tidy the kitchen, much to Jude's annoyance. They cleaned in silence for the most part, Jude unable to ask the questions that burned in her mind and Harley staying his usual quiet self.

Eventually, Harley took stock of the kitchen, nodded to himself and left the mess. Jude breathed and turned to Kai to find their passenger watching Harley leave. She glanced at Jude and went back to cleaning the worktop.

'You get used to his silences,' Jude said. Kai smiled and put her dishcloth away, looking around the kitchen.

'Would you like a drink?' she asked Jude.

'No. Thank you. You're off duty now. Relax.'

Kai's shoulders lowered and she plonked into

one of the chairs at the table, leaning back with a light groan. Jude pulled up a chair nearby and leaned her elbows on the wooden top. 'It would be good if you could take Bucky up on his offer.'

Kai smiled and stared down at the table. 'And if you go back to your aunt?' Jude continued. 'What happens then? Will the people you're running from keep tracking you down? I don't know if you'd be safer here—'

'I could be. He knows my aunt's ship. He'd expect me to leave you as soon as I could.' Kai frowned, still looking down at the table. 'But if that was him shooting at us…'

Jude shifted her position and leaned back, clearing her throat.

'I hate to say it this way, but if you signed on with us as a merc, Bucky would protect you.'

Kai met her eyes and Jude shrugged. 'We would protect you whatever, but you know what I mean.'

'He'd have an investment in me.'

'Yeah.'

'But you can't afford another crew member.'

Jude turned away and took a deep breath.

'Maybe. Maybe not. Often you have to invest in order to win the jobs, though.'

Kai nodded.

'How long have you been together? As a crew, I mean.'

'Four years, or maybe it's five now. Probably five since Bucky got The Magpie.' Jude looked around the mess fondly. 'Maybe four since Crash joined us. And Harley.'

'They were the last to join?'

'Yes. Bucky found Seph first, then I joined.

Then Crash and Harley. He found Crash in a bar, would you believe. Overheard someone talking about her racing days. She was looking for work but she was drunk and, well, you've met Crash sober. You can imagine her drunk. Harley was more official. He practically interviewed Bucky, as well as some other captains.'

'He rents his cabin?'

Jude moved to fill a glass with water.

'He does. Bucky found Seph on a landing pad. Similar to how you found us, I guess. He was looking for work, pretty desperate to get away.'

'How come?'

'I don't know. Seph hardly talks. I asked once. I would say I can't tell you, patient confidentiality and all that, but the truth is he never told me. We don't know much about Seph.'

'What about Harley?'

'Harley's on board in a professional capacity. It isn't our place to ask about him.' Jude could have sworn Kai rolled her eyes, but she hid it well. Jude frowned and sat back down.

'What about you?' Kai asked. 'You're Bucky's sister?'

'I am.'

'How did you end up on board this ship?'

Jude smiled.

'You know, I don't think any of us came here as a result of something good happening. I sometimes wonder what that means. People pulled together into tiny living quarters after their lowest moments, or something terrible happening.' Jude looked Kai up and down, remembering Kai's wedding dress, wondering what the truth was behind those stains and tears, and the bride who ran away.

'I guess that's why most people don't want to talk about it,' Kai murmured. She looked at Jude sideways. 'What's your story?'

Jude smiled.

'I don't think anyone's ever asked me that. Well, anyone except Crash. Crash asks everyone. Has she asked for your story yet?'

'She has.'

'Did you tell her?'

Kai hesitated.

'Was that a mistake?'

'It depends. I don't think so. Crash has a mouth on her but her heart's made of gold. I don't think she's told anyone what I shared with her.'

Kai watched Jude and Jude could feel the questions hanging heavy between them. Her lips almost moved to give the answers. She pressed them together. Kai wasn't part of the crew. Not yet. If Kai wasn't going to stay, where was the harm in telling her? Or in asking questions.

'Who are you running from?' Jude asked gently. As the silence dragged on, Jude looked up to find Kai smiling at her.

'That's the game Crash played,' said Kai. 'A question for a question. An answer for an answer.'

'I'm not playing a game,' Jude told her, keeping her voice soft. 'I'm a doctor.'

Kai leaned her elbows on the table.

'How long have you been a doctor?'

Now Jude smiled. This girl was clever, she thought. Clever and a good shot. She wondered if she would truly be a help or a hindrance in the crew. It might not do to have a merc on board who was a match for Bucky.

'I've always been a doctor,' said Jude. 'Since I left school. It was always a given.'

'A doctor on a ship like this?'

'No. I started in a hospital.'

'Whereabouts?'

Jude studied Kai.

'Where are you from?'

Kai sat back.

'I thought we weren't playing that game.'

Jude sighed.

'Diathan Falls. I was a doctor at the largest hospital.'

Kai considered this.

'That must have been good money. Why would you leave?'

Jude looked down at the table, memories nudging at her.

'Because not everything is about money. Yes, the money was good, but wealth doesn't mean you're healthy. Wealth doesn't mean you're happy. Wealth isn't a good reason to stay.'

Kai nodded.

'I get that.'

Jude narrowed her eyes.

'You do? How come?'

'The man I was supposed to marry is wealthy.'

Jude leaned forward, her elbows on the table.

'What does he do?'

'Well, he's not a doctor. That's a stressful job, I imagine. If you're in a big hospital.'

'You have no idea. Mix that together with a high profile fiancé and a massive reputation to maintain, and you'll be closer.'

'Sounds like an enviable life to some,' said Kai carefully.

'I think that was the problem,' murmured Jude. 'I was in an enviable position. People wanted to be me. Do you know what that's like? Everyone either treated me with disdain or wanted a piece of me. A piece of my time or advice or approval. And it was constant. Even when I was at home, the messages would come through or I'd have to lock myself away to write paper after paper. My fiancé was a psychologist, the best in his field. I was expected to spend every spare moment furthering my career and reputation, because that's what he did.' Jude looked up into Kai's eyes. 'I can understand the need to run away from a marriage, but I've never been sure if I was running away from him or the work.'

'The captain didn't have that pressure?'

Jude gave a small laugh.

'No. Bucky's the second born. The baby. I'm the first born. Our parents knew what I would be while I was still growing in our mother.'

Jude expected Kai to be disgusted or shocked. That was the usual reaction. Instead, Kai nodded knowingly, smiling to herself as she stared down at the wooden table top. 'You're not shocked by that?' Jude asked tentatively.

Kai met her eyes.

'No. It's not just people in Diathan Falls who have their children's destinies worked out before they're born.'

'No? What did your parents want you to be? They wanted you to marry this man?'

Kai looked away.

'My mother died a few days after I was born. My

104

father didn't want to decide who I was going to marry. He didn't want to decide anything about my future. He said that was up to me.'

'I'm sorry. About your mother.'

Kai didn't respond.

'How did you end up in that wedding dress if your father didn't want you to marry?'

Kai looked back up at Jude, her eyes hard and angry.

'He didn't get a choice. None of us did.' Her gaze softened. 'But you did. You made a choice to leave your fiancé?'

Jude nodded.

'Bucky turned up one day and told me he'd got this ship.' She gestured at the mess. 'I always could talk to him. About anything. So, I told him what I'd been thinking, what was going on, and he gave me an out. Because that's what we've always done for each other. We look after each other. He asked me to join his crew.'

'That's how you became a ship's doctor.'

'I guess.' Jude frowned to herself. She'd never considered herself a ship's doctor. She was a doctor. It didn't matter where she saw her patients, or who she was helping, as long as she was helping someone.

'Do you miss him?'

Jude looked up into Kai's eyes. Kai avoided her, still staring down at the table.

'My fiancé?'

Kai nodded.

'Sometimes. I loved him. A part of me will always love him. We had a wonderful romance. At the beginning, at least.' Jude left a few beats of silence. 'Do you miss yours?'

A smile spread on Kai's lips but it was sad and a little sickening. Jude swallowed.

'No.'

'Did you have a romance?'

Kai barked a laugh and then pressed her lips together tight.

'No.' She met Jude's eyes with a fierce stare. 'There's nothing good to miss. There was no love there. I barely knew him.'

'That doesn't sound like the basis of a good marriage,' Jude murmured. She reached out, as if she would touch Kai's hand but then changed her mind and withdrew. 'We won't let him find you. We'll do everything we can.'

Kai's eyes softened.

'Thank you. But you can't promise that, not really. Only the captain can promise that, and to him I'm just a passenger, soon to be out of his way.'

'Unless...'

'Unless I join the crew.'

Jude's shoulders dropped.

'This is a good crew.'

Kai looked shocked.

'I know. It's just... I wanted to go home. That's all.'

Jude stood and made her way into the kitchenette, refilling her water.

'And if you have a home to go to, that's what you should do. But the captain is offering you a new home, you know, in case the one you're heading to doesn't suit anymore. Or isn't safe anymore.' She turned back to find Kai staring thoughtfully at nothing.

'Would you go back? Given the chance?' she asked.

Jude's chest fluttered.

'No.'

Kai glanced at her.

'You must have left people behind. Other than your fiancé.'

Jude shrugged.

'My parents. That's all.'

Kai went back to studying the table. 'You have a lot of thinking to do,' Jude said, unwelcome memories of her old life swirling around her mind. 'And you have time to do that thinking.'

Kai gave a nod and then stood, stretching her arms above her head.

'I feel like I haven't slept in days.'

'No. You have catching up to do on that too. And you should do it here, while you're safe.'

Kai gave her a sideways look.

'What if my groom comes back and attacks the ship?'

Jude spluttered on her water. Wiping the droplets from her chin she gave a weak smile.

'That was a while ago now. I doubt he's followed us.' She ignored Kai's narrowed eyes and cleared the last of the water from her throat. 'I think I'll retire for the night too. I'll see you in the morning.'

'Right. Breakfast will be ready.'

Jude went to complain, to tell Kai to take it easy, but Bucky wouldn't approve of that. Kai had to pay her way, that was the arrangement, so Jude just gave a nod.

'Wonderful. Good night.'

'Good night.'

Jude left the mess and didn't look back. She stopped in the med bay to check everything was in its rightful place. It was, like always. Then she settled in her cabin, easing herself onto her bed, over the covers and blinking hard to disperse the memories.

Kai

The voices were loud but muffled. Still, she knew that echo. She knew those accents. She was back there, sitting on a bed. Kai took a deep breath and looked down, but there was no wedding dress. Not this time. What there was, however, was blood.

Kai dabbed the tip of her finger into the red patch and held it up, frowning. There hadn't been blood.

'No,' she whispered. This wasn't a memory. This wasn't one of those types of dreams.

Kai looked up as the voices grew louder. They were coming from outside the room. She strained to make out the words, to work out if she recognised them. There was a vague familiarity. She'd heard them before. They were the same men as before, but she couldn't hear *his* voice. She was glad of that.

The voices stopped on the other side of the door but didn't come in.

Kai moved to stand but as she did, the world shook. She fell back onto the bed, holding her head, her eyes screwed shut as the world shuddered loudly around her.

When she opened her eyes again, as her body became still, she found herself looking up into his eyes. He watched her with disinterest, his eyes grazing over her body and lingering between her legs.

Kai clenched her thighs together.

'You don't have to do this,' she told him. He met her gaze.

'Apparently I do. You could make this easier. Give yourself willingly.'

Kai shook her head without thinking.

Again, the world shuddered. It roared. He was on top of her, pinning her down and there, above them, ripping through the stone of the walls, was a large white monster.

It lowered its giant head to them, looked him in the eye, opened its mouth and gave a deafening high-pitch call.

Kai woke screaming and thrashing.

Tangled in her bed sheet, sweat covering her body, Kai sat up and looked around. She waited for her heart to stop pounding, concentrating on breathing slower. Still, her hands trembled as she lifted them to push back her damp hair.

She stopped and held her breath.

Had she screamed? Had she been loud?

Had the others heard?

She listened for the tell-tale footsteps. None came.

Kai laid back on her bed in a rush of exhale. She sat bolt upright again as there came a knock on her door.

'Kai?' came Jude's hushed voice. 'Kai? Are you okay?'

Then there came footsteps. Heavy. One of the men.

Kai groaned and took a moment to lament what was about to happen. She climbed from the bed as Jude knocked on the door again.

'What's going on?'

Bucky's voice. Damn, thought Kai, pulling on some clothes.

'You've heard as much as me,' said Jude before knocking again. 'Kai?'

Kai took another moment to take a deep breath and then she opened the door.

Bucky and Jude both immediately studied her, searching for any obvious injuries or explanations.

'Are you okay?' Jude asked, holding out her hand as if Kai might fall.

'I'm fine. I'm sorry. I didn't mean to wake anyone up.'

'Then don't scream in the middle of the night,' said Bucky. 'What happened?' He looked behind her and into her cabin.

Crash and Seph appeared behind the captain and, from the other direction, Harley slowly made his way up.

'Everything okay, Captain?' the lawman asked.

Bucky waved Harley away.

'It's fine. No intruders?'

Kai shook her head.

Bucky turned to Harley. 'It's fine. Everyone get back to bed.'

'Sounded like she was being killed,' Crash mumbled before yawning.

'I'm sorry,' Kai told them all, hugging herself. Opening the cabin door had allowed the cold air of the ship through her light cotton clothes, hitting her sweat and making her shiver. Jude watched with concern. 'I didn't mean to wake everyone up. Or anyone, for that matter. I'm sorry. It was a bad dream. That's all.'

Bucky scoffed.

'A bad dream?'

'Pah!' Crash turned to leave. 'You gonna cook another damn Aegirheim meal tonight, New Girl? Or is it someone else's turn? I like chocolate cake. That's the only thing that'll make me forgive you for getting me up in the middle of the night because you had a fuckin' bad dream.' Crash wandered back to her cabin before Bucky could chide her.

'Right. Everyone back to bed.' Bucky gave Kai one last look before nodding to Jude and herding Seph away. Harley lingered, averting his gaze from Kai and eventually turning and leaving.

Jude offered Kai a smile.

'Must have been some dream. Come to the med bay. Let me check you out.'

'I'm fine,' said Kai, hugging herself tighter.

'Really? Because that looks like blood.'

Kai looked down at herself, where Jude had pointed. There, in the exact same spot as in her dream, was a growing patch of red on her shirt. Dumbfounded, Kai dabbed at it with her finger.

That had never happened before.

'Med bay. Now,' Jude ordered, turning to lead the way.

Kai hesitated. She'd much rather stay put and investigate the bleeding herself but after a moment she silently followed Jude.

'You must have done this to yourself?' It was definitely a question, giving Kai the opportunity to say it was done to her, but there was only Kai in that cabin. Who else could have done it?

'I guess.'

Kai lay on the table, looking down at her own bare stomach where someone—presumably her—had created enough of an incision for it to bleed profusely.

'Why?' Jude gently cleaned the last of the blood away and peered closely at the cut.

'I don't know.'

Jude looked up at her.

'Do you do this often?'

'First time,' said Kai, completely honestly. She was as confused about it as Jude was. 'I must have done it in my sleep.'

'What was your dream about?'

Kai snapped her mouth shut before the words tumbled out. She shrugged.

'I don't really remember. I just remember being scared.'

Jude waited for Kai to continue. When she didn't, she straightened and fetched a large piece of gauze which she began patching over Kai's cut.

'You can talk to me, you know. About anything. It won't leave these walls. Bucky will never hear it.

I promise.'

Kai gave Jude a small smile.

'Thank you.' Still, she'd rather not share so much. Jude didn't seem to have a clue about the truth behind Kai's dream and Kai preferred it to stay that way. She moved to jump off the table.

'No!'

Kai froze.

'You stay there. Maybe get some sleep here.'

Kai stared wide-eyed at Jude.

'I'm fine. Honestly. I just want to go back to bed.'

'So you can do more damage to yourself? Open up that cut? Bleed some more?'

'I think the dream is over,' Kai lied.

'Better safe than sorry.'

'I'm not staying here.' Kai eased herself from the table and winced at the ache in her abdomen. 'What time is it? I'll go start on breakfast. That way I won't be sleeping. Okay?'

Jude considered this.

'It's too early.'

'Yeah, well, we don't exactly have a lot of food. I'll need time to figure out how I'm going to make it stretch,' Kai mumbled, wincing again.

'Don't move so much. And be careful. And if you start bleeding again, you come right back here. Or if the gauze falls off. Or—'

'Right. Will do. I'll be fine.' Kai went to leave but stopped and turned back to Jude. 'And thank you. I appreciate it.'

Jude gave her a nod.

'It's what I do.'

Wasn't that the truth, Kai thought as she made her way to the mess. Jude cared, and Kai couldn't help but wonder if she cared a little too much. That way would lead to a lot of stress, especially on a ship of crew members who weren't entirely law-abiding and were prone to getting shot at.

Standing in the doorway of the dark mess, Kai studied the shadows of the large dining table, the breakfast bar and the near-black kitchenette. In this low light, at this early hour, Kai could believe she was home. She half-expected her aunt to appear behind her, commenting on how she was up too early and had she had another bad dream? She saw her old crew's faces around the table and quickly shook her head, dispersing them. She didn't want to see them. Not now. Not like this.

But this might be the only way she saw them again.

Kai bit hard on her lower lip, until tears welled in her eyes but the thoughts were banished.

She couldn't go back to them, she realised. Turning on the light, she padded through the mess. Sitting at a stool at the breakfast bar, she tried to remember every aspect of her dream. Her stomach twisted.

Those hadn't been memories. Which meant that he was coming for her, and when he caught her, it was going to be bad.

She frowned at the memory of the large white beast. What had that been? She'd never seen anything like it, or heard of anything like it. It's roar had been alien enough to have made her scream without the thought of her groom-to-be pressing down on her from above.

Perhaps it was a representation. That could happen. A large beast symbolising her fear and pain at being caught again, at not being able to escape this time. That was the only explanation that made sense.

And that meant she couldn't go back. If that was her fate, then she could only fight it. But she couldn't bring her aunt and crew back into that chaos and danger.

Kai slid off the stool and made her way into the kitchenette, opening and closing cupboards. The cupboard with the dodgy hinge gave a creak and rattle. Kai held it up, making sure it wasn't about to clatter to the floor.

Dammit, there was hardly any food. There were only so many times she could ask Bucky for funds, for someone to go out and buy provisions while they were on the ground.

She wondered if his stance would change if she accepted his offer of joining the crew as a mercenary. Kai stopped and placed her elbows on the counter, her chin in her hands.

Should she accept? Could this crew help to protect her if she told them the truth? Well…most of the truth. Enough of the truth.

They had a lawman on their side. Harley alone could be enough. But they would be outnumbered. Kai sighed and straightened. She needed more information about Bucky and his intentions, not to mention more food to fill the cupboards.

There had to be a way to get more food.

Of course, there were always ways.

Kai wondered just how unlawful this crew really

was. Seph wouldn't talk and she could hardly ask Harley. Going to Bucky might be too much too soon, but Kai knew someone in the crew who talked easily. Someone with the brains to help her work this out and the passion to put it before Bucky. Yes. Kai smiled, reaching into the cupboards and pulling out what was left of the flour and sugar. Digging deep into the back, she found an old tin of cocoa powder. The small print said it was a few years old, but Kai was sure cocoa powder couldn't become toxic. The milk and eggs were a problem, but she'd just have to find a way to do without.

First, Kai made a fresh pot of coffee, strong and black. Then, she started baking, taking her time and turning the ideas over and over in her head.

Crash

'Oh, New Girl, don't toy with me,' said Crash, gliding into the mess with her nose in the air and taking deep breaths. She stopped as Kai struggled to keep the smile from her face. 'Is that a chocolate cake baking or am I dreaming?'

'It's a chocolate cake.'

Crash gave a whoop and landed on one of the bar stools, pouring herself a cup of coffee. She hesitated and sniffed it.

'This is stronger than before.' Crash looked up at Kai again, narrowing her eyes. 'This is exactly how I like it.'

Crash sipped at the coffee. The new girl wanted something but Crash wasn't the type to pass up on all her favourite things. It wasn't often that people lavished her with strong coffee and chocolate cake.

Actually, that had never happened. She eyed Kai warily.

'Good.'

'Why?' Crash hadn't meant to ask. She'd meant to simply enjoy it, but the question fell out of her mouth before she had time to think. Like most words did.

'I want to accept the captain's offer to join the crew.' Kai spoke carefully. Crash waited, knowing there was more to come.

'But?'

'I think I need more information about Bucky first.'

Crash sipped her coffee. It warmed the inside of her mouth, then throat and stomach as she swallowed. It was damn good coffee.

'What kinda information?' Crash glanced up at Kai. 'You into him?'

Kai's eyes widened.

'No! Not that kinda information. More like…' Kai waved her arms around as if she could pluck the right words from the air. Her arms dropped as she sighed. Crash watched her.

After a pause, she said, 'Is that cake ready yet?'

'No. Not yet.' Kai leaned on the worktop. 'I'm in trouble, Crash. I can't go home. I can't take this back to my aunt. It'll be worse if that trouble catches up to me and I'm there instead of here. So I'd like to stay. But if that trouble does catch me up…' She looked up into Crash's eyes.

Crash's heart fluttered.

'You think we wouldn't protect you?'

Kai shrugged.

'The trouble chasing me? It has money, and it

seems the capt'n doesn't. So…'

Crash faltered.

'Capt'n is some things,' she told Kai. 'But he would never sell out his own crew. Not Bucky Winters. That man's as loyal as they come to us. You don't know yet, 'cos you ain't officially one of us. But you join us, join the pathetic payroll, and you'll see it.'

Kai still looked worried. Without looking at Crash, she turned and opened the oven. Crash's stomach grumbled as the strong smell of cooking chocolate filled the mess. Kai put the cake on the worktop, gave it a prod and then left it to cool. Crash didn't think it needed cooling, years of coffee abuse meant her mouth could cope with food straight from the oven. Still, she let it settle, turning her attention back to Kai.

'What trouble're you in? This about that man you were supposed to marry?'

Kai nodded.

'I think he's coming after me.'

'Well, yeah, he shot at us.'

The shift in Kai's expression was subtle but Crash saw it. 'You don't think that was him?'

'He's not the type to put effort into chasing a person, shooting at them and not taking them down, or getting what he came for. It just…it doesn't feel right. But maybe. I guess. What do I know.'

'You know the man,' Crash pointed out. 'Hell, we've never met him. We don't even know his name. But you do. You know him. Even if you don't love him or whatever. Even if you hardly knew him before they chucked you in that wedding dress. You still know him better than us. And if you don't think he'd come after us, then there it is.'

In which case, thought Crash, who had been shooting at them?

'I guess,' Kai murmured. 'What if he does come? What if it's less trouble for the capt'n to just hand me over?'

Crash's features darkened. There were a lot of things in this world that twisted her gut and one of them was the soiling of Captain Bucky Winters' name.

'He's not that man. He's a good man and a good capt'n. Best I've ever known. Plus, he wouldn't just hand over the best shooter on the ship,' Crash added.

Kai smiled.

'Seph's good.'

'Meh.'

'Harley's good.'

'He's technically not crew.'

'You're good.'

'Yeah, I am. And yet you didn't say me first.'

Kai laughed.

'No. Sorry about that. Guess I'd rather you were flying us away from trouble than us all shootin' at it.' She glanced back to the cake. 'So, am I forgiven? For waking you up?'

'I dunno. Haven't tasted it yet.' Crash flashed a grin at Kai. 'What was the dream? Can't say a nightmare's ever made me scream before. Must have felt real.'

Kai's eyes flickered down. Crash waited, taking a gulp of coffee.

'Just a dream.' Kai looked back up. 'Shall I make you some breakfast?'

'You already have.'

'You want cake for breakfast?'

'Yeah, I do. 'Cos some new girl woke me up by screaming her lungs out. Not the best way to be woken.'

Kai smiled at her.

'If I join the crew, will you stop calling me "New Girl"?'

Crash grinned and topped up her coffee.

'Oh no. Not until you've passed your probation.'

'There's a probation?'

'Nah. Not with the capt'n, but with me. Give it a month, maybe less, and you won't be a new girl anymore.'

Kai screwed up her lips, as if holding back from pulling a face at Crash.

'What was scary about the dream?' Crash tried again. Kai had been quite open, considering. Crash thought it strange that she should clam up now, all because of a dream.

'Memories,' said Kai. 'That's all. Memories.'

'Of the trouble following you?'

Kai nodded.

'Memories and my brain playing tricks on me. Nothing really.' Kai's hand went absent-mindedly to her stomach. Crash watched, frowning.

'You okay?' she murmured.

When Kai met her gaze, Crash indicated her hand on her stomach.

'Oh. Oh, yeah.'

'Did he… ?' Crash didn't finish the question. She'd never been good with this stuff, but it turned out she didn't need to be. Kai knew what she was asking.

'No. He hurt me, but not like that. I, erm…' Slowly, Kai lifted her shirt.

Crash moved to the edge of her seat, her mind whirring with the possibilities of what Kai was doing. She relaxed when she saw the gauze taped to Kai's abdomen, then she shifted to lean closer.

'I hurt me,' Kai told her. 'During the bad dream, I must have scratched it. Or something. I dreamt of blood and then I woke up bleeding.' She dropped her shirt and shrugged.

'Well.' Crash sat back. 'That'd sure make me scream.'

There was a pause as Kai turned to cut the cake. Crash waited, trying to slot Kai mentally into their little family. A plate with a slice of chocolate cake was slid over to her and Crash looked up, giving Kai a grateful smile. Kai handed her a fork.

'Take the capt'n up on his offer,' said Crash, sliding the fork into the cake. 'Do your job, join our family and we'll protect you. Can't say fairer than that.' She popped a forkful of warm sponge cake into her mouth.

The taste of chocolate spread over her tongue and Crash couldn't contain the smile as she swallowed, lifting her fork for the next mouthful.

'You're forgiven,' she said.

Kai laughed.

'Well, thank the gods for that.' She leaned her elbows on the worktop and watched Crash eat.

'How long has the crew been low on funds?'

Crash paused in her eating, meeting Kai's eyes.

'You mean, can the capt'n afford to pay?'

'I mean, how long are we gonna be flyin' for? You said something about us needing an engineer.'

'An engineer, some parts, yeah. One or the other, at least.'

'Is this a one-off, or are we always about to fall out of the sky?'

Crash chewed her cake slowly and swallowed, trying to judge what response to give.

'Not always, but sure, this situation has been going on for some time. That ain't the capt'n's fault though. Our old engineer left us high and dry, no warnin'. He just left the ship one day and didn't come back. Took stuff with him, too. Tools, money, stuff we needed.' Crash took a gulp of coffee and filled her fork with cake. 'Nuffin' we could do about that. Other than keep workin'. That's what we're tryin' to do. That's where you can help. The pay ain't great but you get a roof over your head, food in your belly, Capt'n always makes sure we're provided for. There's a lot to be said for family.'

Kai nodded.

'I know. I'd choose a safe place over good pay every time.'

Crash watched her carefully.

'Capt'n says we just need one big job. Just that one job and we'll be back on track. He'll pull us out of this. You'll see. But we'll need you for that job.'

'And that job will pay to fix the engine, fill the cupboards and pay for an engineer as well as your new merc? That's gotta be one big job,' Kai pointed out.

Crash shrugged.

'Maybe. But I'd forfeit my salary if it'd fix the ship. To pay for that engineer. I bet others would too. Doc certainly would. Seph don't care much about the money. Capt'n can use our salaries from that one job to get us sorted if he wanted.'

Crash frowned. She hadn't ever given serious consideration to giving up her salary, although she was sure she'd mentioned it to the captain before. Maybe after a few too many beers. She couldn't remember Bucky's response. 'But like I say, we'd need you on board to get that job done quickly and right. We'd need your aim.'

'I do that, I help you get the job done and the ship fixed, and then I'm part of the crew. And you'll help keep me safe?'

'I guess.' Crash stared down at her cake and coffee. There was so much to consider and Kai was asking all the wrong questions. Unless she was keeping something from them. Crash blinked. She hated secrets, they exhausted her and were unnecessary. She looked back up at Kai. 'So, you're gonna join?'

'Probably. One more question.'

'Go on.'

'Why work the jobs? If you're that desperate to fix the engine and put food in these cupboards, and you lot are what you say you are, why not just steal the money?'

Crash stopped with the fork halfway to her mouth.

Kai had a point. Why hadn't they stolen the money? Crash was pretty sure Bucky was hiding things. They had never been the most honest crew, so why not do the most obvious thing?

Crash ate the forkful of cake and chewed thoughtfully.

'You know what. You have a good point. Why don't we just steal it?' She swallowed her mouthful.

'Good cake, New Girl.' Crash pushed the empty plate back towards Kai and then dabbed up the last few crumbs with a finger which she stuck in her mouth. 'Maybe I should ask the capt'n about that.'

Kai blinked at Crash.

'Oh. No. I didn't mean to cause trouble.'

Crash hesitated, wondering how true that was. Still, Crash made her own decisions. No one could make her do anything, and what Kai had said was true. Why couldn't they just steal the money?

'No trouble. Just a little chat with the Capt'n, that's all.' Crash gave Kai a smile, she could already feel her blood pumping.

All this time, all this trouble, all these worries, and Bucky could have fixed this with such ease. There would have been work to find the right target, but Bucky could have done that. That was what he did. He found the jobs, he brought the money in.

Crash slid off her stool and skulked out of the mess as Kai watched. Harley bumped into her as he appeared in the doorway. She mumbled what should have been an apology but the words got lost in her busy thoughts. Harley stood aside to let her go and she made her way straight to the captain's office.

Bucky

'Capt'n?'

Bucky flinched and stopped writing at the sound of Crash's voice. She stormed into his office, flinging the door open and standing over him. He looked up at her, placing down his pen.

'Yes, Crash? What's wrong?'

'I have a question, Capt'n.'

'That's a mighty entrance for one question.'

'It's a mighty question.'

Bucky leaned back in his chair and crossed his arms.

'Go on then.'

'We can't afford an engineer.'

'You know we can't.'

'And we can't afford a new coil to fix the ship.'

'Not right now.'

'And the passenger's on about our cupboards being empty.'

Bucky rubbed the back of his neck.

'It's true that we're a bit low on food right now. But that'll change soon.'

'Will it? How soon?' Crash crossed her arms, tapping her toe on the floor. Bucky looked her up and down, pursing his lips.

'Soon.'

Crash tutted and leaned down, palms flat on the desk.

'When though, Capt'n? You've been sayin' soon a long time now. You keep sayin' just one more job. Well, we just did a job. And you said you've got another job. Surely, we've got enough for somethin' now? Even if it's just fillin' the cupboards?'

Bucky exhaled hard through his nose and looked down at the open ledger on his desk. It was filled with numbers.

'If we wait until we finish this new job, we could afford the coil and the engineer, and all that food.'

'And when will we finish that?'

Bucky sighed again.

'Soon.'

Crash muffled a scream. It came out as a growl. Bucky didn't react, he was used to Crash having these tantrums, and he could understand this one. Crash was right. He'd been looking at the figures, and he could have filled the cupboards and paid their salaries with their latest payment. But the ship could still fall out of the sky at any moment.

'When, Capt'n? I don't ask for a lot—' Bucky stifled a laugh. '—and I don't think I'm askin' for a lot now. Just a timeframe.'

'I don't know, Crash. Not long.'

''Cos we don't have long, Capt'n.'

'I know, I know. Why are you suddenly here saying all this, anyway? What's gotten into your head?'

Crash relented a little, standing straight and looking for the chair that usually sat opposite Bucky's desk. She collapsed into it, crossing her legs and examining a fingernail.

'Nuffin'. Just been talking to Kai. The new girl.'

'I know who Kai is,' Bucky muttered.

'Yeah, well, she mentioned how we still don't have much food, and…'

'And?'

Crash avoided Bucky's gaze. 'Crash. If you know something, you should tell your captain. Come on. And, what? Is it about how she woke us all up last night screaming the ship apart? I mean, what in the gods was that about? What does that girl dream?'

Bucky had been thinking about Kai's rude awakening since he'd returned to his cabin. He hadn't been able to get back to sleep, and his thoughts twisted and turned from Kai's scream to the ship's finances. That was nothing new. No matter what there was to think about, his mind would always return to the ship's finances.

'She dreams horrible things, Capt'n, 'cos she's been through some horrible things.'

Bucky met Crash's eye.

'What's she told you?'

'Not for me to say, Capt'n.'

'Fair enough. So, all this because the cupboards are bare?'

Crash shifted in the chair. That obviously wasn't all. 'Crash. Tell me what's going on. That way I can tell you the same thing I've been tellin' you all this time and we can both get on with our days.'

'She says she wants to join the crew, as a merc, but she needs protection,' Crash blurted. She snapped her mouth shut, her cheeks flushing. That, along with the soft blonde hair cut up in spikes, almost made her look cute. If you liked that sort of thing.

A small voice in Bucky's mind, most likely his libido which was admittedly a little starved these days, considered Crash. It instantly dismissed her.

'Protection from the man she stood up?'

Crash's features darkened.

'You don't know what that man did to her, Capt'n.'

'Do you?'

'Not my place to say.'

Bucky gritted his teeth.

'Any idea who this man is? Does he have any power?'

Crash shrugged.

'She wouldn't say.'

'Not sure how much protection we could offer then.'

'Maybe talk to her then? If you're sayin' we need a good shot for this next job, then we should have her. And all she wants is the promise that we'll protect and defend her. Far as I can see it, best we can do is try. You know, not knowing who this man is, and all.'

'She's such a good shot,' mused Bucky. 'Why didn't she shoot him? Why didn't the crew that taught her to shoot kill him? Shouldn't they have protected her? Maybe this man isn't just a man, maybe he has a crew of his own.' And I bet they don't have financial problems, thought Bucky, his gaze flickering back down to the ledger.

'What if he never comes?' Crash offered. 'We'd get one hell of a merc.'

'What if he does come?'

Crash leaned forward in her chair.

'That was him shooting at us before, huh?'

Bucky blinked. Did she know? How could she?

'I don't know. Who else could it be?'

'Dunno, Capt'n. You tell me. It seems to me that lately there's being secrets kept on this ship, and I don't like it. I don't like secrets. New girl's got 'em, but right now she's allowed 'em. Maybe she'll come clean if she joins us. But you, Capt'n. I thought you'd tell us if something came up. I thought we had a mutual respect thing goin' on.'

Bucky's fingers ached to punch something. He needed time to think this one through, but that was something Crash was never able to give. Where was Jude when he needed her? Or a welcome distraction, just a little one, that was all he needed. He waited, just in case.

Nothing happened.

Should he come clean? He tapped his fingers on the desk.

'Capt'n, what's going on?' Crash murmured. He'd expected her voice to be sharp and demanding but instead she sounded scared. He looked up at her. 'We got no food, we're about to fall out of the sky and now you're keepin' secrets? What've you got to lose by tellin' us?'

Bucky smiled.

'Everything,' he told her in almost a whisper. 'My ship. My crew. Everything.'

'Capt'n, we fall out of the sky, you lose all of that anyway.'

Bucky leaned forward and ran his fingers through his hair. The woman had a point.

'So, Kai's in trouble. Well, she ain't the only one,' said Bucky, still unsure of how much he was going to share. For once, Crash kept quiet. Patient, even. 'We're in the red. No money whatsoever. Well, that ain't strictly true, we got enough to put some food in our bellies and for me to pay your wages, from that last job. But that's it. And the food won't last. Been this way for a while, if I'm honest, but I didn't want to say.' He waited to see if Crash would ask why, but she remained quiet, watching him, waiting for more. 'This new job I got, it's a big one. I've said that before, I know. Usually a big job pays for a few months of food and salaries, maybe fix the engine once, keep us re-fuelled. All that. This job is bigger than that.'

Crash's eyes widened.

'Will we stay flyin' long enough to finish it?' she asked.

'That ain't the question,' Bucky told her. 'The question is whether we'll… The question…' Bucky sighed, not sure how to finish that sentence without Crash leaving in a fit of rage and running to tell the crew. 'This job is trouble, Crash. Big trouble. Kai might not be the only one in need of protection, and we've got no one to ask for help.'

Crash took a moment to think and Bucky waited. Eventually, Crash smiled.

'What?' Bucky asked.

'Ever thought to ask your crew about this, Capt'n?'

Bucky sighed long and deep, closing his eyes.

'Was scared you'd all run.'

Crash barked a laugh.

'Run! Where're we gonna go?' She was grinning now. Bucky didn't know whether to take comfort from it or to feel mocked. 'Capt'n, no one's runnin'. We're family. You seem to have forgotten that somehow. You could've asked us. We could've helped. This could've been over long ago.'

'Oh yeah? You got contacts you've been holding back on?'

'Well, no. But it sounds to me like we need protection, say, from a sharpshooter. Seems like we got one of those in the mess. And it sounds to me like she needs protection, from a crew. Seems to me like she's got one right here waitin' for her. I don't see the problem.'

Bucky opened his mouth to tell Crash that it wasn't that easy but he stopped, slowly closing his mouth, his gaze going distant. Could it really be that simple?

'Sounds like there's detail missing,' he suggested.

'Detail's the stuff you figure out as you go,' said Crash. 'Life's too short for detail.'

Bucky nearly laughed. Instead, he kept it behind a smile.

'True. True.'

'So, this big job that'll fix everything might take some time. Capt'n, why don't we just steal the money? We can take it off a bigshot or somethin'.

Why ain't we ever tried that?'

Bucky looked at Crash curiously.

'It crossed my mind, a few times. There's a big bank in Diathan Falls that's askin' for it. Other places that are easier but smaller targets.'

'So?'

'So, this big job we've got, it's not the type of job where you draw attention to yourself. A robbery could go wrong in so many ways, and if it does, the authorities will know us, maybe even catch us. We won't be able to do this job.'

'So, the client will find someone else.'

'No, Crash. That's what I'm sayin'. They'll find someone else, sure, but they'll find us along the way and make sure we don't talk. About anything. Ever again.'

Crash blinked at Bucky.

'What kind of job is it?' she asked, her voice getting higher.

'Like I said. Trouble.'

Crash gaped.

'We could have just gone robbin'!' she squealed, standing up.

'Crash. Calm down.'

'If we got caught, we'd be locked up, sure, but we'd get out. You can't get out of being dead!'

'Crash. Calm.'

'And what about—' Crash leaned back down on Bucky's desk, lowering her voice. 'What about Harley?'

'Well, he's not going to find out, is he? You're not going to tell him, are you?'

'But you're gonna tell Seph. And Kai. And offer Kai that damn job and protection. I assume the doc

134

already knows, seeing as how she knows everythin' before us.'

'Jude knows. I'll tell Seph.' He would be easier to tell than Crash in many ways. For one, he wouldn't scream in Bucky's face. 'And I'll talk to Kai. Okay?'

Crash straightened and thought it through, her lips tight.

'I guess that's okay.'

'Good. Okay. Go make sure we're on course. I'll let you know when we need to change direction.'

'Where're we goin'?'

Bucky closed the ledger.

'We need supplies, so we'll be landing at Northhold before we start. I'll talk to Seph and Kai before then, don't you worry. Just go do your job and I'll do mine.'

Crash narrowed her eyes.

'Make sure you do, Capt'n. Worries me when I have to come remind you how to do it.'

Crash turned on her heel and left the office as quickly as she'd entered. Bucky collapsed back into his chair with a rushed exhale.

That wasn't quite how he'd envisioned that going, but all in all, it hadn't been too bad. Maybe he needed to give Crash more credit, talk to her more often. If this worked, that was. He stood, wondering if Seph was up yet.

Harley

Harley hadn't spoken. It had been roughly eight minutes since Crash had walked into him as he'd entered the mess. He'd gone with the idea of grabbing a coffee and getting back to his cabin to do some work, but something had made him sit at the breakfast bar. He sipped his coffee in silence. It was too strong and the mess smelled of warm chocolate.

Kai had given him a smile as he'd arrived and poured his coffee. She glanced at him every now and then but was otherwise preoccupied.

He cleared his throat.

'I'm sorry,' she said before he could find his voice to ask what she was doing.

'What for?' Harley pulled a face at his coffee as he swallowed another mouthful, the bitterness twisting his lips.

'Last night. I didn't mean to wake everyone up.'

'It's okay. You couldn't help it. Are you okay?'

Kai glanced over her shoulder to him with another smile.

'I'm fine. Thank you.'

'It was a bad dream?'

'Yes.'

'Is there any milk?'

Kai turned to face him, following his gaze down to the coffee.

'Oh. Right. Sorry about that.' She passed him a light carton. There wasn't much milk left. When was Bucky getting more provisions? Harley poured a minimum amount of milk in, just enough to make it bearable.

'Did Crash make this?' he asked. He looked up, wide-eyed as Kai laughed. She stopped when she saw his expression.

'Sorry. No. I made it, but I made it with Crash in mind. Sorry about that.'

'No problem.'

There was a pause. A silence. Drawing out awkwardly as Harley considered different questions he could ask. He wasn't used to this on this ship. It was something of a novelty, having someone he could talk to. He talked to Jude sometimes, but she could be so serious. Not that that was bad. There was something about Kai's smile, though, that made Harley miss sharing a joke. It had been a long time, it seemed. It almost made him want to go find Crash, to let her talk at him. Almost. Harley didn't move. He stayed in the mess, alone with Kai, trying to work out what to say to her. He took a deep breath to sigh and the heavy smell of baked chocolate filled his nostrils.

'It smells of chocolate in here.'

'Is that a bad thing?'

'No. It's just…unusual.'

'I baked a chocolate cake for Crash. She said she'd forgive me for waking her up if I baked her a chocolate cake.'

Harley grinned. He hadn't smiled that hard in a long time, he realised, and his mouth ached with the effort. Still, it felt good, amazing even, as if the grin started on his face but eventually filled his whole body.

'That's good of you. Taking her seriously.'

'It's not that good. I also wanted a favour from her.'

'Oh. What was that?' Harley hadn't meant to pry but asking questions came naturally.

'Just some background. About the capt'n's job offer.'

Harley watched Kai as she went back to whatever it was she was doing. He guessed she was preparing some sort of breakfast for the crew. She wasn't slight, as such, but neither was she big. She didn't look particularly strong, either. It was a genuine shock that she was such a good shot. Harley wouldn't have pegged her for a fighter. A cook, maybe, a bride, definitely—she was pretty, her golden red hair bouncing around the pale skin of her cheeks and bare shoulders—but not a fighter. Harley smiled to himself. Watch out for the redheads. That's what his mother had once told him. Kai glanced back at him and Harley sharply averted his gaze, back down to his coffee.

'Are you going to accept the captain's offer?'

'I don't know.' Kai stood in front of Harley, thoughtfully wiping the worktop. 'What do you think I should do?'

'It's a good crew.'

'You've never had any problems with them?'

'No. The opposite, actually. Bucky kinda saved me.' Harley snapped his mouth shut and then drank from his coffee cup to make sure no more words slipped out. Kai eyed him curiously.

'Funny, that. He kinda saved me too.'

Harley relaxed a little.

'Pretty sure he saved Jude. And Seph and Crash.'

'That's what this crew is then? A group of misfits that the capt'n collected outta the goodness of his heart?'

'And they just so happen to be the best doctor, the best pilot and one of the best mercs. Not a bad crew to join, if you ask me. I'd probably accept, but then, I'm not running from the same things you are.'

'What are you running from?'

Harley flinched. Crash had asked him about his past a few times but he'd learned that if you left a long enough silence, she'd be forced to fill it and the conversation would move on. Jude had asked, but only politely, followed by stating that he didn't have to share. It was as if they were scared to ask. Everyone was always scared to ask. Or ashamed.

'My old life, I guess,' he said, thoughtfully. 'I don't know. I've been running so long that maybe I've forgotten.'

'I doubt you could forget.'

Harley looked into Kai's eyes. They were green, bright and deep at the same time.

'No,' he murmured. 'I could never forget.'

Another long pause as they stared at one another. Harley allowed himself to wonder if this could mean something. He hadn't been with a woman since he'd been freed, he'd forgotten the rush of meeting someone. Was this what that was?

'What about you?' he asked. 'You're running from a man.' He regretted the words as Kai looked away.

'You could say I'm running from a fate, or am I running to my family? No. I was runnin' to my family. Now I don't know where I'm runnin' to.'

'I guess this crew have that in common too. They don't seem to know where they're heading.'

'But you do.' Kai looked back to him. 'You're a lawman. You have a purpose.'

Harley lifted his shoulders in a shrug.

'I've spent my life lost. Now I'm finding myself.'

'Same as us,' whispered Kai, giving him a private smile.

Harley smiled back.

'You're a good cook,' he murmured. 'That cake smells good. Couldn't have been easy. I'm told we don't have much by way of ingredients.'

'No. Crash seemed happy with it.'

'So, when are you going to cook us something from your homeland?'

Kai snapped round to look at Harley.

'I hope the meal I cooked was okay, from Aegirheim.'

'My mother couldn't have done better. That's why I ask. You're getting to know us, but if you're going to join the crew, we should get to know you.'

Kai looked away, returning to tidying the kitchenette.

'I'm sorry. I didn't mean to pry.' Harley sat back. He'd said too much. It wasn't a common complaint of his; he was usually so good at feeling his way through a conversation, taking what he needed, giving as little as possible. Could it be, he thought, that Kai had broken that in him. He'd already revealed more to her than to anyone else.

'Maybe. One day,' she murmured.

She was from somewhere small then, he realised, if she couldn't even tell them where without them guessing things about her.

'You're not of Aegirheim too, are you?' he asked, studying her again. Her red hair meant that she could be. His people were on the fair side, even if their skin was usually a little darker.

'No.'

His mind raced through other countries, cities with troubled pasts.

'Surely, it can't hurt to tell us where you're from?'

Kai twisted her lips.

'No. No, I suppose not. It's such a small country, most people haven't even heard of it. And even if they have, many don't know its history.' She looked up into Harley's eyes. 'I'm from Decima.'

Harley remained quiet a moment, working through what he knew of the country. It was tiny, he knew that. So tiny that it consisted of one city of the same name, nestled inside a valley with sides so high and thick with forests that the country was effectively cut off from the world. That was how it had stayed so different, out of the control of main governments. It had no financial worth, not that anyone knew about anyway. He met her gaze.

'I've heard of it. But you're right, I don't know much about it. What's the main dish there?'

Kai relaxed, smiling and shaking her head.

'It depends on the family. The poor tend to eat mushrooms and pork. We raise good pigs and we're surrounded by forest where we get a lot of food.'

'I'd love to try some.'

Kai shook her head again, this time without the smile.

'I couldn't get the right mushrooms. Or pork. But I suppose I could make a variation.'

Harley nodded.

'You should.'

'Okay.' Kai glanced back to the hob. 'What would you like for breakfast? We don't have any eggs or porridge, but there is some bread. It's going stale but I could toast it. I do have some meat, but I wanted to save that for tonight and tomorrow.'

'Toast is good,' said Harley.

Kai set to work preparing it, lighting the grill and placing slices of bread beneath it.

'We were close to Decima when we picked you up,' mused Harley, still thinking, watching her. 'Had you come from there? Is that why your dress was torn? You'd been running through the forest. You knew the way out because you'd grown up there.'

'No. I didn't grow up there. I left when I was six. The paths are obvious, I just had to hope I was taking the right one and I would find some sort of vehicle or civilisation. Eventually I made it to Valkwick and the landing pad.' Kai turned her back on the grill and crossed her arms. 'But yes, I had to run through brambles at one point, and through a river. Thankfully not too deep.'

Harley rubbed at his blonde beard, twirling one of the beads braided into the hair as he thought.

'Why did you leave when you were six?'

For a moment, Kai appeared caught, as if realising what she'd said.

'My father thought it would be best, and my aunt offered to take me.' She turned back to the grill, taking out the toast and finding some of the cheap butter Bucky had bought a while ago.

'Why?' Harley watched her. Everything about her told him that she didn't want to talk about it, but Harley couldn't help himself. Kai sighed, her shoulders heaving. She turned back and handed him a plate of buttered toast.

'You know, I was told when I got on this ship that no one would ask questions.'

Harley smiled.

'Sorry.'

'You're a detective. I get it. But I'm not someone you're investigatin'. You don't need to question me.'

'It's not about that,' Harley told her. His mind screamed at him to quieten, he was going to share too much again. 'Back before we were freed, we had our own community. A sort of village. There were injustices, of course. People often came to me to fix them.'

'You brought justice?'

Harley took a bite from a slice of toast.

'I just wanted to protect people.' He swallowed. 'That's what your father was doing?'

Kai hugged herself.

'I was betrothed before I was born. It was seen that I would give the… That I would have a son. So I was betrothed.'

'Seen? By who?'

Kai's lips twitched.

'My mother.' She turned away and began cleaning the already clean worktop. Harley chewed his toast thoughtfully. He could have asked more, he could have persisted, but he didn't need to. Enough had been said. He picked up his plate.

'Thank you, for the toast. I'm sorry to pry.'

'No.' Kai turned back to him. 'No, it's okay.'

'I best get back to work.' Harley offered her smile and then left without looking back.

Jude

Jude slammed the drawer of her desk shut as there was a rap on the door. She turned, swallowing, to find Harley stood in the doorway.

'Harley. Good morning. Is everything okay?'

If Harley noticed Jude's panic, he didn't say anything.

'Do you have a moment?'

'Of course. Come on in. Close the door if you like.'

Harley did so. He didn't sit but stayed by the chair and crossed his arms against his chest.

'What can I help you with?' Jude asked when Harley didn't appear forthcoming. She leaned back in her own chair.

'Kai. The passenger. Has she told you anything about her dream last night?'

Jude narrowed her eyes and leaned forward.

'I can't tell you that, Harley. You know that.'

'Even as professionals?'

'Even as professionals.'

'Even if her life depends on it?'

Jude blinked.

'What do you know?'

'I couldn't possibly tell you, Doctor, you know that.'

Jude twisted her lips. Damn him. Everyone on this ship thought Harley to be quiet, a ghost. They didn't know him like she did.

'How manipulative of you,' she muttered.

Harley's expression didn't change. He pulled himself up onto the surgery table. He was so tall that the toes of his boots grazed against the floor.

'Okay. What do you know of Decima?'

Jude frowned.

'Not a lot. It rings a bell. What of it?'

'It's where Kai was born. Where she ran from.'

'Okay. And?'

'It's a small country, one of the smallest. It has one settlement, a city. They have a royal family, probably the last place on the continent that does.'

'Fine. What does this have to do with Kai?'

'Their religion isn't a religion as such,' continued Harley, as if not hearing her. Jude sat back again, biting on the inside of her cheek, running her tongue over her teeth. 'They have priestesses.'

'How do you know all this?'

'I met a man from there once.'

Jude blinked. Where could he have met a man from Decima? 'He told me about these priestesses.

He'd not lived there for a good few years at that point and was beginning to see his homeland in a different light.'

'And what does this have to do with Kai?'

'The priestesses are important because they're known to see the future. They call them the Visionaries.' Harley paused, watching Jude. She watched him back. Was that it? Was she supposed to understand what he was talking about?

'So?' She gave another sigh. She hadn't even had breakfast yet, not a proper one. Harley had an empty plate in his hand, she noticed, crumbs stuck to it. 'You've just been talking to Kai?' she asked.

Harley nodded.

'She told me something, so I was wondering if she told you anything.'

'Patient confidentiality. Even if she has told me anything, I can't tell you.' Plus, she didn't know which bits would interest Harley. Her stomach grumbled softly.

'Okay. If I tell you what I know, could you tell me if you know anything?'

'No. That's not how this works, Harley. You know that.'

'She wants to join the crew. To take up Bucky's offer. She's going to be part of your crew, don't you want to know this about her?'

Jude rubbed at her forehead, her stomach grumbling again.

'Do you know where Seph is from?'

Harley hesitated.

'No.'

'Do you know why Seph is here?'

'No.'

'No, neither do I. But I still treat him when he's ill or shot. He's still part of the crew. And you haven't shown any interest in him.' Ah, thought Jude. That was it. Was Harley developing a soft spot for their passenger? She gave Harley a smile. 'Is this because she cooked that meal for you?'

Harley's features darkened. He slipped off the table and towered over Jude. She looked up at him, unconcerned. She'd been around the tall, broad man often enough to know that he wasn't a threat. At least, not to her.

'The priestesses see the future. Kai said her mother foresaw that Kai would bear a son, and so Kai was betrothed to someone. The man who she was running from, I assume. Her mother foresaw it. And if her mother had the gifts of a Visionary, then there's a chance that Kai does too. Did she tell you what she saw that made her scream last night?'

Jude stared at Harley.

'She can see the future?'

'Maybe. I didn't ask her about her dream. I'd already pushed her too far.'

'She cut herself,' murmured Jude. 'Her stomach was bleeding. She said she dreamt of memories.' She focussed back on Harley. 'That's not conclusive, is it?'

'No. She seems a good liar.'

Jude stood up.

'I have to talk to Bucky.'

'No.' Harley blocked her way. 'No. Not yet. We don't know enough and, like you said, we have professional confidentiality to consider. This wasn't my story to share with you. Talk to Kai, if you must, but not with Bucky.'

'Then why come here?' Jude threw up her arms, sitting back down. 'Why tell me this?'

'Because she might open up to you. She's scared, Jude. Someone's after her and there are things she's not telling us. You need to protect your crew.' Harley closed his mouth, as if he was about to continue but stopped himself.

'If Bucky knew that Kai is—what did you call her? A Visionary? Then he might not want her on the crew.' That wasn't true, thought Jude. Bucky would definitely want a crew member who could see the future. He wouldn't see past that, but Jude could. Jude could see the trouble it might bring. 'No wonder her groom wants her back,' she murmured.

Harley gave a nod.

'It suggests the man she's running from is powerful.'

'And dangerous,' Jude whispered, looking up into Harley's blue eyes. 'I have to talk to Bucky.'

'No. Talk to Kai. We might have got this all wrong.'

Jude nodded.

'Right. Yeah. I'll talk to Kai. I need breakfast anyway. She's in the mess?'

Harley nodded and turned to leave. He stopped and looked back to her.

'She cut herself?'

'Hmm? Oh. Yeah. She seemed shocked about it too.'

Harley remained expressionless. Jude waited, chewing on her cheek.

'She did it in her sleep?'

'Hmm.' Jude stood, hoping that Harley would take the hint and leave. He glanced at her and seemed to wake from his thoughts.

'I don't suppose you know whether she dreamed of cutting herself? Or being hurt?'

'I don't know, Harley.'

Harley left without another word or even an acknowledgment. Jude sat back down, shaking her head and exhaling through her teeth. When she could no longer hear footsteps in the corridor outside, she turned back to her desk. Opening the top drawer, she pulled out a chocolate bar and reopened the wrapper. It was half-eaten. She finished it in three bites, hardly tasting it. She dropped the wrapper in her bin and brushed her hands.

She was itching to find Bucky. She remembered hearing something about the Visionaries, but as a myth. A fairy tale told to children about a culture lost long ago. Apparently, not as lost as everyone thought.

After a moment, Jude stood and reached for the shelf above her desk where books were neatly stacked on it. She took down two piles and behind them was a smaller stack of just three thick books. She took these down carefully, placing them on her desk.

The first book was about the human body, the first medical book she'd ever owned, given to her by her father. She lovingly placed it to one side. The next book was a gift from her mother, a biography of a Lady Katherine Jayne, who had led the fight for women to vote, and in doing so had started the fight for women to work the same jobs as men. As pilots and navigators, as politicians and leaders, and as doctors. Again, she carefully placed this book to the side, placing it on top of the medical book. The third book, she picked up and began gently leafing through the pages. It had grown yellow with age, but that was because it was second hand. Actually, given its age, it was probably fifth or sixth hand. Not that Jude minded. Some pages had annotations from previous owners and she'd often studied them, wondering who had scribbled them. Some in ink and some in pencil. One was obviously an academic, the words used were complicated and the pencil scratchings twisted with curls and passion. The pages themselves told of stories from across the continent. Some were folklore, others were myths and some were steeped in history. They told of mermaids that sunk ships that sailed on the oceans and great monsters that lurked beneath the water, of giant beasts that lived in the mountains and great reptiles that hid away in secret caves, sleeping on gold stolen from kings of the past. Others mentioned the gods and goddesses from different cities, different cultures, different times.

Jude turned to the front and the page that listed each story in the book. There, *The Visionaries of Decima*. A bubble of nerves formed in Jude's stomach, mixing with the chocolate and filling the gaps left by the absence of breakfast. She flicked through to the beginning of the story and began to read.

The book had also been a gift, this time from Bucky. He'd left home before her, to go exploring, working on a ship, learning all he could as the captain's boy. He'd found the book in a market in a small town Jude had never heard of, and he'd thought of her, stuck in a sterile city and trapped between the walls of the hospital, as he'd put it. So he had bought her a book of adventures. Something he wanted to share with her.

She had no idea if that's what he'd meant by the gift but that was how she'd interpreted it and as such, she treasured it. Just as much as the other two books, which is why they were kept close but hidden. She didn't want the rest of the crew knowing of their existence.

Her eyes scanned the words of the history of the Visionaries and as she did, the story came back to her.

The country of Decima was old, and due to being lost deep in a valley, it hadn't developed and evolved with time as the countries around it had. Obviously some left, forging their own lives in the rest of the continent, as Kai's aunt had. Others spent their whole lives in Decima, perhaps not knowing any different, perhaps not wanting to.

The country was run by a monarchy, a crown that was passed down through bloodlines.

When monarchies had been popular, before they were overthrown by governments, they had their own group of advisors. Decima was no different. The monarch had two male advisors, one for the defence of the country and one for the economy and financial matters. All matters, however, were often brought before the Visionaries, who guided the monarch in the matters of his people, the country and his family. They told him who to marry, who would bear him a son—Jude pulled a face, could it be?—when to go to war, when to harvest, what to do with those who committed crimes.

They were all women.

Visionaries were born and the gifts, or so the story told, were passed down through the mother's blood. They were kept in their own house next to the spring that provided the tiny country with water. Kept separate from the rest of the country's people, the lower Visionaries were seen only by the king. The high priestesses, top of the order, were allowed out, however, for the simple reason that they could control their gift and were therefore not a threat to the people.

Jude frowned. A threat? She read on.

The Visionaries worked hard to control their gifts because they were given only glimpses of a future. This usually came in the form of dreams but sometimes also brought on seizures, involuntary noises and acting out what they saw. Which could, understandably, be terrifying for the everyday person who might pass a Visionary on market day.

Jude finished the story. It told the tale of a young Visionary learning what she could and could not control, the monarch being an aspect of life beyond her control which was to be respected and served at all times.

She closed the book and placed it down on the desk. As hard as she might try, she couldn't stop the story lining up perfectly with everything she'd witnessed of Kai. Seizures were no problem for someone like Jude, nor were the involuntary noises and actions, but Jude had to wonder at how Kai had come to be injured. She couldn't get the word "threat" from her mind.

Kai

Kai sat at the dining table. Seph had just entered the mess, taken the breakfast Kai had served him and immediately left without a word. She leaned her elbows on the table and sighed. She was getting far too much thinking time on this ship. It had been different on her aunt's ship. There was always something to do, whether that was doing her own job or helping another. She would finish whatever task her aunt had set her and would then go and find someone else to help, to talk to. That was how she learned more than just cooking, and it was how she'd grown into the family.

She just couldn't see that happening here. Perhaps with Crash. Piloting would certainly be a good skill to learn and was one she hadn't picked up on her aunt's ship, but she couldn't spend the majority of her days with Crash. For one thing, her ears might be talked off. The other problem was that she found herself opening up to the pilot, which was not something she should be doing. Not yet, at any rate.

She was certain Bucky would chastise her for offering to help Harley, he'd probably refer to it as interfering. Seph didn't talk so that seemed fairly pointless, and Jude was just so full of worry that Kai struggled to be around her for long.

No. She sighed, placing her chin in her cupped hand, she was stuck in the mess, alone with her thoughts. She had a lot of thinking to do, but Kai was tired of thinking. She'd been trapped for only a few days before escaping but it had given her plenty of chances to think. Both panicked and calm, collected thinking. Kai was sick of it. Making big decisions was exhausting but this wasn't over yet.

If she joined this crew, it might be over. She could settle down, rebuild her life, forget about what had happened. If he wasn't following her, that is.

'I hear you've been considering my proposal.'

Kai jumped out of her chair and spun round but it was only Bucky. He stopped mid-step, staring at her with wide eyes. He held up his hands. 'Didn't mean to scare you.'

Kai exhaled and moved into the kitchenette.

'Sorry, Capt'n. I was miles away. Breakfast?'

'Please.'

'We have toast and toast.'

'Sounds good.' Bucky pulled up a stool and sat at the breakfast bar. 'Miles away, huh? Thinking of taking up my offer?'

'Actually, yes.'

'But something's holding you back?'

Kai placed two slices of stale bread under the grill.

'How do you know that? No. Wait. Crash talked to you?'

'She did. I'd have thought you'd have learned by now not to talk to that girl about anything important.'

Kai gave Bucky a smile.

'Or maybe that's exactly why I talked to her.'

Bucky cocked his head at Kai.

'You wanted me to come talk to you?'

'I needed to know what kind of man you are.'

'Thought you'd already figured that one out?'

Kai shrugged, checking on the toast.

'You take on freed men like Harley, that's says a lot about you. You have two women on your crew already, that says a lot too. Then you go and agree to take me on as a cook.'

Bucky grinned.

'What can I say? I got a heart of gold.'

'You're also in debt.' Bucky's grin fell. 'And I know, I think,' Kai continued, 'that that wasn't Bran shooting at us when you picked me up.'

'Bran?'

Kai snapped her mouth shut, swearing to herself and turned back to the toast. There was a pause as she removed the toast from the grill, buttered it and handed it to Bucky.

'Two more slices, please,' said Bucky. 'And Bran is the name of the man you're running from. Your groom?'

'He's not my groom. He's the man trying to

force me into a marriage.'

'Same thing.'

Kai gave Bucky a look before turning to put two more slices of bread under the grill.

'That wasn't him shooting at us, was it?'

Bucky took a bite of toast and shrugged.

'Can't really say who it was, can we?' He chewed. 'And yes, I'm in debt. But we have a new big job and I'm in need of another mercenary to make it work.'

'No. You're not. Otherwise you wouldn't have taken the job. A mercenary would make it easier, though.'

'Same thing.'

Kai crossed her arms and sighed at Bucky.

'And what if I say yes, join your crew, help you do this job, whatever it is, and then what if Bran does find me? He'll come with men. What would you do?'

Bucky gave Kai a smile.

'What did we do when we thought that was your fella shootin' at us? Did we turn around and hand you over?'

'No. Because you knew that wasn't him,' said Kai quietly. Bucky's smile fell and he took another bite of his toast.

'Not a word of that to the others or the job offer won't exist anymore,' he growled around his mouthful.

Kai stood firm.

'Who was it?' she asked.

Bucky studied his toast. 'I won't tell anyone. Otherwise the job offer won't exist anymore, right? And if there's something I need right now, it's a safe place with something to do. If you can offer me that, Capt'n, I'll join the crew. I'll help you do this job. But in return I ask for protection and honesty. I can't trust you if you're not honest.'

Bucky studied her in silence, long enough that she began to feel uneasy. Shifting from one foot to the other, she suddenly remembered the toast and broke away from his stare to retrieve the bread before it burned.

'Is he likely to come, this Bran?'

Kai shook her head.

'I don't know.'

'How much does he need you?'

Kai met his eyes, wondering how much to share. How could she ask him to be honest if she wasn't honest with him?

'Honestly? A lot. But that doesn't mean he won't find someone to replace me. So, again, I don't know. There's a good chance he'll come after me, chase me down. There's a smaller chance he'll just find someone else, someone less trouble than me.'

Bucky gave a nod and let Kai slip the additional two slices of toast onto his plate.

'How many men would he bring?'

'Twenty at the most.'

Bucky nearly spat his toast out, coughing a piece up.

'Twenty?' he hacked. Kai cringed.

'Yeah. I know. But his ships are old fashioned. We do this job, you get this ship fixed, maybe an engineer, we'll outrun them easy. And maybe if I can talk to him, I can talk him out of it. Maybe. But outrunning might be good enough.'

'If you cause him enough trouble, he might

decide you're not worth it?'

'Exactly.'

Bucky took a big bite of toast and chewed thoughtfully.

'And if we don't get the job done? I guess then I'll just have to hand you over. Given the job, you might prefer that.'

'No.'

Bucky looked up at Kai and she tried to make herself tall and defiant. 'The conditions of me taking on this job and helping you is that you offer me protection. If you fail to protect me, then fine, but you have to try. I'll be part of your crew. You can't just hand me over. And no pretending to try, either.'

'Or what? What will you do?'

Kai gave a slow smile that made Bucky stop chewing.

'I'll destroy you,' she murmured. Bucky narrowed his eyes. 'I know this ship. It's already falling apart. It won't take much.'

'You're not an engineer.'

'You need an engineer to fix a ship, not break it.'

'You'd destroy us for not protecting you?'

'If you don't protect me, you'll be destroying me. Seems fair.'

They stared at one another. After a moment, Bucky shook his head.

'Twenty men, Kai.'

'I know. All twenty come at us, I'll do the honourable thing. But I'll make that call, okay?'

'Awful lot of trust you're askin' for there.'

Kai tilted her head towards the captain.

'Speaking of which, who was shooting at us?'

'The people we're doing this job for,' said Bucky, shoving the last of a slice of toast into his mouth. Kai leaned back.

'We gonna be breaking the law?'

'Yup.'

'Could we all get killed?'

'Yup.'

'And I'm not to tell the crew?'

'Nope.'

'And you'll do everything you can to keep me safe from Bran?'

'Sure.'

'Deal.'

'Really?' Bucky swallowed and looked at Kai's outstretched hand.

'Yeah. I thought you meant a big job in the sense that there was a lot to do. Sounds more like it's a big job in terms of danger. In which case, you'll need my aim. So, I'm in. Everything we just discussed. Deal?'

Bucky nodded and took Kai's hand. They shook once.

'Deal,' he said. 'I'll get something written up, let you look it over before you sign. Actually, I won't remember all that. Come with me to my office and we'll get it written up now. 'Fraid I can't pay you immediately.'

'That's fine. Having a safe place is more important right now,' said Kai, walking through the kitchenette to join him. 'Did Crash mention to you she'd be willing to sacrifice her pay to help us stay in the sky?'

'She said that? She didn't say it to me. I don't think. Well, that's good to know. You watch though, this job will turn our fortunes around.'

'If we survive,' Kai murmured, following Bucky out of the mess.

Kai returned to the mess two hours later to find Jude stood in the kitchenette.

'Oh, Jude. I'm sorry.' Kai rushed forward. 'I didn't make you any breakfast. It's only toast, I'm afraid.'

'Oh. Oh, it's okay. I made myself some. No bother.'

But it looked like it was a bother. Jude avoided Kai's eye contact, keeping her gaze low as Kai moved back into the narrow, small space of the kitchenette.

'Everything okay?' Kai asked. 'I'm sorry I wasn't here. I don't know if I should mention this now, but I just signed up to the crew. Me and the Capt'n were just making it all official. That's good of him, you know, drawing up a contract and all.' She studied Jude. 'Are you okay?'

'Are you a Visionary?' Jude blurted.

Kai rocked back on her heels.

'What?' she hissed, coming closer to Jude until their faces were close enough for Jude to try and take a step back.

'You are, aren't you?'

'What makes you say that? How do you even know that word?' Kai whispered. She checked over Jude's shoulder but they were still alone.

'I'm sorry. I don't mean any harm,' said Jude, stepping away. Kai let her, feeling her panic subside. 'But your dream and the wound on your stomach.'

Kai's hand instinctively went to her abdomen and her wound pulsed in response.

'Are you?' asked Jude.

Kai didn't respond. She was too busy thinking as fast as she could. 'It's not a problem if you are. But I think we need to know if you are. I need to know. Visionaries can have seizures. I need to know if someone on board this ship is prone to seizures. And you say you're part of the crew now?'

Kai couldn't argue with that.

'I don't have seizures,' she murmured.

'But you hurt yourself, when you have bad dreams.'

'That's the first time that's happened.'

'So, you could have a seizure?'

Kai studied Jude's eyes, her vision going blurry as tears welled. Jude softened.

'I'm sorry, Kai. I'm sorry. I just…I needed to ask and I didn't know how. I'm sorry. Come. Sit down.' Jude led Kai to the dining table and the women sat. Jude leaned forward, waiting for Kai to tell her the truth.

Kai took a deep breath.

'If I am what you think I am, would Bucky kick me off the crew?'

'If you are a Visionary and can see the future, I doubt Bucky will want to lose sight of you.' Jude gave her a hopeful smile.

'Even if it's the reason I could be bringing a bunch of trouble your way?' Kai held her breath. Jude's smile faded.

Seph

Seph stacked the two empty crates on the back of the Bumblebee. Crash was already in the driver's seat, bouncing a little, impatient to get going. Seph placed a collection of bags into the top crate.

'How's it going?' Bucky asked, walking over and patting Seph on the shoulder. He gave the captain a nod. Bucky lingered a little on him. Seph maintained eye contact, his way of telling Bucky that the man had nothing to worry about. They'd been working together long enough for Bucky to understand and with a single nod, he turned away and approached Crash.

Seph allowed himself to slow a little. They'd landed in Northhold an hour earlier and Seph had been tasked with prepping the Bumblebee to head into town so the crew could restock. The others, except for the eager Crash, were nowhere to be found yet and Seph wasn't in a rush to get into the town. In fact, he would rather not be going into the town at all.

He trusted the others not to question his nerves. They never did. They knew not to. Except this time, there was Kai.

Newcomers always made Seph a little nervous. What if she asked? What would he say? He'd come up with a number of reasons, practised them, but still he knew he'd trip over them if asked.

Thankfully, Bucky had given him a great excuse not to go into town this time. He had to refuel the ship. As soon as everyone left, Seph would be in charge of refuelling and cleaning the outside of The Magpie. Those were tasks that suited him.

'Can't wait to get some fresh air, Crash?' Bucky asked, patting the bonnet of the Bumblebee.

'Doubt it'll be fresh. You seen how many folks there are out there? It's heavin', Capt'n. Last fresh air we got was when we were shot at. I think we're due. Maybe after this job we could stop somewhere nice?'

'Where's nice, then?'

'Somewhere with fewer people. Maybe some mountains.'

'Mountains?' Bucky gave Seph a look. 'Never took you for a girl who liked looking at mountains. Took you more for a girl who liked finding a pub.'

'There are pubs in the mountains. Just have to find the right mountains.' Crash flashed a grin over her shoulder to Seph.

Seph gave them both his usual small smile. Five years ago, he would have joined in, mocking Crash, winding her up alongside Bucky. That was before he'd joined the crew. Before he'd had reason to join the crew. Now, he kept quiet, head down as he tied the crates to the vehicle.

'Deal. We do this job, we'll go find a pub in the mountains. Engineer first though, otherwise we'll be stuck in the mountains.'

Crash laughed.

'That's if we stay flyin' long enough to finish the job.'

Bucky gave Crash a warning look and then patted the Bumblebee again.

'We nearly ready to go?'

'Ready, Capt'n,' said Seph, giving the straps one last tug to check them. The crates didn't move. 'Bags are in the crate,' he told Crash. 'For food and anything else small enough.'

Crash gave him a nod.

'That'll be for Kai. She's comin', right?' she asked Bucky.

'Yup. Where is she? And Jude? And Harley? Thought he was poppin' out too.'

'Well, he hasn't been off the ship since we picked up Kai. Those two missed all the fun last time. Good thing though, I guess, considerin' they saved our arses.'

'You can stop rubbin' that in,' Bucky muttered. 'Ah! The women have arrived,' he cried as Jude and Kai entered the loading bay. Jude narrowed her eyes at her brother.

'You waiting on us?' she asked.

'Not anymore. Now we're just waitin' on Harley.'

'Here, Captain.' Harley appeared from the other

direction with a bag slung over his shoulder. Bucky looked him up and down.

'You stayin' or comin' back?' he asked. Seph remembered a time when Bucky was more formal with the lawman, but Harley had been with them long enough now to be talked to like any other member of the crew. Even though he wasn't a member. Seph frowned. Sometimes that was hard to remember.

'Coming back,' said Harley, taking a seat in the back of the Bumblebee. Jude sat beside him, Kai beside her. Bucky climbed in the front and Crash started the engine.

Wiping his hands on his trousers, Seph moved to the control panel.

'Wait. Hang on,' said Bucky. 'Crash, turn this thing off. We're not goin' just yet.'

Crash gave a loud groan and switched the engine off.

The crew all looked to Bucky expectantly.

'Got a few announcements and things to say before we leave. You won't be able to hear me with the doors open.'

'Go on then,' said Crash.

'Right. First of all. Everyone back to the ship by four o'clock. We're leaving at four fifteen. Don't get lost, drunk or otherwise lose track of time. Everyone has their jobs to do. Oh.' Bucky fished into his pocket and pulled out a small purse which he dropped into Kai's lap. 'Kai, you're being tasked with buying us some food. That's your budget. Seph's put bags in the back for you to shop with. Shop wisely.'

Kai gave Bucky a nod, shoving the purse into her

pocket.

'Yes, Capt'n.'

'Good. Everyone else know their jobs? Seph is cleaning and refuelling, he'll be stayin' here. Any trouble, run to Seph. I'm gonna be startin' our new job, and no I don't need a hand,' he added to Jude who closed her mouth. 'Jude, you're hunting out any medical supplies we need and Crash is gonna see if she can find that coil we need at a good price. You know how much you can spend, don't go over. That's not a try not to go over or please don't, that's a don't. Go. Over. Got it?'

Jude nodded and Crash gave a salute.

'Four o'clock. That goes for you too, Harley. If you're comin' with us. Right. Good. Now, one more announcement and we'll be on our way.' Bucky grinned and a bubble of nerves in Seph's stomach grew. It had to be something about Kai, he thought.

'I'm pleased to announce that Kai has agreed to join the crew as our new merc. She'll be joining forces with Seph, keeping us safe. Never had a sharpshooter on board, I'm fully expecting our income to rise exponentially.' Crash raised her hand. 'It means a lot, Crash.'

'I know what it means,' Crash snapped, dropping her hand. 'Just wanted to ask about how you're payin' for a new crew member when we couldn't afford a new crew member a few days ago. You know, that engineer we need to stay flyin'?'

'She's working for free, Crash, for the time being. Kai's agreed.' Bucky glanced at Kai. 'She's on board with it all. Right. Announcements done. Everyone happy? Four o'clock, not a second after. We'll drive into the town, park up and go our separate ways. I'll be taking the Bumblebee with me, so you'll all have to make your own way back to the ship. It's easy enough to find. Follow the signs for the main landing pad or look out for the bloody great ships. All right? All right.' He sat back down. 'Let's go.' He gave Seph a nod as Crash started the engine.

Seph hit the button and the doors opened.

'You want anything, Seph?' Kai called as Crash carefully manoeuvred the Bumblebee off the ship.

Seph froze and looked up at her. After a moment, he smiled.

'Batter,' he said.

Kai gave him a curious look as Crash drove the crew off the ship and away into town.

Seph watched them go, the smile still on his face. No one had ever asked him that, not since he'd joined the crew. Did he want anything?

He wanted lots of things, truth be told, but seeing as Kai meant food, he'd immediately been reminded of his childhood. Actually, it was something he'd been thinking about since Kai had made that meal for Harley. And then the chocolate cake for Crash.

He hadn't expected anything. Harley was special, marked out as an ex-slave, whether people chose to acknowledge that or not. Crash was loud, it was hard to ignore her. Seph was easy to ignore, that was how he liked it, but sometimes it would be nice to be noticed. It would be nice, he'd thought the night of Harley's meal, as he'd climbed into bed, to have someone make food specially for him.

Did he want anything?

Seph's smile grew to a grin as he ducked under The Magpie's wing to start the job of refuelling.

168

Bucky

Bucky dropped his crew off by the market, reminded Crash again of the time they needed to be back at the ship, and then drove away. He'd been studying the maps of this town since they'd left Valkwick, where they'd picked up Kai. He knew the way, but it was always easier with Crash or Seph driving, so he could have a map on his lap.

It was a stark reminder that they needed a navigator as well as an engineer. Bucky sighed as he made a right turn. Unlike the last job, which was on the edge of a town, hidden away in a warehouse, now he was headed into the town centre. The town itself was still being built. Some buildings were finished and had been in use for some time, but those around them were covered in scaffolding as men lugged up stone and brick and cement. Three men were struggling with a long wooden beam.

These weren't the buildings that were necessary to the survival of the town, the small shops, the lawmen's office, the jail, the mayor's office, the town hall. No, those had been built first, of course, although the main church was made from timber and already too small for a town of this size.

The buildings being worked on now were for the wealthy. Statements to attract the more affluent into the town, to boost its economy. To give them the funds to rebuild that church, Bucky thought, giving it a distasteful glare as he drove past.

It was one of these grand, statement buildings, so close to completion, that Bucky pulled up outside of. The scaffolding had come down but there were two men standing outside the front door, one smoking a cigarette while the other explained something to him, holding a toolbox in one hand and making wild gestures with the other.

Bucky looked up at the building as he climbed out of the Bumblebee. The nerves were building in his stomach, twisting and turning, threatening to bring up breakfast. He probably shouldn't have come alone, but it was too late now. He'd need Seph and Kai for the actual job itself, but this was just a meeting. Just a meeting. Bucky took a deep breath and walked through the front door, between the talking men who hardly paused. Bucky caught something about snagging and faltered. What did snagging mean?

Inside the building was a desk with a woman sitting behind it. She gave Bucky a forced smile as he approached.

'Hi there,' he said, trying hard to sound normal.

'I'm here to see Mr Castell. I believe he's expecting me. Captain Bucky Winters.'

The woman gave a nod and then picked up an old fashioned telephone. Bucky waited while she talked into it in a soft, sultry voice. It was only after she'd given him directions and he'd walked away that he realised how pretty she'd been. He'd hardly noticed her. That's how bloody nervous I am, he thought, can't even see the pretty girls right in front of me.

He wandered slowly up the timber stairs, the scent of newly sawn wood still fresh and sharp in the air. On the third floor, he went through the only available door.

He stopped immediately, the door closing on his back, pushing him forward a step.

It appeared to be some sort of living room. He remembered rooms like this in his childhood home and the homes of his friends. There wasn't much call for them on a ship.

On one of the black leather sofas were two women and a large man with a fat cigar in his mouth. He looked up at Bucky, puffing smoke out of the gap in the corner of his mouth.

'Ah, Mr Castell,' began Bucky, his tongue sticking to the inside of his mouth.

The women either side of the man giggled and the big man gave a hearty laugh. Taking the cigar out of his mouth, he looked Bucky up and down.

'He's in there. Jackass.' He pointed to a door on Bucky's left, put the cigar back in his mouth and sat back, pulling the women with him.

Blinking, Bucky approached the door. The big man at his back, the women giggling, Bucky didn't have time to prepare himself. He pushed open the door, wondering belatedly if he should have knocked, and stepped through.

This was more what he'd been expecting. A large office, decorated in dark colours and stained wood. There was a sofa, empty, and chairs, and in the centre stood a large desk. In one of the chairs sat a thin man, smoking a cigarette. Standing by the desk was another man, stocky but non-threatening as he gave Bucky a wary smile. Sitting behind the desk was a young man in a black suit with black hair. He brightened as he focussed on Bucky.

'Captain Winters?' he asked, standing up and holding out his hand. Bucky, frowning, stepped forward to shake it. This couldn't be Castell. This man didn't look older than twenty-five.

The man laughed.

'Not what you were expecting? Please. Take a seat.' He gestured to the closest empty chair and shooed the standing man away. He moved behind Bucky, sitting on the sofa near the door. Bucky watched him and then sat on the chair designated for him. The man, presumably Castell, sat back behind his desk. 'People don't seem to expect me. Too young. That's what I get told. As far as criticism goes, I'll take it. I guess people think of me as an overnight success, but the truth is I've been in this business since I was a kid. When did you get started, Captain Winters? I was living on the streets when I was ten. By fifteen, I had a little business growing. All this.' Castell gestured around him. 'Took me just over ten years to achieve. And they call me an overnight success.' He grinned, leaning forward on his desk. 'I've heard things about you, Captain Winters. Some good, some not so good. This job you're doing for me isn't one of the biggest, but you prove yourself to me, you show me you're capable, and I could be passing the bigger jobs onto you. How does that sound?'

Bucky considered the young man. He looked harmless, just a boy in a suit, but there was a glint in his eye and Bucky could imagine many men mistaking what that glint meant and paying the price for that mistake.

'Sounds fantastic, Mr Castell,' he said.

Castell smiled. Bucky had given the right answer.

'Well, that's what I like to hear!' He grinned. The two other men in the room laughed but quietened as Bucky looked round at them. He turned back to the boy in the suit.

'You got our message, I take it?' Castell sat back. 'I do hope my boys didn't damage your ship too badly.'

'I got it,' said Bucky. 'And I'll be doing the job right and carefully, don't you worry about that.'

'Oh, I don't worry. You either do it right or you won't be working again.' Castell's features darkened and Bucky pursed his lips, stretching out his fingers to keep his hands from wringing. 'And you have the item in question?'

Bucky nodded.

'Somewhere safe?' Castell asked.

'You wouldn't have hired me otherwise,' said Bucky, biting on his tongue to stop from saying more.

Castell grinned, flashing off teeth that were too white.

'An excellent point. But I have been dis-appointed before and if there's one thing I truly hate…well, that's a lie. There are so many things that I truly hate. But one of those things is being disappointed.'

'I think everyone hates that,' pointed out Bucky.

'But some people expect it.' Castell held up a finger. 'Some people wait for it. Not me. No. I have high expectations, Captain Winters. Very high. This could be lucrative for you. And, from what I've heard, you could do with something lucrative.'

'Oh? What have you heard?' Bucky tensed.

'You've been looking for an engineer for some time. Your ship can't be in great condition. I do hope it survives to finish this job?'

'It will, don't you worry,' said Bucky. And if you know that, try not shooting us outta the sky, he thought, teeth gritted.

'How about I supply you with an engineer, just until the job is finished?'

Bucky narrowed his eyes. He leaned forward in his seat.

'Begging your pardon, Mr Castell, but if you have so little faith in me that you feel the need to place a spy on my ship, why did you hire me?'

There was a tense silence and then Castell leaned back and laughed loud. The other two men laughed with him.

'Another excellent point, Captain Winters. I'm not suggesting I put a spy on your ship, oh no. I was just offering you one of my fine engineers, out of the goodness of my heart, to ensure that the job is completed. That's all. I'm sure you're planning on spending your earnings on an engineer.'

'There seems to be a misunderstanding,' Bucky told him, leaning back in his own chair. 'The reason we are lackin' an engineer is not because of inadequate funds but because we have not yet found the right engineer to join our crew. Once we find the right person, we'll hire them.'

'Well, for now, one of my men will be the right one.'

'Thank you, Mr Castell, but I can't accept. Your man, Crick, made me the same offer, didn't he tell you?'

Castell didn't smile this time.

'He did, Captain Winters, he did. But one of my men saw your crew disembarking from your ship and not one of them appeared to be an engineer. Your ship still appears to be lacking. I rather feel you were lying to Crick. So, now it isn't a question or an offer, Captain Winters. It's now part of the job.'

Bucky sucked on his teeth a moment. The last thing he wanted was one of Castell's lackies on his ship, especially when he hadn't yet told his crew the whole truth. That would make things more complicated.

'Thank you, Mr Castell, for your generosity,' continued Bucky. 'Tell me, if I were to find the right engineer for my crew, would that be acceptable?'

Castell shrugged.

'Good luck finding a skilled engineer in this town that doesn't work for me. So, yes, I can agree to those terms.'

Bucky's insides tightened. At least he had given himself a ray of hope.

'We expect to finish the job imminently,' said Bucky, hoping to change the subject. 'We'll be going straight there. We're just refuelling, getting ourselves ready—'

'Finding an engineer,' said Castell with a snide smile.

'Right. And then we'll be on our way. Ready to meet at the rendezvous point tonight.'

'With the goods?'

'With the goods. Deliver the package and pick up the other.'

Castell nodded, steepling his fingers.

'Excellent. I'll prepare an engineer and send him down to the landing pad. You know, in case you can't find anyone. When are you leaving?'

'Four,' said Bucky.

'Good. He'll be there waiting by The Magpie. A fine ship, Captain Winters, it would be a great shame to let her go to waste.'

Bucky's stomach dropped. He stood, not quite trusting his legs, and went to leave.

'Thank you, Mr Castell.'

'Davey here will show you out.' Castell looked down at the papers on his desk, dismissing Bucky.

Kai

Kai had stuck with Crash and Jude for as long as possible but soon the other women had been swept away, either by the crowds or because the stalls they needed were in the opposite direction. Harley had made his excuses early and ducked away into a pub saying he needed to speak to someone.

Kai was alone, surrounded by so many people her head was beginning to spin.

They brushed against her, talking to one another, voices raised to be heard above the din. As Kai moved closer to the food stalls, the air became thick, not only with the stench of so many people and the overflowing bins and litter that lay strewn behind the stalls, but with the mixed smells of cooking meat, vegetables and bread.

Individually, those smells would have made

Kai's mouth water, her stomach grumble. Especially when her recent diet had been so lacking. But as the heavy spices of one stall mixed with the rich scent of raw meat from another, Kai's stomach turned.

Someone brushed up against her back, prodding her. She gave a yelp and spun round to face them, her hand automatically going to where a gun should have been, if she were still part of her aunt's crew. There was no weapon there now. She hadn't asked Bucky about that. Neither was there an attacker ready to face her. There was only the jostling crowd and a couple of people giving her a strange look. She turned back and kept walking, pushing through the crowds.

In her left hand, she gripped the bags Jude had passed to her as they'd climbed from the Bumblebee. In her pocket was the money Bucky had given her. She had a job to do. The best thing, she thought, was to focus on that job and not on anything else. Forget the smells of food, forget the people, just focus on what she could cook each crew member and the price of it. Figuring out how to stretch the budget should be enough to keep her mind occupied.

She approached a stall of fresh bread and peered over the shoulders of the people in front of her. How much bread should she get? It wouldn't keep long. It was a treat.

Fingers brushed up her legs. Kai gave a squeal and kicked out.

'Oi,' said one man, as she knocked into him. She backed away.

'Sorry,' she murmured. 'Sorry.' Her breath came

hard as she looked around her. Again, there was no attacker, no one sniggering at having touched her. Nothing.

'You all right, love?' the woman in a floury apron behind the stall asked. Kai gave a nod.

'One large loaf, please. White.' White bread would keep for longer.

The woman began wrapping one up for her. Kai nibbled on the inside of her cheek, willing the woman to work quicker. She took a breath, filling her nostrils with the homely smell of freshly baked bread.

It was just the crowds, she told herself, everything was fine. She was safe. Now, what else did she need? She handed the money over to the woman who gave her the bread. With the loaf safely stowed in her bag, Kai moved onto the next stall.

An arm wrapped around her waist, gripping her hand and this time Kai lashed out, hitting a passing woman with the bagged loaf.

'What the—? Hey!' The woman turned on Kai.

'I'm sorry,' Kai said, glancing around her. There was no attacker. This wasn't real, she realised. These sensations weren't real. 'No. Not now,' she muttered with a whine.

'What did you say?' the woman squared up to her.

Kai looked at her, as if noticing her for the first time. She needed to get the food and get back to the ship, away from all these people.

'I'm sorry,' she told the woman, but the woman didn't seem to be in the mood for accepting apologies. Kai put a hand to her forehead. 'I'm sorry. I didn't mean…' she whimpered, pressing her hand to her head and allowing her body to shiver.

The woman took a step back.

'Okay. All right. No harm done,' she muttered, walking away. Kai lowered her hand and looked around. Those who had noticed the almost-fight had lost interest fast and moved on. Kai did so too, ending up at a raw meat stall. She purchased some chicken and beef and then moved on.

Fingers gripped at her thighs, hands pulling on her arms but Kai ignored them. They weren't real. Her mind was playing tricks. She didn't have time to consider why. She stopped at a vegetable stall and filled the bag with an array of fruits and vegetables, enough to keep them going with stews and soups.

Happy that it would be enough and with only a few coins left, Kai headed back to the ship. She turned away from the stall and walked straight into a man. Apologising, she glanced up into his face and stopped. There was Bran's mouth, his lips twisted, and there were his deep, brown eyes. His light brown hair lifted in the breeze created by the people walking past. Her mouth fell open and the bag slipped from her fingers, crashing to the ground, spilling her latest purchases. The man bent to pick them up.

'Are you okay?' he asked, and just like that, he wasn't Bran. He was a stranger with hair darker than Bran's and eyes that were warm and forgiving. Kai blinked and bent to scoop what was left on the ground back into her bag.

'Yes. I'm sorry. I…I'm sorry.'

'It's okay.' The man gave her a smile and moved on.

Kai stayed where she was, allowing the crowds to jostle her. She hardly felt them.

Was he coming for her? Was he here?

She looked at the faces of those walking around her. They glanced back, irritated that she was in the way.

Then, as she stood there, waiting and watching, the noise of the market quietened although everyone kept moving. Above the noise came a loud, high and unmistakable roar.

'The monster,' Kai whispered. It was enough to get her moving. Gripping her bags of food, she pushed through the crowds, trying desperately to remember which direction the ship was in.

Each time she bumped into someone she hoped they would turn out to be Crash or Jude or Harley. Maybe even Bucky. But they were all strangers.

'The landing pad,' she asked at one point. 'Where is it?'

But no one answered.

She found the bread stall, the same woman in her apron stood serving her customers. How had she gotten here? What had she passed?

Kai couldn't remember. The market began to spin around her, everything looking the same.

The pub where Harley had gone. If she could just find that, she would be okay. If she could find Harley, she would be safe, she had no doubt. What had been the name of the pub?

'A pub,' she asked one woman who passed her. 'Is there one near here?'

The woman gave her a disgusted look and moved on.

'Please.' Kai turned to another woman. 'I need to

find my friend. He went into a pub, but I don't remember the name.'

'The Ram, dear? Just up there, on the right.' The woman pointed.

'Oh, thank you. Thank you so much.' Kai resisted the urge to hug the woman and instead jogged in the direction she had pointed. She dodged around people, holding her bag of food close to her.

There, above their heads, was the pub sign for The Ram. Kai grinned. Harley would be in there and everything would be okay. She threw herself through the front door and stopped.

Silence met her as every man and woman inside turned to look at her.

She stood there, breathing hard, gripping her bag to her chest, glancing from one face to the next but she didn't see Harley.

Was this the wrong pub?

As the patrons turned away, going back to their drinks and conversations, Kai made her way to the bar.

'What can I getcha?' the man asked.

'I'm looking for someone. A friend. I think he came in here. Tall, broad, blonde, he has long hair tied back and a beard with beads...' Kai drifted off as the man's expression changed.

'Slave, is it?'

'A man born of Aegirheim,' said Kai, standing straighter. 'There are no more slaves.'

The barman laughed.

'If you say so, love. He was here. He ain't here no more. You want a drink?'

Kai's shoulders sagged, tears pricking her eyes.

'No. Thank you.'

'Paying customers only,' said the barman stiffly.

Kai turned her back on him and left. Standing back out in the throng of people, she moved aside to let two men into the pub.

Where could Harley have gone? Back to the ship, she thought. She had to get back to the ship. Looking around, she recognised a spot over to the right where Bucky had dropped them off. If she turned right here, she would be on the road back to the landing pad.

If she could just get somewhere quiet, her mind might stop. If she could just get back to the ship, she knew she would be safe.

Kai pulled a watch from her pocket and checked the time. There was only half an hour before the crew would have to return. There wouldn't be long to wait, and then Crash and Bucky would take her away from here.

Kai glanced again at the faces of the men passing her. She recognised none but that didn't mean he wasn't here. It didn't mean *someone* wasn't here, looking for her. Head down, Kai began walking again, heading back the way the Bumblebee had come, to where the landing pad should be.

At her back, an unearthly high-pitched call sounded. It echoed around her head but no one else moved. No one else flinched.

It was in her head, it was all in her head. Her mind was pulling her dream into reality and, in Kai's experience, that never ended well.

Cassidy

Cass had been standing at the same stall for fifteen minutes and the owner was getting impatient.

'You wanna buy that?' he asked.

She didn't look up. She turned over the watch, studying the cogs for the fifth time. They would fit, but would they last? If she was having this much trouble deciding, they probably wouldn't. She put the watch down.

'No. Thanks.'

The man gave a small growl but caught himself, visibly taking a deep breath and gritting his teeth as Cass picked up another watch. This one didn't have the cogs on the outside.

'How much for this one?'

'Two gold.'

'That's a lot.'

'It's a good watch.'

Cass looked him in the eye.

'It isn't working.'

'It just needs winding up,' said the man, snatching it away from her and winding it fast. 'There.' He handed it back.

Cass waited as the hands of the watch began to tick time away. The noise was strong. She held it up to her ear, listening to the cogs moving.

'Can you take the back off?'

'What? No. Sold as seen,' said the man. 'You gonna buy it?'

'For one gold, yes.'

'No. Two gold. That's it. If you don't want it, put it down. I got other customers.'

'Then go serve them,' said Cass. The man glared at her but didn't move. Cass listened to the watch again and then put it down. It wasn't worth the risk.

Surveying the stall, she stepped back. There was nothing there that would help her.

'Thank you for your time,' she murmured, moving on as the man rolled his eyes at her. She was used to it. Men always thought they knew better than her. Some even feigned shock at the grease under her fingernails. They didn't feign the shock when she spoke though, usually to tell them where they'd gone wrong.

Cass moved on to the next stall. A singular large table with a red cloth covered in pieces of dirty metal. Cogs, gears and coils, a few small tools, a large capacitor, and at the back, a steel barrel. Cass eyed the barrel before picking up a couple of cogs and feeling the edges with her fingertips.

'Lot of coils you got here,' came a voice beside

her. Cass glanced at the woman, shorter than her with light blond hair that seemed to have been chopped off to make it short and stick up at odd angles.

'You want coils, we got 'em,' said the man behind the table. Cass looked down at the coils. She placed the cogs back and picked up a length of copper wire, twisted into a ring. 'We got lots o' things,' said the man, turning his attention to Cass. She nodded to the barrel behind him.

'How much for that?'

He followed her gaze, looking over his shoulder, and gave a shrug.

'Fifty silver.'

Cass narrowed her eyes.

'Can I look at it?'

'Don't see why not.' He gestured for her to go round the table, which she did, following him towards the back. He left her studying the barrel, turning back to his other customers.

Cass ran her fingers over the steel. It was thin but strong. She could bend it, if she needed to. If this didn't work, then there could be other uses for it. The inside was slightly burned from whatever it had been used for previously and there was a slice cut out along the side. Still, it would do. She straightened, looking for the stall owner.

'Forty silver for this,' she called to him. He wandered over, pursing his lips and studying the barrel.

'Think I said fifty.'

'It's been burned and there's a piece missing.'

'That's why it's fifty.'

'Forty.'

186

The man narrowed his eyes at Cass.

'Forty-five.'

'Forty-five and you throw in a bag of cogs,' said Cass.

The man held out his hand.

'Deal.'

They shook and Cass dug into her pockets, finding the money. Having paid the man, she hefted the barrel and went to collect her cogs.

'What'd you want a barrel for?'

It was that petite blonde from earlier. Cass barely looked at her, nor did she reply. She took a moment to study the cogs as the stall owner handed her a bag.

The woman watched over Cass's shoulder.

'Don't suppose you're an engineer?'

'I am,' said Cass, picking up one cog, studying it and then discarding it.

'Never seen a ship with a metal barrel like that one,' said the woman.

'I'm not a ship engineer.'

'Oh. That's a shame.'

There was a heavy silence and Cass looked up to find the woman studying her. She sighed, closing the bag of cogs and shoving them into her large pockets. 'You're looking for a ship engineer?' The woman nodded. 'I know some. I can give you some names,' said Cass.

To her surprise, the woman pulled a face.

'Why don't you work on ships?' she asked.

'Because I don't.'

'What else is there?'

Cass looked the woman up and down.

'There are plenty of other occupations for an

engineer. Plenty of other types of machinery.'

The women shrugged.

'None as exciting as a ship, though. Or as big.'

'Actually, water ships have been built larger than an air ship. I take it you're talking about air ships?'

The woman grinned wide.

'Best kind,' she said. 'Only kind that really matter. Anyone can make somethin' that floats move, but it takes magic to make it fly.'

Cass hesitated, searching the woman's eyes.

'I like to work on my own projects,' she said carefully.

Again, the woman shrugged.

'Plenty of room for that on an air ship, and no bobbing around like you would on the water. Plus, you know, no drownin' or sinkin'.'

'Unless you crash into the ocean.'

The woman grinned again.

'But with the right engineer, that ain't likely.'

Cass smiled.

'What makes you think I'm the right engineer?'

Now the woman looked her up and down. Cass frowned, crossing her arms against her chest. The woman's eyes sparkled at they met hers.

'Somethin' about you.'

Cass went to move away. 'It's a great ship,' the woman continued.

Cass picked up her barrel and began walking through the market. The short blonde followed her. 'And we're a good crew. Excellent captain.'

'You don't know anything about me,' Cass called back over her shoulder.

'I saw how you look at things. That was enough.'

Cass stopped and turned back.

'How is that enough? What did me looking at cogs teach you about me?'

'You're after somethin',' said the woman, glancing down at the barrel. 'And maybe you're a bit lost.'

Cass's breath caught in her throat and she gritted her teeth.

'That's a lot to get from someone looking at cogs.'

The woman held out her hand.

'I'm Crash. Don't let the name fool you, I'm an incredible pilot. Pilot of one of the best ships around. All we need is a good engineer.'

Cass looked from Crash's face to her out-stretched hand.

'It's nice to meet you, Crash. I'm not looking for work at the moment.' Cass picked up the barrel and continued walking away.

'What do you need?' Crash called after her, jogging to catch up, weaving between people while Cass simply held the barrel in front of her and assumed those walking towards her would get out of the way. 'What do you need that barrel for? I bet we can help.'

'I don't need help,' said Cass. 'Stop following me.'

'We all need help. We've all been lost.'

Cass strode on, determined to lose Crash, but Crash kept on coming.

'I'm not that lost.'

'Okay, well, we're that in need of an engineer.'

'Then let me give you some recommendations.'

'We've had the recommendations.'

Cass stopped walking, placing down the barrel. Crash skidded to a halt behind her.

'So, what you're saying is that you've tried the other engineers and they don't want the job so you thought you'd try your luck at the engineer who doesn't even work on ships that you found at a random market stall?'

Crash opened and closed her mouth, then she grinned and nodded.

'Yup.'

'Which means that either your pay is too low or your ship is falling apart. Which is it?'

'Both. We're special like that.'

'So, give me one good reason why anyone should want to join your crew?'

Cass expected Crash's grin to fade, for her to get angry, but instead the grin stayed put, lighting up Crash's whole face.

'Like I said, we're special. We take what is lost and we make it found.'

'You're bounty hunters?'

'Nah. Not literally. Figuratively.'

Cass was impressed. She had assumed Crash wouldn't know that word, never mind understand its meaning.

'What are you then?'

'We take on jobs. Delivery, mostly.'

Cass raised an eyebrow. She'd heard of independent delivery ships, of course, but wasn't that also the answer that pirates gave when asked what they did?

'Are you pirates?' she asked.

Crash barked a laugh.

'We have a lawman on board our ship. Don't

think pirates do that.'

But there was something about the look in Crash's eyes that said differently.

'A lawman?'

'Detective. He uses our ship as his office, cracking cases, huntin' down suspects. See, we're the good guys.'

'And you're special.'

'Yeah. That too.'

'But you've got no money and your ship is falling apart.'

Crash shrugged.

'She just needs one good engineer to make her sing.'

'Engineers won't work for nothing.'

'Ah,' said Crash, stepping closer. 'But there's more to life than getting paid. Not everyone is after money. There are some things that can be given in place of money that can act as payment. Security, safety, a roof above your head, food in your belly, a place to belong.'

'To be found?'

'Exactly. Where are you stayin' right now? Have you rented a room? Is it nice? We've got an empty cabin waitin' for an engineer. And the engine room, that would be all yours. Capt'n lets the lawman use the loading bay as he likes. Bet he'd do the same for you.' Crash gestured at the barrel. 'The next pay load is just around the corner, but in the meantime, I bet our ship's better than what you got right now. All in exchange for you fine-tunin' our engine.'

Cass crossed her arms again.

'Fine-tuning? And what's wrong with it?'

'Well.' Crash rubbed the back of her neck. 'Hard

to say. I ain't an engineer.'

Cass sighed, looking down at the barrel. It was true that she had rented a room and it was also true that it wasn't a pleasant place. There was a tavern at one end of the street, a brothel at the other. The nights were filled with alcohol-fuelled shouting and the days filled with the grey squalor that came with such a poverty-stricken part of town. People trying to make ends meet with no food in their bellies and nowhere to go.

'Is it fixable?' she asked.

'Definitely.' Crash nodded. 'We're just missin' some pieces.'

Cass raised an eyebrow.

'What pieces?'

Crash shrugged.

'You're the engineer. Why don't you come take a look? Talk to the Capt'n, see the ship, see what you think.'

Cass looked off in the direction of her room, then back at Crash.

'Maybe. Maybe I could talk to your captain. I'm not promising anything. For the right price, I could fix your engine for you before you leave.'

Crash grinned again.

'Yeah. Well. We'll see what Capt'n says. You'll love the ship, she's a beauty.'

'Hmm.'

'We should go to your place, grab your stuff.'

'We don't know I'm staying yet.'

''Course you are, 'course you are. You'll see. Where're we headin'?'

Cass sighed, considering her options.

'I'm not going to win this argument, am I?'

Crash patted her on the shoulder.
'Most don't.'

Crash

Crash practically skipped behind the engineer as the woman led her away. They left the market but didn't walk far. Down a long road were rows of small terraced houses, with a pub at one end which caught Crash's attention. Some of the houses were boarded up, wooden planks over the windows. A couple of windows were smashed. Some children played in the road but stopped when they saw Crash and the woman she was following, watching as they walked up to a blue front door.

The engineer took out a key and unlocked it. She was taller than Crash, with long silver hair, dark green eyes and elegant fingers. Crash watched her hands working the lock.

'What's your name?' she asked. 'Should've asked earlier. When I told you mine.'

'Cassidy,' said Cass.

'Nice name.'

Cass glanced back to Crash and Crash gave her a sweet smile. As Cass turned her back and entered the building, Crash's smile faded. What was she doing? The captain sent her out to find a coil— Crash swore under her breath, she'd forgotten the coil—and instead she'd found a pretty woman who didn't work on ships.

'You have experience of fixin' engines, right?' Crash asked, following Cass up some creaking wooden stairs. Cass didn't respond, instead unlocking a door off the landing and pushing it open. Crash stepped inside and her mouth fell open. 'Shit.'

The room was about the same size as the cabins on The Magpie, which was a good sign. There was a bed with crumpled sheets, a desk and, in the corner, a toilet and shower. At least on The Magpie, the toilet and shower were partitioned off. But it was what was in the middle of the room that had made Crash stop. She approached it, bending to get a closer look.

'What is this?'

'Don't touch it!' Cass was busy shoving things into a bag. Some clothes but mostly pieces of machinery. Bag packed, she stood behind the thing in the centre of the room, next to Crash and exhaled sharply. 'Been a while since I had to move this. It was smaller back then. You'll have to help me.'

'Sure. What is it?'

Cass pointed to where Crash should hold it while Cass slowly took parts from the large machine and wrapped them up in rags. They placed the wrapped pieces into another bag and Cass handed Crash the bag filled with clothes and machinery. Crash slung it over her shoulder, feeling some metal pieces digging into her.

'Can we go now?'

Cass nodded and gestured for Crash to lead. 'So, err, what is it?' Crash asked as they left the house and walked back up the road, past the playing children, and back towards the market.

'A machine.'

'What does it do?'

Cass looked at Crash out of the corner of her eye.

'Nothing. Yet.'

'What will it do?'

Cass gave a small smile. Crash wondered if she was supposed to have seen it.

'Nothing. If I don't get the right parts.'

Crash narrowed her eyes at the bag Cass was carrying over her back. 'It's damn heavy though,' Cass added. 'Sure be nice if we could get to your ship as quickly as possible.'

Crash laughed and lengthened her stride.

Leading the way to The Magpie across the landing pad, bag growing heavier on her back, Crash rushed over to Seph who was waiting under one of the wings. He stepped forward as he saw them coming, his gaze lingering first on the bag over Crash's shoulder and then on Cass.

Crash tried not to drop the bag as they reached Seph and he put out his hands to catch it, so it landed softly on the ground. Crash avoided looking at Cass for a moment but the woman didn't say anything. She placed down her own bag, studying Seph.

'This is Seph,' said Crash. 'This is Cassidy. She's an engineer,' Crash told Seph proudly. Seph gave a single nod. 'Seph is one of our mercs, among other things.'

'Other things?' asked Cass.

'Yeah, like today he cleaned and refuelled the ship while we all went to the market.'

Seph gave Crash a steady, unblinking look. 'No one else back yet?'

'Capt'n's back,' said Seph.

'Where is he?'

'I'm here.'

They turned as Bucky walked down the ramp, looking round to them. Heaving up the bag, Crash led Cass over to him, meeting at the foot of the ramp. Seph took the bag from Cass and went to take Crash's before she dropped it again when Cass stopped him.

'Hang on,' she murmured.

'Capt'n, this is Cassidy. She's an engineer.' Crash stood back while Bucky looked Cass up and down.

'Captain Bucky Winters.' He held out his hand.

'Cassidy.'

They shook hands.

'No last name?'

'Is that important?'

Bucky shrugged.

'Depends. Are the authorities lookin' for you? No point just leavin' out a last name on our ship for that reason. We got a lawman on board.'

'Crash said. That's not the reason.'

'Not got anyone chasin' you?'

'No.'

'Good. Don't need more of them.'

Cass narrowed her eyes. 'What's your experience?' Bucky asked.

Crash held her breath.

'I'm self-taught, been playing with machines since I was five.'

'No formal training?'

'No.'

There was a pause. Crash looked between Cass and Bucky.

'How many years have you spent on ships?'

'None.'

Bucky slowly turned to Crash and raised an eyebrow. Yeah, this was going well. Crash looked down at her boots.

'No,' he said. 'Sorry,' he added to Cass. He turned to Seph and opened his mouth.

'The way I understand it,' Cass said before Bucky could speak. 'Your ship is broken.' She looked to Crash. 'That right?'

Crash glanced at Bucky and found him glaring at her.

'Well, she is, Capt'n. We're gonna fall outa the sky and how're we gonna do that job if we can't fly? We need someone and Cassidy here is a good someone.'

'How d'you know she's good?' Bucky asked, glancing back to Cass as if she couldn't hear him.

Cass looked to Crash. Crash swallowed.

'Well, 'cause she is.'

'Okay, but how do you know?'

'What's wrong with the engine? Do you know?'

Cass asked. Crash snapped her attention to her.

'A coil, or something,' Bucky said. 'Crash knows. She hasn't told you?'

Everyone turned to look at Crash again. Everyone thought Crash liked attention, that that was why she talked so damn much. It was true that sometimes Crash liked all eyes on her, when she was flying or when she was drinking, but sober and on the ground? She shrank back under the glare of their eyes.

'Didn't know if I should, Capt'n,' she murmured.

Bucky's eyes widened in exasperation and he gestured that Crash should tell her now. She faced Cass.

'There's a coil about to snap. It needs replacin'.'

'That's it?' Cass asked, looking from Bucky to Seph to Crash. 'Replace a coil?'

'Yeah, but that takes skill,' Crash pointed out. 'Skill that we don't have. But you do.'

'That's a skill every engineer has.'

'But not every engineer is right for this crew, Bucky told Cass. 'I'm lookin' for a new crew member. If you can give us a quick fix, then great. But we can't pay you right now. We get a new crew member, they'll get paid. You see where my problem is.'

Crash's stomach twisted. What was he doing? She'd found him an engineer and he was going to waste the opportunity.

'Oh yeah,' said Cass. 'I see your problem. You don't have any money.' She glanced at Crash. 'But not everyone wants just money.'

Crash grinned and her heart gave a flutter as

Cass smiled at her. Bucky looked between them, frowning.

'No? And what is it you want?'

Cass looked him in the eye.

'Safety,' she said. 'A safe place to live where I can work on my project here.' She pointed to the bag at her feet. 'I'll need space for it. And to be left alone. In return, I'll fix your ship and keep her running.'

'You've never worked on a ship before,' said Bucky.

'A machine's a machine. An engine's an engine.' Cass shrugged.

Bucky sucked on his teeth.

'C'mon, Capt'n. What we got to lose?' Crash murmured.

'Where'd you find her?' Bucky whispered.

'In the market. She was lookin' at cogs. And a steel barrel.'

Bucky's brow creased.

'You what?'

'That.' Crash pointed to Cass's bag. 'There's a steel barrel in there. She was looking over machinery.'

'That's it?' he hissed. 'You have no idea if she's any good?'

Crash opened and closed her mouth. She could hardly argue, but as she gazed over Cassidy, her silver hair flowing around her shoulders and down her back, she knew she was meant to be part of their crew.

'I say give her a chance, Capt'n. You gave Kai a chance.'

Bucky heaved a sigh.

'That did turn out well.'

'So might this,' said Crash, glancing back to Seph for support. The short man remained silent.

'Cassidy, was it?' Cass looked up at Bucky. 'What's this project of yours?'

'I'd rather not say. That'd be part of the agreement.'

'Okay. How much space do you need?'

Cass looked up at the ship and squinted.

'Looks like your loading bay would be big enough. You planning on having much in there?'

'Not that I know of.' Bucky rubbed his chin. 'Is it legal?'

Cass looked him in the eye.

'It's not not legal.'

Finally, Bucky smiled. Crash relaxed. Everything was going to be okay.

'So, she's in?' Crash asked.

'You fix the engine, keep us flyin', you get to work on whatever it is you're workin' on in the loading bay, you get a cabin and three meals a day, but you don't get paid till we've finished this job we got. And if we decide you're not a good fit, you'll get paid and you can go on your way. Deal?'

'Deal.' Cass held out her hand. Bucky shook it.

Crash bounced.

'We got an engineer!' she shrilled. 'Told you I'd find one.'

'Did you?' Bucky muttered. 'You met Seph?'

Cass nodded.

'Good. We're just waitin' on the others. You got everything you need?'

'Yup.'

'Great. Crash will show you around. Crash, show

her the engine room. I need you both to make sure we got what we need to stay flyin' before we leave. Seph, put Cassidy's bags in her cabin.'

Seph picked up the bags and Cass let him.

'Cass,' she said. 'It's Cass.'

Bucky gave a nod.

'Great. Oh, hold up. Here come the others.' Bucky shielded his eyes from the sun and they all turned to where he looked. Jude and Harley were walking towards them. 'Just waitin' on Kai, now.' Bucky held his arms open as Jude and Harley approached. 'We got an engineer!' he called when they were close enough. Jude smiled, looking to Cass.

'You found someone?' she asked.

'Hmm. Cass, this is Jude, our doctor, and Harley, the lawman who travels with us. This is Cassidy. She'll be keepin' us flyin' and using the loadin' bay for her…machines or whatever.'

'Oh. You build machines as well as maintain them?' Jude asked Cass. Cass cocked her head.

'I do.'

'Fascinating. I'd love to take a look.'

'Maybe.' Cass gave her a short smile and a curt nod to Harley who returned it.

'Kai isn't back yet?' he asked Bucky.

'She's the last to come back. Where did you leave her?' Bucky asked Crash. The pilot shrugged.

'I dunno. We all parted ways but I didn't see her go.'

Harley stared back towards the market.

'Maybe we should go find her.'

'It's not four o'clock yet.' Bucky gave him a pat on the shoulder. 'When she's late, then we'll talk about whether we go look for her or leave her behind.'

Crash and Jude stared at Bucky.

'We can't leave her,' Jude said as Crash yelled, 'We only just got her!'

Bucky blinked at them.

'You can't leave her behind after everything you did to get her on the crew,' Jude reminded him.

'Yeah. We need her, remember? You said so.'

'I did, I did.' Bucky ran a hand down his face. 'But I was clear about today. Back by four. It ain't four yet. She's got five minutes.'

They all glanced back to the market but there was no sign of Kai.

'C'mon,' Crash said to Cass. 'I'll show you the engine room.'

They began to walk up the ramp when Harley yelled, 'There!'

They stopped and looked back.

Walking, nearly jogging, onto the landing pad came Kai carrying full bags. She looked behind her and picked up the pace.

'Is she okay?' Jude murmured.

'Looks spooked,' said Bucky.

Without a word, Harley began walking towards her. As Kai looked in their direction, he held up a hand and waved to her.

'Right. Everyone's here. Crash, wait and introduce Cass to our new merc and then get to the cockpit. I'll show Cass the engine room.'

Crash deflated a little.

'Fine,' she muttered. She folded her arms and stood on the ramp to watch Kai come in.

Harley was still a good distance from her when

Kai stopped.

'What's she doin'?' Crash murmured, narrowing her eyes to try and see clearer.

They watched as Kai looked around and then started jogging towards Harley. Harley hesitated and then picked up the pace.

'What's goin' on?' Bucky growled.

A four wheeled vehicle came speeding from the right.

'Where—?' Crash looked over and saw a tiny ship, a Gallnupper class boat with the ramp down, a figure inside, waiting. 'Capt'n!' she yelled, running down and jumping onto the concrete of the landing pad.

The transport's wheels squealed as it headed straight for Kai. She began running towards Harley. One of the figures leapt from the vehicle while it was still moving. As the vehicle did a tight circle to turn around, the figure on the ground threw itself at Kai and hit her. Tumbling to the ground, Kai screamed, her voice clearly reaching The Magpie crew.

'Seph!' Bucky cried as he started running towards Kai and Harley, Seph close behind.

The figure on Kai picked her up, dragging her to her feet, as the vehicle pulled up beside them. Kai was put into the vehicle, kicking out at her attackers as her arms were pinned behind her. Harley was almost on them when the vehicle sped away, back towards the waiting boat. Bucky and Seph changed direction to follow, Bucky pulling out his revolver and aiming a shot.

'No!' yelled Jude. 'You might hit her!'

There was no way they could have heard her but

Bucky seemed to have the same thought, holding back from firing his weapon. Harley was faster than the other men, reaching the ship first. He skidded to a halt and yelled as the ramp lifted up. He'd be shouting about being a lawman, thought Crash. Yelling at them to stop and explain themselves and to give Kai back, but she was on that boat now and lost behind the closing doors.

The engines fired up as the doors shut and Harley was forced back, just as Bucky and Seph reached him.

'Shit,' said Crash, as they all watched the Gall-nupper take off, taking Kai with it.

Bucky

'We have to go after them. Right now,' Harley growled, storming up the ramp of The Magpie.

'All right, all right. Calm down,' said Bucky, close on his heels. 'Everyone inside. Crash, get us in the sky, right now. Jude, show Cass the engine room.' He turned on Cass. 'I want that engine fixed. Keep us flyin' or you're off.'

Cass didn't respond but followed Jude as the doctor left to lead her through the ship.

Bucky hesitated as the crew disappeared to their posts. As he hit the button to lift the ramp, he saw a large muscular man with a toolkit heading towards them. The man broke into a jog when he saw the ramp moving. Bucky walked to the edge as the ramp lifted and cupped his hands around his mouth.

'We got an engineer!' he yelled. 'Tell Castell

thanks though!'

The door lifted and shut, sealing Bucky and his crew inside. He allowed himself a satisfied smirk before running through the ship, up the stairs and storming into the cockpit.

'I'll give you co-ordinates,' he said.

Crash turned on him.

'We follow that boat?' she said, pointing out the window as the ship holding Kai rose further into the sky.

'Crash, we got a job to do and a time limit on it.'

'We're going after her,' said Harley from behind him. Bucky held in a sigh but moved so he could see both of them as they crossed their arms simultaneously. Bucky pursed his lips.

'We have to get this job done,' said Bucky. 'Crash, get us in the air.'

'I can't until Cass has fixed the engine.'

Bucky snapped up to look at Crash. They rarely heard her stern tone, but there it was. He knew what that meant. If he wanted to fly off in the opposite direction to Kai, he'd be the one doing the flying.

'Fine.' Bucky turned and walked straight into Jude entering the cockpit. Seph was behind her.

'Cass is looking at the engine now. She spotted the problem immediately, said it's an easy fix. She even has a part in her bag. We are going after Kai, right?'

'We have a job to do,' Bucky growled at her.

Now Jude crossed her arms. Bucky looked at each of his crew members, all staring him down, arms tight across their chests. Seph stood behind Jude, his arms at his sides but his eyes told Bucky all he needed to know.

'Oh, for the love of—we have to get this job done.' He looked to Jude for help.

'She's part of the crew, Bucky,' she said. 'You have no idea what they're going to do to her. She was scared of them. They'll force her into a marriage and a marital bed. Do you want that on your hands? Because I don't.'

'You're outnumbered, Capt'n,' murmured Crash.

'And bound by law, Captain,' Harley pointed out.

Bucky glanced at him.

'What law? There's no law that says I have to go after her. There's a code, but that's not legal. You want to go after her, that's fine, there are smaller ships here you can rent. Go after her.'

'Then we'll all go after her,' Crash told him in her cold monotone.

A shiver ran through Bucky.

'No. You have a job to do.'

'So, do you. You're our captain. You're her captain.'

Bucky rubbed his forehead, Kai's words echoing through his mind.

'You don't understand…'

'So tell them,' said Jude, her voice softening. She dropped her arms and stepped closer to him. 'Tell them the truth.'

'Truth? What truth?' Crash's arms fell and she looked between Bucky and Jude. 'What truth?'

Behind her the intercom crackled.

'Engine's good to go,' came Cass's voice. 'Hello? Anyone reading me? We're good to go. Start her up.'

Hesitantly, Crash went to the intercom.

'Thanks, Cass. Might want to come to the cockpit. Don't get lost.' She faced Bucky. 'What truth?'

Bucky sighed. So it was going to be like this, in the small cockpit where they only just fit. He cleared his throat.

'Fine. Here we go. We don't have any money—'

'We know that,' Crash interrupted.

'It's worse than you think.'

'Worse than not being able to buy food for a while?'

Bucky nodded, noting Cassidy approaching the cockpit and standing behind Seph, looking at each crew member, trying to catch up. Bucky took another deep breath.

'We haven't had any money for a while now.'

Seph frowned but said nothing.

'Except enough to buy the food we've been eatin'.'

'No, Crash. I stole that money. To buy food, to pay your wages. It's why we couldn't afford to fix the engine. I mean, look at that. That took, what? Five minutes?' Cass nodded. 'Yeah. Couldn't even afford that. Never mind replace our engineer and navigator.'

'I said we should steal!' Crash threw up her arms.

'Stealing from our clients,' Bucky explained. Crash's eyes widened.

'What? Why? That's stupid.'

'I was desperate. So I pickpocketed our clients.' Bucky glanced at Harley but the lawman didn't respond. 'That job was goin' to be our last. We had nothin' lined up. Until…'

'Until?' Crash prompted after Bucky didn't say anything for a while.

'I thought that if things carried on and I didn't find more jobs you'd disband. Leave me on this ship alone. And I couldn't for the life of me find any more jobs. So, I went lookin' where I shouldn't have.'

'What did you do?' Harley asked. It wasn't really his place, Bucky thought. Harley wasn't part of this crew. This didn't affect him. It was bad enough that Bucky was confessing to crimes in front of the lawman, even if he wasn't technically an official lawman, yet. Bucky closed his mouth. Harley let his crossed arms fall and leaned against the wall of the cockpit.

'I'm not going to arrest you, Captain.'

'Thought you were all about justice and doin' the right thing.'

Harley shrugged.

'Sounds like you were too. You were trying to keep a roof over your heads, you were looking out for your crew, and yourself. I doubt you stole enough to ruin anyone's life. And I know a lot about that.'

Bucky gave Harley a small, appreciative smile. Yes, that was why he let Harley on his ship. Sometimes he forgot what a good man he was.

'Is this about the big job we got, Capt'n?' asked Crash, bringing the conversation round. 'It's why you don't want to go after Kai?'

This was it. Bucky took another deep breath. Now or never.

'I took a job from Castell. You heard of him? He's not what you expect, except he's much worse.

210

I took the job. It's dangerous, it's illegal.' Bucky glanced back to Harley. 'And we have a time limit. We don't get it done, we're dead.'

Crash's mouth opened but Jude was the one who punched Bucky's arm.

'You didn't mention that,' Cass murmured. Bucky gave her a fleeting look.

'When do we need to get the job done?' Crash asked, recovering quickly.

'The first part is tonight.'

'Where?'

'West Vale.'

'Shit.' Crash turned her back on the crew, facing out of the window. The boat carrying Kai had vanished. 'We have to go get her, Capt'n,' Crash murmured.

'I can help,' said Harley. 'With the job, too. Whatever I can do'

'You're not part of this crew,' Bucky told him. 'It's not your responsibility.'

'He's part of the family,' came Crash's voice. 'And so is Kai.' She turned back. 'We face this shit together, and you said yourself, that job will be easier with someone like Kai.'

'We need a sharpshooter, Capt'n.' They all turned to look at Seph. He shrugged. 'We do.'

Bucky turned to Jude.

'They're going to do things to her, Bucky. I can't…we can't…'

Bucky groaned.

'Fine. Fine. But we have to go quick.'

Crash bounced into her seat and started the engine.

'We don't know where we're going,' Jude said

as Cass turned to rush back to the engine room, Seph close on her heels.

'Back to Valkwick, where we found her,' Bucky told them.

'They're taking her to Decima,' Harley said. 'I sort of know where that is.'

'Great. Crash, meet your new navigator.'

Bucky left Crash and Harley to it, losing his footing a little as the ship took off and then accelerated. He held onto the wall as he went, walking as fast as the ship would allow him to his office. He closed the door and leaned on his desk, fighting the tightness in his chest.

Behind him, the door opened and closed.

'Can I just have a moment, Jude?'

'She's a Visionary.'

Bucky straightened and turned to face his sister.

'What? What's a Visionary? What are you on about?'

'Kai is a Visionary. I shouldn't be telling you this, but I think you need to know.'

'What in the gods is a Visionary?'

'I've been reading up on it. All the evidence pointed to it. Where she's from, what she's been going through. That dream. So I asked her and she confirmed it.'

'I swear, Jude, just get on with it.'

Jude sat down.

'A Visionary is someone who gets visions of the future. Kai can see into the future. That's what she dreamt about that night she woke us all up. Something scary and something to do with her life back in Decima. Maybe she saw those men taking her, I don't know. She wouldn't tell me.'

Bucky leaned back and sat on his desk.

'She can see the future? Then why didn't she avoid being taken? Or getting into that wedding dress?'

Jude shrugged.

'It takes a lot of training to be a Visionary. They're all women and they're born into it, it's passed on through the blood. Her mother would have been a Visionary. But Kai was brought up by her aunt on her ship, wasn't she. So I doubt she got any of the training. I don't know what that means, exactly. Whether she doesn't know how to interpret the visions or the visions just aren't clear enough. Maybe she just gets bad dreams.'

'So, why do I need to know this?'

Jude searched Bucky's eyes.

'Because, little brother, the sharpshooter and cook you just employed and then lost has the ability, even if she requires some training to do it, to see into the future and I think that might be quite useful. You know, for jobs, like, for example, this big job we're doing in a rush after we get Kai back. Or future jobs. Or hiring engineers and navigators. Or, whatever. Don't you think?'

The possibilities had been whirring through Bucky's mind as Jude had spoken and now they gathered speed.

'I wonder what she's like at gambling,' he murmured.

'She can see the future, Bucky, she's not a mind reader. And we don't know how it works. But, in case you needed another reason to go get her, to fight for her, well, there it is.'

Bucky nodded, staring into space at his thoughts.

'Yes. Yes, that is useful. Yes. Okay.' He stood and clapped his hands once. 'Let's go get our girl back.'

'We can't just go in all guns firing,' Jude told him, not moving. 'We don't know the place and we don't know where they've taken her.'

'No, we'll need to be subtle, I guess. We don't know how many men this groom of hers has.'

'Exactly.'

'Fine. Seph is with Cass, right? I'll go have a word with him, see what weapons we have and make sure Cass is doing okay. You go to the cockpit, keep an eye on Crash and Harley.'

Jude stood.

'All right. And I'm coming this time.'

Bucky looked up at his sister.

'You want to come with us?'

'To get our girl back.' Jude nodded.

'You want a gun?'

Jude hesitated and then gave a slow nod.

'Yes.'

Bucky grinned and patted her shoulder.

'Well, this is goin' to be fun.'

Cassidy

Saying the engine room was hot would have been an understatement. Cass's skin prickled with sweat as she stepped inside and a smile grew on her lips without warning. Engines always had that effect on her. Absent-mindedly, she ran her fingertips over a metal pipe than ran from the ship into the engine, feeling the heat threaten to burn her skin.

'What can I do?' Seph murmured, breaking Cass from her reverie.

'Nothing. I've fixed the broken coil,' Cass told him, looking around the room, eager for him to go. 'I'll need to keep an eye on it, in case it has a wobble.'

Seph didn't respond but neither did he leave. He stepped further into the engine room, glancing around and finding the newly fixed coil.

'Looks like it's holdin'.'

'Yup.'

There was an awkward pause.

'Been with this crew long?' Cass asked.

'Yup.'

A moment later, realising Seph wasn't going to add to that response, Cass wandered further inside, her back to Seph. The room was a mass of copper and steel, of cogs and gears, turning, coils and hinges, and various sized cylinders filled with the bubbling sounds of the fuel moving through them. A large piston pumped as Crash sped the ship up and, instinctively, Cass put out an arm to steady herself as the ship shifted right.

'You've never worked on a ship,' Seph said, which Cass assumed was a question.

'No, but I've flown in them. By myself.'

'Must have been a small ship.'

'It wasn't, actually.' Cass stopped to check on the main cylinder. She didn't glance back to Seph or wonder if he was impressed. She was more interested in the copper wire, cogs, and broken cylinders and hinges she'd just spotted piled in the back corner. She ducked under the main cylinder and hovered over the pile, rolling a copper cylinder back with the tip of her boot.

The ship moved to the left and both Seph and Cass went with it.

'What's your story?' Cass asked, leaning down to pick up and examine a short cylinder. There was a thin crack along it, easily fixed. She wondered why it had been thrown into what was obviously a pile of rubbish. Had the previous engineer created the pile? Or had Crash?

'Nothin' much,' Seph mumbled. 'I needed work, Capt'n hired me.'

Cass caught Seph's eye and raised an eyebrow. 'That's it?'

Seph gave a deliberate nod. 'Fair enough.' Cass held up the cylinder. 'Your previous engineer chuck these out?'

'I guess.'

'This can be fixed.'

'Capt'n'll be happy to hear it.'

Cass glanced at Seph again.

'Don't say much, do you.'

'Not paid to talk.'

'I didn't realise this was that type of crew. I'm not sure I'm gonna be paid at all.'

Seph gave a small smile.

'People on this ship are usually runnin' from somethin',' he told her.

'But you're not gonna tell me what you're runnin' from?'

'And I won't ask what you're runnin' from.'

Cass grinned.

'Oh, I'm not running away from something. Oh, no. I'm running towards something.' She gripped the broken cylinder and studied the rest of the rubbish pile. There was so much material just sitting there, going to waste.

'And we're takin' you there?'

'Maybe. Guess it depends on how this goes, doesn't it. How long has this Kai been on the crew?'

'A week.'

Cass lowered her hands, the cylinder falling to her side as she stared at Seph.

'She's been on the crew a week and she's already been kidnapped? And we're going off course to get her back?'

Seph nodded.

Cass looked back down at the cylinder. She imagined it looked like she was reconsidering joining the crew, or was perhaps concerned for Kai. Instead, she was planning on what she would use this cylinder for. The crew obviously didn't want it and if they had no use for it, she certainly did.

'The man she was runnin' from caught up with her,' Seph said. Cass snapped away from her plans.

'Guess it was hard to fly fast enough when your engine was faulty. Good thing Crash found me, huh? Got you back flying so you can go get her. She's a mercenary?'

Seph held eye contact, his dark eyes intense with the monotone quiet of his voice.

'Our cook.'

Cass frowned.

'You called her a sharpshooter.'

Seph turned around and began to walk out of the engine room.

'You know how the intercom works. Press one for the cockpit, two for the loading bay, three for the med bay. I'll go see if Crash needs a hand.'

Now he was leaving? Cass moved to follow him.

'She's a cook and a sharpshooter?'

'She joined as a cook. If we get her back, she'll be our sharpshooter.' Seph paused and looked at Cass over his shoulder. 'We need her back.' Seph left the engine room.

It took Cass a moment to tear her thoughts away from Kai and realise that she was alone among the heat and metal. She smiled, looking around.

She should have thought of this before. Joining a crew, living on a ship. To be honest, she'd always considered working as a ship's engineer to be beneath her. She could just about admit that she hadn't considered she would have a whole engine room for herself, a large engine that was hers to keep running, and spare, broken parts that would be hers to use.

It was probably a concern that Kai had only been part of the crew for a week before trouble had found her. Not that it was much of a problem for Cassidy. She wasn't running from anything and was happy to go along with wherever the crew took her, as long as she could have the freedom to make her own designs. As long as they didn't get caught, as long as she wasn't put behind bars and her tools and materials taken from her. That was the only way this could go wrong.

She grinned to herself, throwing the cylinder into the air and catching it. This had the potential to be a good gig. Once they had Kai back, she'd have to start setting up in the loading bay. In the meantime, the engine was running smoothly and she had a pile of discarded parts to sort through.

As she turned back to the rubbish, the intercom on the back wall buzzed. Cass made her way over and pressed the button.

'Yes?'

'Cassidy? How's it going?' came Crash's crackling voice.

'All fine and dandy,' Cass told her, glancing back to the engine. 'Any problems your end?'

'Nope. Flyin' smooth, now we got a headin'.

Flyin' smoother than we have in a long time. I guess that's thanks to you.'

'Why you hired me.'

Cass waited a moment but Crash didn't respond. With a small shrug, Cass went back to the pile of discarded metal in the corner. It was difficult to know what was going on when in the engine room. There were no windows and the only sound was the almost deafening pumping of the cylinder and grinding of the gears. A rush of steam would shoot out in some places every now and then, and the main cylinder would give a rattle. That might cause some concern for other engineers but after a few seconds of observation, Cass spotted a lose screw that was supposed to be holding the cylinder still.

Absent-mindedly, she stepped over, pulled a screwdriver from her pocket and tightened the screw. The rattling stopped immediately.

The intercom buzzed again.

'Hello, again,' said Cass, holding down the button.

'We need to go faster,' came Crash's voice. 'Their ship is so much smaller, it's zipped away. Doc wants us to gain some ground. Anythin' you can do?'

Cassidy glanced around the engine room.

'Give me a moment.'

She let go of the intercom and moved around the engine, ducking under pipes and tracing her fingers along the curves as she studied the intricacies of the machine. It had been designed well but it was outdated. Whatever engineer the crew had had before had not only thrown away good materials, they hadn't kept the ship up to date. Those engineers that had come before her hadn't had the know-how. She wondered if they'd blamed it on lack of funding from the captain.

Cass flipped the cracked cylinder in the air again and caught it. Well, she had the know-how and the parts. What she was lacking was the time.

She looked down at her right wrist to the large copper watch that sat against her skin.

'I could use a hand,' she murmured.

The watch, its face larger than the width of her wrist and showing not just the current time, but the time in three other places, began to glow blue.

Kai

The boat was small, even without comparing it to The Magpie. There was a tiny cockpit with one pilot and then two parallel rows of seats along the length of the ship, towards the tiny loading bay which only had room for the vehicle they'd used to snatch her. As far as Kai could see, that was it.

She sat on one side, her wrists bound behind her back, her feet tied together. The bags of food she'd bought at the market sat on the bench next to her. Opposite were the two men who had grabbed her. They sat, legs open, grinning silently. Kai glared at each of them in turn.

'We were getting a day off, you know,' said one of the men. He had long dark hair that he had to keep blowing out of his eyes in exhaled puffs. Kai didn't know how the man next to him didn't smash his fist into his face each time. 'And then you had to go and run away. Like a coward. I mean, you ran from a cushy life. What's wrong with you?'

'What's wrong with me? I didn't want to marry a man I don't like,' growled Kai.

The long-haired man laughed.

'It's not like you'd have to clean the house much!'

The other man chuckled to himself. 'You just have to open your legs to him every now and then and go around looking pretty and having visions. How hard is that?'

'I don't know. Why don't you open your legs and bend over for him and we'll see.'

The two men stopped laughing, their smiles fading. The long-haired one's neighbour pulled out a blade and pointed it at her.

'Careful what you say, miss. You're not married yet and until you're married, you're not safe from us.'

'You cut me, you'll have to pay for it. I'm guessing Bran wants me in one piece. Hard to pull off the whole harmonious married couple when one of us is sliced open.'

'Not if I slice where they can't see.'

Kai pulled at her wrists.

'Go on then.' She wasn't sure why she'd said that, the words just slipped out of her mouth, confident and proud.

The man hesitated and then sat back, lowering his blade.

'It's not worth the bother,' he mumbled.

Kai, heart pounding against her ribs, tried to relax a little. She needed to conserve some energy if she was going to get out of this.

And how was she going to do that? She blinked back tears. Last time she only escaped moments before the wedding ceremony because that had been the only opportunity to present itself. There had been so much chaos, so much confusion, that they had taken their concentration from her for one second. It had been all she'd needed.

She needed to learn from that, to take her time.

Except, she doubted there would be any time. They wouldn't wait for her to escape again, and everything was already prepared. All they needed to do was get her back in a wedding dress, tell the guests and drag her into position.

Kai unstuck her tongue from the roof of her mouth.

'Got a new dress for me, have they?' she asked, her voice low to keep it from breaking.

The long-haired man shrugged.

'Would serve you right if they made you get married naked.'

The man with the blade grinned.

'Oh, don't you worry, they'll have another dress. Can't get married without a dress, can you? Not a woman of your stature. Not with all those people lookin'. That's why it'd be so easy to cut you. No one would know. That dress would hide so much.'

'Until Bran takes it off me,' Kai told him.

He shrugged, turning away from her.

'Will you get a day off again?'

The long-haired man barked a laugh and Kai's stomach turned as Crash's smiling face appeared in her mind.

'We're workin' now, ain't we? So much for a

day off.'

Kai gritted her teeth. She'd been right. They wouldn't wait to hold the wedding, although she hadn't been expecting it to happen so soon.

'Today? The wedding's today? I won't have time to freshen up.' She tried to pull against the binds around her wrists without moving any part the men could see.

'They'll scrub you clean. Didn't think you cared so much,' the bladed man grumbled.

Kai cocked her head at him. He was older than the long-haired one.

'You got children?' she asked. He didn't look at her. 'You've got daughters, don't you?' She leaned towards him. 'You don't have to do this, you know. You could help me. Imagine, imagine if this was one of your daughters sat here. One of your daughters about to be forced into marriage to a man she didn't like. Your daughter forced to open her legs and bear his children.'

He slowly made eye contact, his expression hard.

'Shut up,' he growled.

'It ain't his daughter, though, is it,' said the other man. 'It's you. He's not stupid enough to go and get one of the High Priestesses pregnant. So it never would be one of his daughters.'

Kai stared at him steadily.

'You can't help who you fall in love with,' she murmured. 'Am I really so different from your daughters?' she asked the man with the blade. He turned away.

'Yeah. You're older, marrying age, plus you're a Visionary. His daughters'll get to marry whoever they want. There's plenty of differences.'

Kai kept her attention on the older man as the other exhaled in a puff, blowing the hair from his eyes.

'Will you stop doing that?' the bladed man turned on him. 'Or it's you I'll cut.'

The long-haired one sank back, glaring at Kai.

Great, she thought, get him all angry. There's only one person on the boat he can take that anger out on.

The ship dipped and her two captors looked up, reaching up to grab hold of something and steady themselves. The longer-haired one grinned at Kai.

'We're home,' he sang.

Kai's chest fluttered, her stomach turning, threatening to bring her breakfast back up. The lowering boat didn't help, as her insides were forced up. Kai closed her eyes and tried to think steady thoughts.

The ship landed with a light bump and the two men were up in seconds, yanking Kai to her feet before she had time to take a deep breath and swallow the rising bile.

The men pulled her from the ship. Her arms screamed as their fingers dug in but she let her feet drag. The long-haired man swore, his chipped fingernails pinching her skin, but still she wouldn't move her legs. He dropped her, making the older man stumble.

'Stand up and walk properly,' the long-haired man growled. Kai glared up at him.

Out of the corner of her eye she could see that they weren't on the normal Decima landing pad. They were on the royal landing pad, the boat they'd arrived on sat next to the king's large, sleek ship.

That meant that there weren't just some people around, there were guards around.

Kai didn't speak, neither did she move.

'Stand up. I'm not draggin' you,' the man spat. The older man sighed and went to pick her up.

Kai shifted, tucking her legs under her, leaning away from him.

'Hard to walk with my legs tied together.'

'Not impossible,' the younger man said.

'What's going on?' came a clear voice. Kai looked around the men to see two of the castle's guards approaching.

'We have Miss Summerbee,' the older man said, lifting Kai easily and placing her over his shoulder. She wriggled and spat curses at him, exposed and helpless. He put an arm across the back of her thighs to hold her in place as he walked towards the guards. 'Tell the king. Oh, and we want our reward.'

Reward? Bran had put a reward out for her? Kai stopped struggling. There really had been no chance of her escaping.

One of the guard's faces appeared in front of her. He studied her and then turned and nodded to his colleague.

'Bring her this way.'

'Nice to see you too,' Kai mumbled, gripping onto the shirt of the man who carried her.

The castle hadn't changed, but why would it after only a week? The walls were made of stone with large tapestries thrown over them. The inhabitants were glad of those in winter, they kept in the warmth from the great fires lit in the hearths in each room. But in summer, when the sun beat down relentlessly over Decima, it all became a bit much.

Sweat trickling across her back, the stench of the man carrying her permeating her nostrils, Kai was placed almost carefully into an armchair.

'This way, gentlemen. The king has been notified and will want to thank you.'

The men left the small room, containing only two large, leather armchairs and the great fireplace. Kai watched them go, trying to find a more comfortable position despite her wrists and legs still being bound. The older man glanced over his shoulder to her, and then they were gone, along with the guards.

Kai held her breath.

She was alone. She stood, a little shakily, and looked for a window. There were none. It would have to be the door. Beside the fireplace was a small coal shovel and a poker. She picked up the poker and tested it, both hands gripping it, swinging it through the air with a satisfying swoosh.

Her teeth gritted, she moved towards the door, which opened, revealing a man whose eyes widened at the sight of her.

There was a moment of hesitation from both of them and then King Bran laughed. He gestured for the guards behind him to leave as he entered the room and shut the door. Kai stood, poker still in her hand, wondering how much force she would need to knock him out, and whether he'd have a blade she could use to free herself.

'Hello, Kai,' he murmured, taking a seat in the armchair opposite the one she'd been dumped in.

'You're looking well, considering.' She turned to face him, her hair sticking to her neck and cheeks as the sweat beaded on her skin. 'What were you planning, exactly?' he asked, a frown playing on his brow as he looked her up and down. 'To escape with your legs tied together and nothing but a poker?' He looked up into her eyes, a bemused smile twitching at his lips.

Bran wasn't bad looking, in fact many women in Decima considered him handsome. He wasn't necessarily a bad man, either. He was kind to his people and there were rumours that he had a fondness for animals. Kai had believed the whispers when she'd first been brought to the castle. She'd explained that she didn't want this life, that she didn't want him, that he could easily find someone else.

She thought he would let her go, release her to live her own life. Except, as he had pointed out, their marriage had been foreseen, as had their child.

'Please don't do this,' she murmured, not dropping the poker.

The humour drained from Bran's face and he rubbed at his dark eyes.

'I don't have a choice, Kai. You haven't given me any choice. I thought we had a deal? I thought we'd discussed this? You seemed happy.'

'Well, I wasn't.'

'I didn't realise I was asking so much.'

'You asked for my body, Bran. That's too much.'

'One night, Kai. And one child. You don't even have to stay here to raise the child. You never have to see the child again. We'll tell everyone you ran away and died, which I suppose is more believable now. I'll have my heir and you can go do whatever it is you want to do so badly.' Bran looked her up and down again. 'Be a pirate on your aunt's ship. Is that it? You want to be a pirate, instead of the wife of a king.'

'I want my freedom, Bran. I want to make my own choices.'

'You see, this is why you should have stayed in Decima. If you'd stayed, received the proper training as you were supposed to, we'd be happily married by now.'

Kai lowered the poker and laughed.

'Why? Because I wouldn't have tasted freedom? Because I wouldn't know what lies beyond our valley? You admit then, you want me to be a prisoner.'

Bran's eyes softened.

'I don't believe anyone could imprison you, Kai. You've never been the type.' He sighed and stood. 'Are you having visions? Did you see this coming?'

Kai didn't respond. 'I'll take that as a yes, then,' said Bran, studying her eyes. 'I've known you since we were children, Kai. Remember? Two children, playing together. I saw the fire in you then, and your inability to lie. I do wish you'd agree to this marriage and stay.'

'You're asking me to bear a child for you and I won't do it,' Kai hissed. 'You don't have to do this.'

'Apparently I do. You could make this easier. Give yourself willingly.'

'No,' Kai murmured as a shiver of déjà vu ran through her.

230

Bran heaved another sigh.

'You know I don't have a choice.'

'You're the king, Bran. You have all the choices. You can change this tradition. Find a woman who loves you, and who you love.'

Bran frowned and stepped over to her, gently taking the poker from her hand.

'Didn't you hear me? I thought it was clear. You're the one, Kai, you're the woman I love. Ever since we played together as children. Ever since I saw that fire in you.' He opened the door, revealing the guards stood outside. 'Take her to her room, see that her handmaid knows she's returned.' He glanced back to Kai. 'And tell the staff to prepare for our wedding.'

He walked away, still holding the poker, disappearing from sight as the guards approached Kai.

Crash

Bucky stepped into the cockpit to find it already quite crowded. Harley stood near the doorway, large arms crossed against his chest, and Seph sat in the co-pilot's seat staring at some maps that none of them could fathom.

'How we doin'?' Bucky asked Crash, sitting in her chair, leaning forward to stare out of the large window. Bucky glanced around at the vista.

'We're here, Capt'n. Did you ever doubt me? C'mon, you hire the best pilot there is, she'll get you here.'

Directly below them was a large, green forest and there, just over the tops of the trees, were the turrets of a castle.

'What the hell is that?' he grumbled.

'Well, see, here's the thing, Capt'n,' said Crash.

Bucky sighed and crossed his arms, mirroring Harley beside him.

'Go on, what now. Did we lose her?'

'No, no. She's down there. If I lift the ship up a bit, you'll be able to see that little tugboat of a thing they took her away on.'

'So, what's the problem?'

'Well, Capt'n, the problem is that if I lift The Magpie up to show you said tugboat, there's a good chance we'll be shot at.'

'Shot at?' Bucky approached the control panel, leaning his hands between the buttons and reaching to look out of the window, to get a better and wider look.

'Yup. Can't see 'em from here, seeing as they can't see us from here, but they're there. Trust me.'

'So, Decima has good security,' Bucky murmured. 'Doesn't bode well.'

'We can't go storming in,' said Harley, stroking the braids of his beard.

'Right. Crew meeting. Everyone in the mess, now. I'll tell Jude, Crash, you get our new engineer.'

'Aye, aye, Capt'n.' Crash gave a salute and hit the intercom button.

Crash put her feet up on the dining table in the mess and caught herself glancing into the kitchenette. Kai had been on The Magpie for a only a week and yet her absence could be felt. There was a Kai shaped hole in the mess. Crash looked at each of the crew in turn, wondering if they felt it too. She ignored Harley. She was pretty sure he'd been feeling it since the second Kai had been snatched.

Seph looked mildly uncomfortable, but he was a man who was hard to read. Jude was wringing her hands, she was worried. Nothing new there, and Crash shared her anxieties this time. Cass sat back in her chair and Crash let her gaze linger on the engineer. Her long silver hair fell down the back of the chair. She didn't know Kai, so Crash could forgive her for not feeling the same as the rest of the crew. Kai hadn't had a chance to cook for Cass yet. But she would, Crash told herself, biting her lower lip. They'd get Kai back, introduce her to Cass and Kai would make something that would burn her onto Cass's heart. Crash blinked. One week, she thought. It had to be the fastest time anyone had become so much part of the family.

'Right. We need a plan. Does anyone know where we should be headed? Where will they be taking Kai?' Bucky asked, looking between them all.

'The temple,' said Jude, catching Harley's eye. 'Maybe.'

Harley narrowed his eyes.

'Maybe. It's all we have. It's a good place to start.'

'Great. Anyone know where the temple is?' Bucky looked around again but no one responded. 'Well, I guess we go in and find out.' He clapped his hands. 'We'll go in on the Bumblebee, keep it low key. We're there as traders, looking for good deals. I'll go with Seph and Harley. Rest of you stay here.'

'What?' Crash screeched at the same time as Jude yelled, 'Absolutely not!'

The women glanced at each other.

'We're coming with you,' Jude told the captain. 'We're all in this together.'

Bucky shook his head.

'Nope. This is a scouting mission and we don't know what's waitin' for us. We'll figure out where she is, send word to you and then you come join us. If we need you.'

'Is this because we're women?' Crash asked as she, Jude and Cass all glared at Bucky. The captain took a step back, remembered himself and stepped forward, clearing his throat.

'Absolutely not. I need someone who can fly the ship in case it needs moving or we need rescuin'. I need someone in the engine room to help you out, just in case. And I need the medic on standby.'

'I'd be more help if I came with you,' said Jude.

'And if there's trouble, you'll be in the way. You can't shoot.' Bucky held up a finger as Jude opened her mouth to argue. 'That's final.'

Jude closed her mouth.

'We don't even know if Kai is in trouble—'

'She was being forced into marriage,' Crash interrupted.

'Yeah, but she won't be forced into it today, will she? For all we know, she's in a plush room—'

'Being kept against her will,' said Jude.

'True, but in luxury and we're comin' to get her, aren't we.'

Crash crossed her arms and exhaled hard.

'And what if they're doing things to her?' Jude asked. 'Punishing her for running away? I should come along. Just in case.'

Crash had to give Bucky his due as he considered this for a moment.

'No. Nope. Still too dangerous. We go in, find out where she is, assess the situation, and—'

'We then come in, guns blazin'and save your asses?' Crash offered.

Bucky clicked his fingers and pointed at her.

'Close enough,' he said. 'Everyone know what they're doin'?' He clapped his hands. 'Good. Crash, get back in the cockpit so I can contact you if need be. Jude, get some supplies together in case there's an emergency, and, erm, Cassidy, err…'

'The engine is all ready to go,' said Cass.

'She can keep me company in the cockpit.' Crash grinned but her shoulders sagged as she saw the expression on Cass's face.

Bucky gave a nod.

'Whatever, figure it out, just be ready if we need you.'

'*When* you need us,' Crash mumbled.

The men followed Bucky out of the mess. Jude stood and faced Crash and Cass once they were alone.

'You don't want to wait in the cockpit?' Crash asked Cass while she had the chance, before Jude could speak.

Cass frowned at her.

'What? No, I don't mind.'

'You pulled a face.'

'Did I? Sorry. I was just thinking, if we had time to spare, I could be setting up one of my projects. Or unpacking. You know.'

Crash narrowed her eyes and then shrugged.

'Fair enough. Except we don't have time.'

'No. I'll go get my supplies, then shall I join you in the cockpit?' Jude offered.

236

'Can do. Or we can wait in the loading bay. I'll get the radio down there workin' so Capt'n can contact us. Then we'll be ready to go in and get 'em.'

'How many vehicles do you have?' Cass asked.

'Just the one.' Crash rubbed the hair on the back of her head. 'They got a landin' pad here. If need be, we'll land there, make up some rubbish to give us the all clear or somethin'.'

'I don't like this,' murmured Jude. 'We should all be going together. This is just going to take too much time. We don't know how much time Kai has, if she has any at all.'

'What do you know of the folk that live here?' said Cass.

'Nothing,' Jude told her. 'Why?'

'Just that you're making them out to be violent, untrustworthy scumbags when actually you don't know a thing about them.'

'The bloke she was being forced to marry is some rich guy with men workin' for him. Men who kidnapped her,' Crash told her.

'You can't tarnish the whole country with that brush.'

'It's a small country no one's really heard of,' Crash argued. 'Chances are they're a bit backward.'

'The same can be said of Diathan Falls.' Cass shrugged. 'I think that whole country is backward. The rich waste their food and are bored with their lives while the poor work themselves to death if they don't starve first. You can call any country or town backward if you don't know enough.'

Jude was nodding.

'I'm from Diathan Falls. She has a point.' She

looked up at Crash. 'And I'm pretty certain that the man Kai's being forced to marry is the king.' Crash and Cass stared at Jude but she continued before Crash could speak. 'Once the men are gone, why don't we get to the landing pad? You can tell Bucky where we are when we get there. That way we're ready to go. No wasted time. Well, no more than we have to.'

Cass glanced between Jude and Crash.

'Who's second here? Who's in charge when the captain's gone?'

Crash looked at Jude and beamed.

'Doctor Jude Winters is,' she told Cass. 'And the Doc just gave me an order.'

Crash sat in the chair in the cockpit and watched the Bumblebee drive through the forest, disappearing amongst the trees. Bucky was driving, a little too carefully and slowly for Crash's taste, but they'd always had different styles. Harley was next to him and even from this distance, Crash could see him fretting. Girl makes him one nice meal and he goes all funny, she thought. Seph was in the back, holding on, unreadable as always.

'Ready?' Jude appeared behind her. 'Where's Cassidy?'

'It occurred to me that we're in a massive forest,' said Crash.

'And? Is Cassidy in the engine room?'

Crash nodded.

'But even with all those trees, this ship's still gonna make one helluva racket when we take off. Capt'n's bound to hear.'

Jude plonked herself into the co-pilot's chair.

'Good point. So, we shouldn't do it?'

'Well, you're in charge, Doc, so I hope you don't mind but I used my initiative and asked Cass if there was anything that could be done about the engine noise.'

'Oh?'

'She said probably not but that she'd take a look. Somethin' to do while we wait for the Capt'n to gain some distance.'

Out of the corner of her eye, Crash saw Jude smiling at her.

'Done the best I could.' Cass appeared behind them, making them both jump.

'That was quick.' Crash looked back to the engineer. Cass was wiping grease from her fingers. 'How did you do?' Crash forced her eyes back up to Cass's face.

'Not much I could do. We'll still be loud, but not as loud. I imagine they'll still hear us.'

'Well.' Crash turned to her controls. 'One way to find out.' She kicked the engine on and felt The Magpie shudder to life around her. Pushing the stick in front of her forward, the ship roared and lifted from the ground.

It only took a few minutes before the radio buzzed.

'Crash? What the fuck is goin' on?' came Bucky's voice.

'Nothin', Capt'n. Just movin' the ship, is all,' Crash told him, raising The Magpie and setting her on course for the landing pad off to the left, on the outskirts of the tiny country that was the size of a city. Crash shook her head. How could a country be so small?

'Movin' her where, Crash?' Bucky sounded angry. Crash smiled.

'Not far, Capt'n. Will let you know when we touch down.'

There was a growl through the radio as Bucky told them to be careful through gritted teeth, and then they were alone again.

'I'll pay for that,' Jude muttered.

'He'll see sense,' Crash told her. 'Once we have Kai back.'

The landing pad was small compared to others belonging to cities, and considering it seemed to be the only landing pad for the entire country.

'Does this place not trade with the outside world?' Crash muttered as she got permission to land.

'They better do, or Bucky and the boys' cover will be blown immediately.'

'They don't have many fields,' Cass pointed out. 'They must import some food. They can't grow enough here.'

'Makes you wonder why they ain't been taken over yet,' Crash mumbled, landing the ship with a gentle bump. 'We're here. Shall I let the Capt'n know?'

Jude nodded.

'I suppose I best go fill out the paperwork.' She stood and went to leave. 'It's been a long time since I did that without Bucky.'

Crash let Cass and Jude leave as she tried to get hold of the captain. She quickly told him where they were and as he was asking why they'd gone against his orders, she made a crackling noise into the microphone and switched the radio off. She'd switch it back on when she got down to the loading bay.

By the time she got down there, the doors were open and at the bottom of the ramp, Jude and Cass were talking to a man with a large belly. Crash switched on the radio and ambled over.

'Everythin' okay?' she murmured to Cass. The engineer didn't respond.

'They want to charge us double for parking here,' Jude told her. 'We're lucky to get a space apparently.'

'Oh? Why's that?'

Jude caught Crash's eye and the worry in that one look made Crash's bowels loosen.

Bucky

Bucky stomped a little too hard on the brake and the Bumblebee stopped with a shudder, sending Harley and Seph falling forward. Harley straightened, shooting Bucky a look.

Bucky ignored him.

They were parked on a side street, having entered the city from the forest. Homesteads had given way to a proper road and buildings on either side, growing closer together until they'd reached what sounded like a market ahead.

The sun beat down and Bucky was glad to find some shade in the shadow of the buildings.

'They'll be ok,' Harley told him as they climbed out of the vehicle. Seph jumped down, looking around. Bucky huffed, making sure his weapon was concealed under his coat.

'Disobeyed an order,' he grumbled.

'Technically, you didn't order them to keep the ship where it was.'

'I told them to stay put,' Bucky told Harley as they looked out across the street. 'That'll be Crash. That woman can't take orders.' He gave Harley a warning look as the man opened his mouth to protest again. Bucky took a deep breath, trying to compose himself, and pulled a face. 'Funny smell in this place.'

The others stopped and sniffed.

Most of the cities Bucky had been to in this part of the world were often cold and wet. This sun and blue sky were common but only in the peak of summer, which was now over. The smell wasn't of the heat or of the rain. Bucky checked the road and around his feet but there was no sign of sewage, although that wouldn't have surprised him given how small and isolated this country was. They reached the main road, the sun bearing down on them again, and Bucky stopped, looking around, sniffing. He stopped as he turned to his right, his arms falling to his sides. Seph and Harley reached him and followed his gaze.

'Nice castle,' Bucky murmured.

In front of them, rising from the edge of the city, was a turreted, grey brick castle with high walls and small, stained glass windows. 'Wonder if that's still in use.'

'Excuse me.'

Bucky turned to Harley who had stopped a woman. Her long brown hair was flecked with grey and she was wearing a silk blue dress. She held no bags or evidence of the market Bucky thought they were headed towards. 'We're new in town, looking to trade some goods,' Harley told her. Bucky held back, so as not to intimidate the woman as she glanced at him and Seph. 'I've heard there's a lovely temple here, I was wondering if you could point me in the right direction?'

The woman looked Harley up and down and Bucky wondered if she'd talk to him.

'Well, you picked one hell of a day,' she said with a smile. Bucky relaxed a little. If she did recognise what Harley once was, it didn't seem to bother her. It hadn't bothered Kai either, maybe that was how these people were brought up. In which case, Decima wasn't such a bad place after all.

'Why's that?' Harley asked.

'There won't be much trading to be done today, I'm afraid. You might want to find a couple of rooms for the night, the markets will be back to normal tomorrow. Back to business as usual tomorrow. We sort of had it sprung on us only a couple of hours ago. Still, there was enough time for me to get my dress ironed.' The woman swished the hem of the blue dress and then looked back up at Harley.

'Had what sprung on you?' Bucky asked, feeling a little nauseous.

'The royal wedding.' The woman beamed.

Harley shot Bucky a look.

'Sounds like a good party,' said Bucky. 'I didn't realise you had a royal family here. Up at the castle?' Bucky gestured to the turrets. The woman nodded.

'We've always had a royal family. You didn't know that? Where are you boys from?'

'Diathan Falls,' Bucky said before Harley could respond.

The woman studied each of them in turn.

'I've heard of it. Is it nice there?'

'It is. It's…different to here,' Bucky told her. 'More buildings, more people, fewer trees.'

'Oh, that does sound lovely.'

Bucky smiled although he didn't exactly agree.

'Who's getting married?' Harley asked.

'King Bran. He hasn't been king for long, only a few weeks. We had his coronation after good King Drest sadly passed away, then he was supposed to get married only a week ago but unfortunately the wedding was postponed.'

Bucky's stomach twisted.

'Oh? Why was that?'

'The poor bride was taken ill, apparently. Poor love.'

'And she's better now?' Harley asked.

'I hope so. Otherwise they wouldn't be holding the wedding, I guess.' The woman smiled. 'Been a long time since we had so many celebrations, and such a wedding that brings the whole country to a standstill for a day. You never know, fingers crossed there'll be another celebration in about nine months' time.' The woman gave Harley a wink and a darkness came over the lawman's features.

'Thank you, ma'am,' said Bucky. 'The wedding's taking place at the castle? I sure would like to see that.'

'It is. I must get over there myself. My family's waiting for me, saved me a spot. You might have trouble getting a good view now, most of the country's over there. The wedding happens out of view, of course, but King Bran and his wife will come out afterwards so we can see her dress and watch them kiss.' The woman gave a small bounce. 'Excuse me, sirs, enjoy the party.' She walked away, giving them a wave.

'Bucky,' Harley growled, approaching the captain. Bucky held up his hands.

'I know, I know. Sounds like our girl is about to become a queen.' He pulled up his sleeve and hit the button on his leather bracer. The speaker whirred and buzzed as it connected. He held it up to his mouth.

'Crash? You there?'

'Yes, Capt'n,' Crash's voice crackled through.

'Where are you?'

'Landing pad. Where are you?'

'You see the castle from where you are?'

'Castle? No. Err…I see towers. Is that it?'

'Maybe. Okay. We need to get to the castle and quick. Where's the landing pad?' he asked Harley.

'Back that way.' Seph pointed in the opposite direction to the castle.

'Shit. Right. Back to the Bumblebee.' He spoke into the radio beneath the speaker on the bracer, 'Crash, there's too many people here. Get The Magpie going, we're headin' to you. We need to get to the back of the castle, under cover.'

'Right, will do. What's goin' on, Capt'n?' 'Tell you when we get there. Just get the engine goin'.' Bucky clicked the communicator off and pulled down his sleeve. 'You heard that? C'mon.' Bucky jogged back down the side road towards the Bumblebee, happy to be back in the shade again. He jumped into the driver's seat and started the engine as Harley and Seph took their places. Pulling out onto the main road and heading for the landing pad, Bucky pushed his foot down on the accelerator as far as it would go.

'He must be damn desperate to get married,' Bucky said into the wind. 'They must have only just got her back here.'

'We sure it is her, Capt'n?' Seph shouted from behind.

'Who else could it be? Surely he'd want to invite people from other countries. Dignitaries, make political alliances, that sort of thing?'

'There's something else going on,' shouted Harley. 'Unless all those special guests stayed put for a week.'

'Shit.'

'No wonder she wasn't open about who she was going to marry,' said Harley.

'How does a girl who grew up on a ship run by outlaws come to marry a king?' Bucky growled, trying to push his foot down harder. 'And where's her family? Why aren't they stopping this? Why is this down to us?'

Bucky tried to ignore Harley glaring at him. It was easy to keep looking forward, watching the road, although there was no one around. No, everyone must be at the castle. Bucky gripped the steering wheel tighter.

'We need her, Capt'n,' Seph said in his ear. Bucky nodded.

'I know, I know.'

'And her family aren't here, as far as we know,' Harley added.

'I know, I know. We're gettin' her back, okay?

You don't need to convince me. I've heard what the royals used to do. Back before we got rid of most of 'em,' Bucky shouted into the wind. 'I've heard the stories.'

The others didn't respond, but they didn't need to. Bucky shut his mouth, he needed to conserve his energy for what was to come.

There was a sign for the landing pad and then the open gates came into view. Bucky didn't slow down. Someone screamed at them as they roared onto the main tarmac. There was his ship, over on the left. Bucky pointed the Bumblebee towards The Magpie. Jude was waiting for them. She ran up inside and out of the way as Bucky powered the Bumblebee up the ramp and slammed on the breaks. The nose of the vehicle smashed into the crates at the back of the bay and Bucky thanked the gods that he hadn't stored any goods in those particular crates.

Harley and Seph had leapt from the Bumblebee as it had arrived on the ship. The engines roared to life around them.

'Get us in the air,' Bucky yelled as Jude slammed her fist on the button to raise the ramp and shut the loading bay door. Harley ran in the direction of the cockpit while Seph went to the right, pulling out a crate that was strapped to the wall and lifting the lid to reveal their ammunition stash.

'Bucky.' Jude followed him as he took the steps two at a time. 'Bucky. They're marrying her today. It's today.'

'I know. We know. It's at the castle.' Bucky stopped and turned on Jude who skidded to a halt.

'She's marrying the king, did you know that?'

Bucky didn't wait long enough to see Jude's reaction. He continued striding through the corridors, heading for the cockpit as the ship lifted and banked.

'Wedding's today, Capt'n,' said Crash as Bucky entered the cockpit followed by Jude. Bucky stood by the co-pilot's seat, staring out of the window at the large castle that now dominated the view.

'I know, Crash. Did you know she's marrying the king?'

'Well, she did say he was some powerful man.'

Bucky sighed.

'Guess we're goin' in the castle.'

Crash looked up at him with a grin. Bucky placed his hands on the control panel, leaning forward. 'Looks like we might miss the drop for our job,' he murmured. 'You realise what that means?'

Kai

Kai paced the bedroom. It was the same room they'd kept her in before, with a large soft four-poster bed, a dresser and full length mirror, and wardrobe that was empty. Kai had checked. There was no sign of her old clothes she'd abandoned the day she'd run away and no sign of a new wedding dress. Kai reached the one small window and glanced out. The room was at the back of the castle, looking out onto a steep cliff and bare rock that banked down onto the small landing pad where servants came and went from the kitchens. Now, they were bringing in large pots of ornamental flowers.

Kai shivered and turned to pace back across the room.

There had to be a way out. There just had to be.It was ironic, she thought, that if her mother hadn't died, Kai would have been partially raised in this castle. She would have known every crevice and turn of corridor, she would have known of any secret passageways. She would have known of multiple ways out.

Kai stopped and sighed, wondering where her father was.

She sat on the bed and for a moment, as she sank down, she was overcome with an urge to lie back and go to sleep. She fought it, sliding to the edge as her mind drifted to The Magpie. Bucky had a job, they wouldn't be coming for her. They had more important things to be doing. What about her aunt? She wouldn't know about the wedding, she hadn't been there at the first one.

With a groan, Kai lay back on the bed. The mattress and sheets swallowed her. Fighting her way back up, Kai returned to pacing, stopping by the heavy oak door and listening. There were no muffled voices, no sign of anyone on the other side. She glanced down at the door knob but she'd already tried it, more than three times. The door was definitely locked.

Kai's chest tightened, her breath coming quicker as she paced back to the window.

She jumped as the door knob turned and span round to face whoever was entering, her chest aching, her fingers curling around a weapon that wasn't there. There was nothing around her that could be used in a fight, they'd been careful about removing anything that she could pick up and use to hit.

A young woman came into the room with her head down. Past her, Kai could see two large men dressed as guards stood by her door. They really were taking no chances this time.

The door closed and the woman bustled past Kai to the bed where she lay down something long and white.

Kai held her breath as the woman opened the cover and revealed a new wedding dress of ivory and lace.

'No,' said Kai, crossing her arms against her aching chest and pounding heart. 'I'm not putting that on.'

The woman finally lifted her eyes, giving her such a look of pity that Kai's knees weakened. The woman gave a small curtsey and left the room, closing and locking the door behind her.

Kai slowly walked over to the dress on the bed, eyeing it suspiciously, as if it might burst into flames.

The lace was exquisite, covering the shoulders and arms, while thick silky ivory material made up the body of the dress. It was long, it would likely trail along the floor. Kai flinched away from it, and then the door opened again.

'Good morning, Miss Summerbee, how lovely to see you again. It's a beautiful day. Are you ready to put your dress on?'

Kai glared at the older woman who entered, flanked by young maids.

'You know I'm not,' she growled. 'You think I wanted to come back? You can't do this to me.'

'I'm sorry you feel that way, Miss Summerbee.' The older woman stopped by the dress and looked Kai up and down. 'The people are excited to have you as their queen.'

'Are they? I won't make any difference to their lives.'

The woman frowned.

'Oh, but you will. They are excited about having a new baby in the castle. You'll give King Bran an heir, don't you realise how important that is?'

Kai shivered, hugging herself.

'Please,' she tried, lowering her voice. 'Please, help me.'

The woman blinked and then approached Kai.

'Do you really think that you're the first woman in this room who hasn't wanted to marry the king? Do you really think you're the first woman in this room who wanted a different life? There were many before you, Miss. There will probably be many after you. After you give King Bran his son, who do you think will be forced into this room and into marriage with him?'

Kai's breath caught.

'All of the women in our royal family, forced into marriage and into bed,' she murmured.

The woman shrugged and turned back to the wedding dress.

'Not all of them, but most. All of them think that they are different, that they can get away from it. You managed it once, and maybe that makes you a little different, but you weren't good enough to not get caught again. I'm sorry, Miss Summerbee, but this is life. This is your life. Now, shall we get started? Take off your clothes and we'll get this dress on you.'

'What are you going to do? Force strip me? Absolutely not. Not before I talk to Bran. Let me talk to Bran.'

'It's bad luck for the groom to see the bride on before the ceremony.'

Kai burst out laughing.

'Bad luck!' She stopped before she said any more. The other women who had stood where Kai stood now may have wanted to escape, they may have pleaded and begged, they may have asked to speak to the man who would become their husband, and they may have even grown to love him. But none of them, Kai was sure, had grown up on an outlaw ship. None of them, as far as Kai was aware, had learned to shoot to kill at such a young age. Kai was more than different to the women who had come before her. She was a life changer, and sometimes a life ender.

There was no escape from this, nowhere to run and no point in fighting. No, she would save her strength and her words.

Kai sniffed, letting the tears prick at her eyes as she submitted and began to undress.

The older woman nodded.

'Good.' She turned to pick up the wedding dress. 'We'll probably need to make alterations and we'll have to be quick. It's such a shame you lost your original dress. That was an antique, you know. The king's mother wore that dress on her wedding day.'

Kai remembered the old queen consort, her eyes dull and usually down on the ground. It made sense now, how forced her actions were, how rigid her posture next to Bran's father.

A conversation with Bran came back her. Her aunt had brought her home on her twelfth birthday, to see her father, and she'd ended up spending a day with Bran.

Kai and Bran had ridden through the kingdom, talking, climbing trees. Bran had tried to catch fish with his bare hands while Kai laughed at him. He had asked about her life away from the kingdom, growing up on a ship surrounded by criminals. She had asked him about life in the kingdom and in the castle, and there the memory turned vivid as the sadness in him had overwhelmed her.

That had been the moment she'd sworn never to marry him, never to give him the child she was supposedly destined to bear for him. She couldn't put her child through that sadness.

Kai allowed herself to be dressed. The women bustled around her, pulling on her and scratching her as they got the wedding dress into place. The older woman then got to work lifting the hem as one of the maids began brushing Kai's hair. She tutted as she pulled on a stubborn knot and Kai swore.

'They'll be none of that, Miss Summerbee,' said the older woman, around the needles between her teeth. 'A queen does not curse.'

'I bet they do,' Kai muttered. 'Let me get the knots out.' She pushed the maid out of the way before the girl could respond and began teasing at her hair, pulling gently at the knots and running her fingers through.

The older woman glanced up as the maid went back to running a brush over Kai's head.

'You have beautiful hair,' she sighed, taking a needle from her mouth and placing it in the dress. 'Just like your grandmother.'

Kai looked down at her sharply, the brush tugging painfully as it caught. Kai winced.

'You knew my grandmother?'

'Your mother's mother.' The woman nodded. 'A fine lady. She took over as the High Priestess in the same week I joined the staff here, back when I was very young.' The woman glanced up at the maid brushing Kai's hair with a smile. 'I remember, she would visit the castle and the queen often. King Bran's grandmother always welcomed her. They would have afternoon tea together. She had long hair, longer than yours, and slightly darker than yours. Hers was the colour of a sunrise, the queen often said. Yours, my dear, is more the colour of gold. Quite fitting for a queen. I sometimes caught parts of their conversations. They would talk of family, of the king of course and their children, of your poor mother, but also of you.'

'Me? How could they talk about me? My grandmother was retired when I was born.'

'Yet still, she talked. She was the High Priestess, gifted with visions of the future.' The old woman stood and looked Kai in the eye. 'Just like your mother. Just like you.'

Kai chewed on the inside of her lip.

'I didn't think Bran would want me, you know, as I haven't had the training,' she murmured.

'No. That is a shame. But that's not what's important. King Bran has the current High Priestess for that job.'

'Right. My job is to smile and give him a son. I get it,' said Kai through gritted teeth. The woman smiled at her.

'You'll do a fine job, I'm sure.'

Kai shrugged and the maid fixing beads into her hair gasped and tutted.

'Not sure why I'd want to do a good job for

him.'

The woman studied Kai and then laughed.

'You think yourself a caged bird, don't you? Poor girl, given what you consider freedom from such an early age and then forced into a marriage. You think you'll fly away one day? Let me tell you something. The best thing you can do for yourself right now, what every successful queen consort in Decima has done, is to accept your fate with dignity, embrace it and enjoy it. You're about to become royalty. Your son is the future king. You should hold your head high and be proud of that. Be proud of what you will provide for this country.'

Anger roiled and burned in Kai. She clenched her fists but didn't respond, instead looking away from the woman to the wall in front of her.

The silence stretched out as the woman began fretting over a veil.

'Some birds,' Kai said softly, 'are dangerous when caged.'

The woman either didn't hear her or chose to ignore her, stepping around the maids to fit the veil over Kai's head.

'There. Beautiful. Now, we must see to your bridesmaids and make sure everything is in order. There will be someone on the door, should you need anything. We'll be checking up on you. It won't be long now.'

The woman let the two maids out and then she closed the door, leaving Kai alone in the bedroom, standing in a wedding dress, her veil hanging down her back and curling on the bed. She sat down with a huff and gave a small squeal as the veil caught and the pins in her hair dug into her scalp.

She flexed her fingers as her stomach churned, tears pricking at her eyes. There was nothing left to do but wait.

Seph

Everyone expected mercenaries to be tall but Seph found being short to be a great advantage. First off, no one thought of him as a mercenary. They assumed he was the engineer, so they didn't expect him to have a weapon. It also meant that when they were trying to blend into a large crowd outside a castle, he didn't stick out as a traditionally large, muscular mercenary would. Seph weaved between the people jostling and waiting, all staring up at the castle, and no one suspected that he had a shotgun, pistol, knife and two additional rounds of ammunition for each gun hidden under his coat.

In front of him, two women were talking. It was difficult to make out full conversations in a crowd of this size, filled with such excitement, but still, Seph caught bits of it.

'I wonder what she'll be wearing,' said one.

'I heard she lost the dress. They can't have made her a new one so soon.'

'What do you mean?'

'Well, she ran away, didn't she.'

'Where did you hear that?'

'Careena. Her daughter works in the castle, doesn't she. In the kitchen. That dress was a family heirloom.'

Seph stopped listening as Bucky joined him. The captain was wearing his usual long coat but now he had a hat on, covering his eyes. He kept his head down but gave Seph a nod as he reached him, a sign that Seph could move on. Seph scoured the crowds as he went. Bucky was taller than him, he stood out, people noticed him. Seph didn't need a hat to hold off suspicion, not here at least. If they were in a different town, a different city, then Seph might think twice.

Over to their right, Crash and Cassidy were also pushing through the crowd. Crash had her head down. Seph could just make out the sharp edges of her hair as she bobbed along, and on the edge of his hearing was her voice, swearing and yelling at people to get out of her way.

Crash had never been one for subtlety.

Cass glided along behind her, taller than Crash, searching the crowd. Her gaze met Seph's and she gave him a nod before turning to look up at the castle. She had the least reason to be here and yet Seph had a good feeling about her. She was making all the right moves as she followed Crash. Bucky had even given her a revolver, despite none of them knowing how good she was with a weapon. Judging by how she'd turned it over in her hand, she didn't know how to shoot it but it was obvious she knew exactly how it worked. If one of their guns was smashed into tiny pieces, the look in Cass's eye gave Seph full confidence that she'd be able to put the damn thing back together again.

Bucky placed a hand on Seph's shoulder and the mercenary stopped and turned back. Harley, a hood over his blonde beaded hair and beard, stood behind Bucky, gesturing at the castle. They needed to get closer.

Seph turned and began to weave his way through the crowd, towards the castle. This time, pushing between people instead of around them. They met Crash and Cassidy, and Bucky gestured for them to do the same.

'They could have given us more warning,' grunted one man as Seph passed. 'I've had to close my shop. Wife said I had to come. Guess she's right. There won't be another wedding for a long time.'

'You won't be moaning later when the party's started,' said his friend.

Seph didn't hear the man's response, he'd already pushed past.

'We need to speed this up,' came Harley's voice from behind. Seph's lips twitched. He could quicken his pace, but he didn't want to draw attention to them.

'Hold up,' said Bucky.

Grateful, Seph stopped and turned back to the crew. Crash and Cassidy joined them from the side.

'Harley's right. We need to get inside, soon, as in, now.' Bucky looked up at the castle. 'And I don't think from the front is good idea. Back's no good either, judging by all the movement we saw.'

Crash sighed and opened her mouth to speak.

'Excuse me,' said Cassidy as Crash drew breath. A group of women beside them turned to the engineer. 'We're supposed to be delivering some favours for the wedding, but I'm afraid we've gotten turned around. I don't suppose you happen to know the way into the castle?'

At the mention of the wedding, the women's eyes lit up. One looked Cass up and down.

'What sort of favours?'

'Oh, how exciting! There's a side door over there, I bet you'll be able to get in that way.'

'Deliveries go round the back.'

Cass eyed the woman who'd said that until the woman seemed to back down. Seph raised an eyebrow.

'Thank you, so much,' she said before throwing Bucky a look and leading the group towards the side door the excited woman had pointed to.

They had to push hard through the crowd, with Crash exclaiming loudly every few steps that they had a delivery for the wedding and didn't these people realise how important they were?

Seph could feel Bucky bristling and tensing, but he didn't stop Crash. It was working, the crowd parting and letting them through. As the men followed the women, the side door came into sight.

Right beside the wooden door was a guard.

'Great,' Bucky muttered.

Harley pushed past them and headed for the door.

'What's he doin' now?' grumbled Bucky, following.

'Err, hi,' said Harley, approaching the guard. 'We seem to have been turned around. We have a delivery, for the wedding?'

The guard narrowed his eyes and looked at them each in turn.

'What are you delivering?'

A chill ran over Seph and his fingers curled, ready to reach for a weapon.

'A gift, from the Aegirheim embassy,' said Cassidy.

After a beat, Harley removed his hood and the guard relaxed a little. With a nod, he pointed to a clear path that led along the castle wall.

'Guests are welcome through the front of the castle,' said the guard. 'Just show your invitation.'

Seph reached for a weapon.

'Or, you could just let us through here,' Bucky suggested, pushing the barrel of his own gun into the guard's ribcage.

The guard went to speak when Seph pulled out just enough of his shotgun for the guard to see he was outnumbered.

'You could call for help,' Bucky hissed, gesturing to Crash who had also revealed her weapon. 'But you'd be dead before the words left your lips. Or, you could let us pass and live. What do you want to do?'

'I can't let you in,' muttered the guard. His eyes wide, flitting between Bucky, Seph and Crash. 'Please.'

Bucky gave Seph a nod and Seph inwardly sighed. He was always happy when he didn't have to kill anyone, not that it mattered much, but violence of any sort was always a dangerous thing.

He stepped forward and apologised to the guard before ramming the butt of his shotgun into the man's jaw. The guard fell limp into Bucky's arms as Crash stepped forward to open the door. The thick wood creaked and Crash stuck her head through.

'All clear,' she hissed, glancing about them. 'Quick.'

Bucky and Seph lifted the guard inside and Seph tried to position him comfortably on the ground, sitting against the door. The man's eyes flickered as he began to regain consciousness.

'Tough one,' muttered Seph, but at least he hadn't killed the man. 'Gotta be quick, Capt'n.'

Bucky looked over his shoulder to the guard and gave a nod. He shut the door once everyone was in and turned to lead the way but Harley was already jogging down the corridor.

'Shit,' spat Bucky, running after him. Seph followed, glancing over his shoulder once to the guard who was slowly raising a hand to his head.

They followed Harley as the corridor led to a grand hall where they skidded to a halt, one behind the other.

'Now what?' Crash asked, breathing hard, looking around Harley to the people crowded in the hallway.

'The wedding guests,' said Harley. He glanced back to Bucky. 'I guess we try and look like we belong.'

'We're hardly dressed for a weddin',' Bucky pointed out.

Harley took off his coat and rearranged his hair,

tying it back and straightening the braids in his beard.

'You're my entourage. Take that hat off,' he told Bucky. 'Look smart, stay behind me.' He aimed that one at Crash who gave a nod, a sparkle in her eye. That was a surprise, Seph had to admit, that Crash was actually enjoying this.

Bucky tucked his hat into his coat and then held his hands out, unsure what to do with them. Seph made sure his weapons were concealed. Blending in was never a problem, he'd had years of practice.

Crash and Cass were making the same checks. Once Harley was satisfied, he stepped out into the hallway, head held high, and walked into the crowd.

'Stay close,' Bucky hissed to his crew as he followed. Seph let Crash and Cass go ahead before taking up the rear. Some people bowed their heads to Harley in acknowledgement although they were followed with murmurs. Something about the tall, broad man standing tall demanded respect. It was a wonder, Seph thought, that anyone would dare enslave his people, never mind how they'd actually managed it.

Harley was walking straight towards the large staircase that curved its way up to the first floor. As his foot fell on the first step, a guard appeared.

'Excuse me, sir. Guests are not allowed upstairs.'

'I do beg your pardon,' said Harley. 'I was looking for…the…lavatory.' He cleared his throat. A hint of a smile played on the guard's lips.

'Through the large doors, then left.' The guard pointed back down into the hallway full of people. Some of whom were beginning to look.

Seph sighed. There were too many people for

them to take the guard out and, in any case, they were outnumbered. There were guards on every door and at every window. It was almost as if the king expected people to break in. Seph smiled. Or break out.

'Do you not know who you're talking to?' Bucky demanded, stepping aside so that the guard almost turned his back on Harley. Harley went up another step when the guard stopped him again.

'Can I see your invitations, sir?' he asked.

Something in the crowd exploded and screams filled the hallway.

'What the—' The guard turned his back on all of them.

'Go!' Cass hissed before tossing something metallic into the crowd beside them. There was another bang, more screams, silver smoke spiralling up towards the ceiling. The guard stepped away from them, shouting to the others.

Seph turned back to Bucky, ready for orders, and saw that Harley was already running up the stairs.

'Go go go.' Bucky followed, gesturing to the others.

Crash gave a small 'Whoop!'. Punching the air, she ran up the stairs after Harley. Seph glanced back to Cass and saw the newcomer grinning, watching the chaos she had created with a hand on her hip. He tapped her on the arm.

'Come on.'

It took them a moment to catch up with the others.

'How do we know where she is?' Crash asked.

'Easy.' Bucky grabbed a young woman, a maid, as she appeared from a room. The woman squealed and screamed, backing away but Bucky's grip only tightened around her arms. He pushed her against the wall. 'Kai's room. Where is it?'

The woman shook her head, whimpering.

'The bride,' said Harley. 'Where's the bride's room.'

'T-t-top floor,' the woman stuttered. 'Top floor, to the left.' She yelped and cowered as Bucky let go.

'Oh, I'm not gonna hurt ya. Go on. Get outta the way,' Bucky told her as they followed Harley once again to the stairs.

Up we go, thought Seph, taking the stairs two at a time. How were they going to get back down without getting caught?

Kai

Kai heard the explosions as muted bangs although the screaming was louder. She stood by the door, holding up the skirts of her dress, wondering if this was all part of the wedding. It seemed a strange celebration if it was.

Shifting her weight from one foot to the other, she argued with herself.

I should open the door, she thought. If nothing else, I can ask the guards what's going on. That woman and the maids should be back by now.

She looked over to the window.

Was something bad happening? There shouldn't be screaming at a wedding. This could be the moment she'd been waiting for and she was missing it.

What if the castle was on fire? She placed a hand

on the stone wall but it was cold. If there was a fire, she definitely needed to talk to the guards.

Wiggling her fingers in indecisiveness, Kai took a deep breath, ripped her veil off and opened the door.

Poking her head through the doorway, she closed her mouth and held her tongue. There were no guards. Kai stepped forward and frowned. There were no guards and no maids coming to fetch her. The corridor was empty.

'Has it always been empty?' Kai mused aloud.

At the end of the corridor, a guard fell backwards into view and smashed against the wall, sliding down and remaining still. Kai's heart pounded and she instinctively stepped back into the doorway.

Harley jogged around the corner, past the guard, searching.

There was a pause as their eyes met and then Kai gave a loud yelp and shot forward.

Grinning, Harley shouted over his shoulder, 'She's here!'

Kai launched herself into Harley's arms, wrapping herself around him, feeling his large hands take hold of her.

'I knew you'd come,' she murmured into his shoulder. That was a lie. She hadn't known he'd come, but she had hoped and prayed to whichever gods might be listening. Looking ahead, she saw Bucky, Crash and Seph approaching with another woman.

Kai let out a sob, blinking back tears as she dropped back to her feet and pulled herself together. Crash grinned at her, tossing her a semi-automatic pistol, already loaded, which Kai caught and automatically checked.

'Good to see you alive,' said Bucky.

'Good to see you,' she murmured back. Bucky frowned down at her dress.

'Can you run in that?'

'Only one way to find out.'

'Or you could, you know, get changed.'

'Nothing to get changed into, Capt'n. They put a dress on me and took my clothes.' Kai flashed him a grin. 'Not my first wedding, now, is it?'

Crash barked a laugh. Kai looked from her to the strange woman stood beside her, watching without expression.

'Oh, this is Cassidy. She's our new engineer. Cass, this is Kai. Our…erm…cook.'

The women looked one another up and down.

'You spend months looking for an engineer and then find one as you're coming to rescue me? What are the chances?' Kai wasn't sure whether she should be impressed or annoyed. The latter was winning.

'To be fair, Crash found her before you went and got yourself Kai-napped,' said Bucky, waving her away. He looked over his shoulder. 'We need to get moving.' He turned to go back the way they'd come.

'How did you get in?' Kai asked, not moving, glancing up at Harley still standing a little too close to her.

'Practically through the front door,' he told her.

'We told them Harley was an ambassador for Aegirheim.' Crash beamed. 'Cass's idea.'

'That worked?' Kai glanced again at the engineer. She was pretty, slender and tall, her long silver hair somehow sparkling in the meagre light. Kai turned back to look at Crash, staring up adoringly at Cass, and raised an eyebrow.

'Until they asked to see the invite, yes.'

'And all that screaming, that was because of you,' Kai said. That made sense.

'Cass, actually.'

The engineer held up a copper ball she'd pulled from her pocket.

'Basically a small smoke bomb. It doesn't do much damage, but it's enough to create an easy escape most of the time.'

Kai caught herself staring at Cassidy.

'Come on!' Bucky went to go again but Kai stopped him.

'You can't go back out the front door. The back way will be better. Come on.' Kai hitched up her skirts.

'I don't suppose there's a side door we can sneak out of?' Bucky asked.

'Probably but I don't know where. Sorry, Capt'n. I haven't spent that much time in this place, other than in that bedroom. I know of the front door and back door.'

'And last time you escaped out the back door?'

'Yup.'

'And you don't think they'll be expecting that this time?'

Kai sighed and looked up at Harley. The tall man turned to the captain.

'She's right, Bucky. What choice do we have? It's either back door or fighting through guards and guests out the front. And I think they'll notice their princess in a wedding dress, don't you?'

Bucky smiled and looked back down at Kai's dress.

'I'm not a princess,' she said.

'Well, you sorta are,' Bucky told her.

'I'm not.' Kai looked down at herself. Admittedly, it was hard to argue when she was dressed this way. She looked back up and folded her arms defiantly. She was not a princess.

'Don't take offence, Princess.' Bucky grinned and Kai sagged. No, she thought. That was it. She wasn't going to live that down now, was she?

'I think you're focussing on the wrong thing,' she tried. 'Harley said I was right, so, let's go.'

Bucky was still grinning.

Voices came from behind him, male voices, shouting. He glanced over his shoulder and when he turned back to her, the grin was gone.

'All right, Princess, show us the back way.'

Kai gritted her teeth and turned on her heel.

For the second time in as many weeks, she ran through the castle of Decima in a wedding dress and bare feet, heading for the back door. There would be someone there to stop her this time, she knew, but this time she wasn't alone. Kai found the servants' stairs and ran down them, listening to the heavy breath and footfalls of the crew behind her.

'Where's Jude?' Kai called over her shoulder.

'With the ship. Just in case. Plus, you know, the woman can't shoot,' said Bucky, close behind her.

Kai didn't reply. She concentrated on not falling down the stairs, or getting too close to Harley's big boots as he trampled down beside her. He had an arm out, around her back but not touching. Kai decided not to read too much into that right now.

'How far is it?' Bucky asked.

'Err, Capt'n? We're being followed,' came Crash's voice, further behind. Kai didn't risk looking back. There was a chance she'd lose her balance and they'd all fall over her. She kept going, putting a bit more energy into her legs, tapping into everything she had.

They reached the ground floor and Kai gestured for Harley to follow as she wheeled around to the left.

They ran through a corridor, their footsteps echoing around the stone walls, floor and ceiling. The cold grabbed at Kai's feet and she could feel the bruises already developing. Still, she didn't slow. They couldn't afford to slow down.

The voices of the guards behind them were audible now. Shouts reverberating down the corridor as they too reached the bottom of the stairs.

'Keep going,' Kai said, as much to herself as to the others.

She slammed through a heavy wooden door and into the large kitchen. Jumping over a box on the floor, she kept running, holding her skirts higher. Harley was close behind and she heard Crash swear as she tripped over something.

'Not far now,' Kai told them. 'Where's the ship?' She risked glancing over her shoulder and found Harley closer than she thought.

'To the side. We had to keep out of sight,' he told her.

'Jude. Bring her in,' Bucky shouted into the communicator on his wrist.

Satisfied, Kai gave herself another boost towards the large open back doors just off the kitchen, where people were walking in and out carrying boxes and flowers.

All of them stopped when they saw the bride and a group of people running straight for them. A couple moved out of the way.

'Move!' Kai yelled, not hesitating.

A man dropped a box and there was a smash as it bounced on the ground. More people moved but then there were guards and they were closing the doors.

With a scream, Kai pulled out her pistol and aimed. One guard stopped, putting his hands in the air but the other finished the job. Kai stopped running just before she smashed into them.

'Open the doors!' she squealed.

'Do as she says,' said Harley, stopping beside her, his gun aimed.

The hesitant guard looked to his colleague who shook his head.

'Are you always this predictable? Or just when you're desperate?'

Kai span round at the voice, but she found herself facing Crash, Bucky and Cass. They turned.

At the back of the room, between one door that led to the kitchen and another that led to a storeroom, was another staircase and standing on the bottom step, was Bran.

Kai had had to drop her skirts to aim her gun. Now she scooped them up with her empty arm and aimed the pistol at Bran's head, walking through her crew to face him. He watched her without changing expression.

'I thought outlaws had to think quick. I thought pirates were full of surprises. I'm almost disappointed,' he said, looking her up and down.

'I didn't think you'd come,' Kai told him between heavy breaths. 'I just thought you'd send some men. Like you always do. It's bad luck to see the bride before the ceremony.'

Bran smiled at that.

'Well, then, apparently I'm the one who is full of surprises. And it's worse luck if the bride doesn't show up.'

Kai took a moment to try and slow her breathing, to steady her hand.

'You know, outlaws don't just thieve, and we don't just think quick,' Kai told him, levelling her weapon. 'We're also known for killing.'

There was a crack as guns were levelled at them. The guards had surrounded the group and now each one aimed a weapon at Kai or one of the crew. Behind her, Bucky and Crash put their hands up.

'Steady men,' said Bucky, stepping forward to stand beside Kai. 'There's no need for this to get violent.'

Bran ripped his attention from Kai and onto Bucky.

'How rude of us. We haven't been formally introduced. Are you the man who has stolen my bride's heart and has come to rescue her?'

'No. That's him.' Bucky thumbed at Harley whose eyes widened. Kai glanced at Harley and then quickly looked away, back to Bran.

The king raised an eyebrow at Harley.

'Him? A slave. A slave and a Visionary. It sounds like a story my wet nurse would tell me at bedtime. A fairy tale. One of those stories that, when you grow up, you realise could never be true.'

He laughed. 'A slave and a Visionary. What next? Dragons roaming the earth? Trolls under every bridge?' Grinning, he turned back to Bucky. 'So you're what then? His master?'

Kai felt Harley bristle behind her, the air around them changing. He pushed forward, standing level with her, the anger showing in his tense muscles and strained breath.

'Easy,' said Bucky as a heavy silence fell over them.

Seph

Fingers wrapped around the grip of his gun, Seph glanced between his captain and the king. Despite being stood on a step, Seph could tell Bran wasn't a tall man. He wondered if it took a shorter man to recognise a shorter man on a step. It hardly mattered. King or not, Bran had just made the crew of The Magpie angry. Seph turned his eyes to the nearest guards. There were four to his right. Too many. But he had survived bigger odds before.

Bucky took a step closer to the king and the guards shuffled, raising their weapons a little higher in warning.

'No one here is a slave,' Bucky said. 'No one here owns anyone else. And that includes Kai.'

Bran raised an eyebrow.

'You're not from here,' the king said. 'You don't

seem to know who you're talking to, or what you're talking about.'

'I'm talking to the king of a small country who doesn't seem to understand what's going on in the rest of the world and who thinks he's allowed to marry whoever he wants, without their permission, just because some lady says she'll give you a son. How am I doin' so far?'

'Good. But you missed some details. Captain Bucky Winters, isn't it? Oh, don't look so surprised, Captain.' Bran gave a slow smile and then rested his gaze on Kai. 'She's not just going to give me an heir. There are plenty of fertile women in this kingdom who would love to become my queen consort and have their son become the next king. If it were just about a son, I would not be forcing a woman raised as a criminal to become my wife. What sort of queen would that be? No. No, Kai here is important, necessary even, because of her gift.'

'Yeah, she sees the future, but you've got other women for that. That ain't a reason.'

Bran's eyes widened a little.

'You told them what you can do?' he asked Kai. 'No wonder they came after you.' A smile spread on his face. 'This isn't a question of sentimentality, then.' Bran turned back to the captain and stepped down from the staircase, approaching Bucky. 'This is a business deal. You think she will be an asset to your crew, but she is destined to be my wife. What is your trade, Captain?'

Bucky pursed his lips.

'It depends.'

Bran cocked his head and turned back to Kai.

'An outlaw finds another outlaw ship.' He tutted.

'Like I said, predictable. I don't deal with criminals,' he told Bucky. 'Take your crew, get on your ship and get out of my country. She's not going with you.'

Seph jumped as Bucky laughed. He kept his eyes on the guards, although he felt Crash and Cassidy move.

'Oh, your majesty, I've lost too many good crew members to give up on Kai just like that. She may be able to give you a son and whatever Visionaries do for a king like you, but this woman is gonna keep my crew safe, help us pay the bills and she makes a mean chocolate cake—'

'—Hear, hear,' Crash shouted.

'But apart from anything else, this woman is her own and no one else's,' Bucky continued, ignoring Crash. 'You see, that's the code amongst us criminals. Freedom. Something that you in your castle with all your walls probably don't know much about. Not as much as you think. I think Kai's made it pretty clear that she don't want to marry you.'

Bran's features darkened, his eyes becoming hard, his jaw muscles tense.

'You're outnumbered, Captain,' he murmured.

Bucky grinned.

'Never stopped us before.'

A cruel smile grew on Bran's lips.

'It will stop you now. I will give you one last chance but my patience is wearing thin. I have a castle full of guests who are expecting a wedding. Not only that, but they've been let down before. They're impatient and frustrated. They've come all this way.' Bran turned to Kai. 'They've come all this way to see us joined. To let them down could be dangerous for Decima. These are powerful people who represent countries that we have trade deals with, powerful people who make powerful decisions. Kai, your father still lives here. Your mother's family, your father's family. You might not want to be a queen, but it became your birth right as much as mine, which means that the people of Decima are your people as much as mine. These are your people, Kai. And you would abandon them?'

Seph glanced at Kai as she opened and closed her mouth.

'For fuck's sake,' cried Crash. 'She ain't goin' with ya. She's comin' with us. Your people will just have to get over it. You'll find another poor woman to be your queen, your people will be happy with that and we can all get on with our lives. Some other woman will give you a boy. What'd you want a boy for anyway? Why can't a girl be your heir? Hmm? What's wrong with a woman in power?'

'You're hardly building a good case for that,' Bran spat.

Crash let out a small growl.

'Look, you—' Crash stepped forward, but Bucky put out an arm to stop her.

'No, you look,' said Bran. 'I am king here. This is my castle, my kingdom. How dare you break into my home, steal my bride and then act as if I'm the bad person. I have every reason to arrest every single one of you and put you to death.'

'They do that?' Bucky muttered to Kai. Kai nodded.

'Oh yes. We deal with our criminals swiftly. Why do you think Kai's precious auntie isn't here?

She knows what's waiting for her if she returns. You know, the only reason I didn't arrest your father for sending you away is because I wanted to start this marriage the right way—'

'Ha!'

Everyone turned to look at Kai. Her golden hair was a mess, the grip that had held her veil in place was stuck half way out. She still gripped her skirts in one hand, her pistol in the other, held firmly by her side. She was in control, despite her cheeks flushing and her body visibly trembling.

'Is that your new threat, Bran? Hurting my father?'

'Would it work?' Bran asked.

At first, Kai didn't respond and Seph wondered if she was going to relent. She didn't. She held her gun up and aimed it at Bran's head.

'I should have killed you the moment I laid eyes on you,' she spat.

Every guard in the room focussed their weapons on her. Bran stood, relaxed.

'Probably. Now you'll never get that chance.'

Kai gave a small shrug.

'I could kill you now, but then we'd all be dead. I could go with you, to save my crew, to save my father, it wouldn't matter. I'd kill you once we were married, in our marital bed, before you manage to get your limp dick out.' Crash barked a laugh. 'And don't think for a second that I'd need this gun for that,' Kai continued. 'I don't need a weapon to end you. There are so many other ways I could kill you. And then this kingdom would be mine, and that would be the end of your line. The end of you. So, Bran, what are you going to do? What choice will you make? Go through with your threats? Take me into your bed? The only option that leaves with you waking up the next morning is letting me and my crew go with no consequences.'

A silence filled the spaces between them. Bran slowly opened his arms, palms out. Seph shifted. The air had changed. He felt the gun in his hand, measured its weight, tried to keep his eye on every single man there with a weapon, which was impossible. Beside him, Cassidy moved. Did she feel it too?

'That was a nice little speech,' Bran told Kai. 'Speeches like that, with kinder topics, and you'll make a wonderful queen.' He smiled. 'You know, deep down, that there's only one option here. I only have the one option, Kai. You've done well to try and convince me. Your captain here could have done better.' Bran clicked his fingers as Bucky mumbled something under his breath that Seph couldn't make out. 'Ultimately, there is nothing you could say to change this. Unless you choose to come quietly with me. Our marriage is only minutes away.' Bran held out his hand to Kai. She didn't move. 'Come with me or I will shoot.'

A guard handed Bran a small, old fashioned pistol covered in well-polished copper. In one movement, Bran cocked the weapon and aimed it first at Bucky, then at Kai. Seph lifted his gun and aimed, as did Bucky.

Crash gave a scream and moved, and then things got confusing. Seph fired at Bran, as did Bucky, and the king's own gunshot was lost in the chaos.

Kai screamed.

It wasn't a scream of fear, or even of anger. It

was a scream of grief and it was so unexpected that everyone hesitated.

Seph snapped round to her at the sound. The crew followed Kai's gaze as she stared down at Crash's body, crumpled at her feet.

Kai

She raised her gun too late. Shots were already being fired before Kai had taken aim. She should have known, she should have anticipated it. Throughout her life, in all of her meetings with Bran, during all conversations about the king, it had never been mentioned that he knew how to use a gun or that he could aim with such dexterity.

Still, she should have been ready.

Crash had seen it coming before her.

The silence hurt Kai's head and she looked up. Somewhere at the back of her mind, voices were shouting.

Check if she's breathing. She might not be dead.
This is your fault.
You're outnumbered, look around you.
This is your fault.

They're all staring at you. All of them.
This is your fault. Crash is dead because of you.

She only had eyes for Bran who had backed up to the stairs but was now watching them with a worried gaze. The guards circled him, protecting him, but that didn't stop Kai from aiming her gun.

Blood pounded in her ears. She couldn't hear her heavy breathing but she felt it in her constricting throat. Tears burned at her eyes although nothing fell and her vision remained clear except for a rage-filled mist.

She lifted the pistol Crash had given her, aimed it at Bran's head and squeezed the trigger within a second.

A guard pushed Bran out of the way and collapsed, spraying the king with a deep red.

Bran held out his arms in disgust. Glaring at Kai, he went to talk but a cry stopped him.

'Enough!'

It was Cassidy, with a bellow from her gut. She had her hand on a brass contraption on her wrist, which she turned clockwise.

A bright white light shone from the device. Bucky and Seph shielded their eyes but Kai was still blinking back the tears.

Something came out of Cass's wrist. It twisted up, round and round, until it hung high above them. Kai could have sworn it looked down at Cass. It peered at the men around her and then it stopped to study the body of Crash still lying at Kai's feet.

All of them except Cass went down on their knees, hands over their ears, as a deafening scream shook the castle.

Kai knew that sound. It took her breath away.

The white…creature—Kai could just make out the head and gleaming jet black eyes—grew, expanding out until it pushed against the door and wall behind them.

'What the fuck?' Bucky hissed beside Kai. They stayed on their knees as the ground shook beneath them.

Kai placed herself over Crash, pushing her body against the woman. She was still warm and then Crash took a breath.

Kai's laugh came out in a sob.

'She's alive!'

The shaking of the castle walls hid her voice as the bright white light above them grew and burned, emitting another high pitched scream, but Bucky heard her.

'Thank the gods. Keep it quiet.'

'What?'

'Whatever the new girl's doing, it's 'cause of Crash. Keep your mouth shut and keep her safe.'

Kai nodded, repositioning herself to make sure she shielded Crash. She squeezed her eyes shut as stonework fell down around them.

Then the scream stopped, no more stone or brickwork fell.

Slowly, Kai looked up. She blinked, sure she had been hit on the head and was hallucinating or dreaming.

Above them was a large, shining white reptile. It's thick back legs were planted on the ground behind Cassidy, its tall body faced away from the small landing pad, courtyard and steep forested valley wall behind them. The castle wall had fallen, the structure split in half, but there was no debris.

Where was the debris?

Kai kept looking up. Up the thick legs to the slender body and the two wings that ended in long claws held over them. A white shield spread over the wings and on top of that strange, translucent forcefield was the shattered castle wall.

Through a gap between the wing and body, Kai could make out a long, slender head and those jet black eyes.

'What...' Kai breathed, still holding herself low and over Crash.

Bucky was doing the same, looking up at the white creature, as was Seph. Bucky straightened, turning to Cass.

The engineer stood straight, her feet square, her hair flowing behind her. Her eyes were fixed ahead. Kai followed her gaze and landed on Bran, now stood at the top of the stairs, surrounded by his guards, each and every one of them staring up at the white creature looking down at them.

The creature opened its mouth and gave a deafening roar. Again, they all put their hands over their ears.

'Out the back,' said Cass as Bucky stumbled over to her. 'Call the ship and get out of here.'

'Jude!' Bucky shouted into the communicator on his wrist, not taking his eyes from Cass. 'Bring the ship round the back. Quick.'

Kai stood up, keeping her hands over Crash but her eyes on Bran. The king was too busy staring up at the creature, his mouth open, to notice her. It would be so easy, to take up her gun, aim and pull the trigger.

But between them were a handful of guards and a

strange shimmer that drifted down from the wings of beast above her. Something in her gut told her that a bullet wouldn't penetrate it. She had more chance of shooting herself than Bran.

Bucky was shouting orders but it wasn't until he grabbed Kai's wrist that she focussed on what he was saying.

'Seph will take Crash out. Go on, get outta here. Go with Harley. Jude'll be here in a second. Get out!'

Kai looked back to Bran, but there was no way to get to him. She looked past Bucky, to Cass still standing with her arms out.

She left Crash's limp body as Seph approached and she made her way over to Cass, the blood still pounding in her aching ears. Harley followed.

'Crash is alive,' she shouted to the engineer. Cassidy wavered, glancing at her from the corner of her eye. The creature above them didn't move. 'Crash is alive,' Kai repeated. 'We have to go.'

Cass turned to watch Seph and Bucky fussing over Crash's body. Then, the engineer looked up at the beast above them.

With a swoosh, the white creature turned, shaking the debris from its wings. Chunks of stone and brick fell and crashed to the ground around them. With another roar, the creature turned in the air, smashing against another wall before shrinking a little and hovering over Crash. Bucky and Seph fell backwards to get away from it as long claws wrapped around Crash's body and the creature flew off towards the landing pad.

A second later, The Magpie appeared in the sky and landed with a judder and a screech. The loading bay doors opened, the ramp lowering and the creature shrank as it flew on board with Crash.

The rest of the crew stared after it in silence for a moment and then Bucky and Kai turned back to Bran. The king still stood on the stairs, dumbfounded. After a moment, the guards began to murmur and Bran looked about him.

'What have you done?' he asked, staring up at where the walls should have been. 'You've destroyed the castle. This has been standing for centuries, and you destroyed it.'

'Oh, quit your whining, you can rebuild,' Bucky told him.

Harley placed an arm around Kai although he didn't touch her. 'Come on. Time to go.' He leaned over to catch Cass's attention. The engineer was glaring at Bran. 'Come on.'

'What the hell was that?' Bran shouted after them as they turned to leave. All thoughts of keeping Kai had apparently escaped him.

'Wrath,' Cass told him, turning her back and silently disappearing onto the ship.

The king remembered himself.

'Wait!'

Kai lifted the pistol still in her hand and aimed it at him.

'What?'

Bran shook his head.

'You owe me what was promised.'

'No such promise was made. I know how it happened, Bran. Your father demanded, my mother did not promise. I owe you nothing.'

'You owe me a son.'

'You'll find a son elsewhere.'

Kai considered shooting, but looking around at the carnage and the old castle walls destroyed so quickly and easily, she lowered her weapon. There had been enough damage done today to last Decima a lifetime. 'Don't follow me,' she told Bran before she, too, turned her back and followed Cass onto the ship.

'Not unless you want the rest of your castle flattened,' Bucky called, following Kai with Harley and Seph aboard The Magpie. They stood in the loading bay as Bucky raised the ramp and called for Jude to take off, and fast.

There was no sign of a white winged beast, but on the floor at Cass's feet was Crash, her chest fluttering in short breaths.

Bucky

They stood in silence as the ship shuddered and lifted. As The Magpie levelled, Bucky turned on the crew in the loading bay.

'What the fuck was that? What was that?' He turned to Cassidy who was bent over Crash.

'She needs the doctor,' Cass told him.

'Jude, get your ass down to the loadin' bay. Crash is hurt. Stick The Mag on autopilot and get here right now,' Bucky shouted, holding down the button that opened up the intercom. Then he immediately turned back on Cass. 'Now, what the fuck was that?'

Cass, one hand on Crash's shoulder, looked up at each of them in turn.

'That was Benny,' she said, averting her gaze.

Bucky opened and closed his mouth, looking

around at his crew who stared back at him with wide eyes.

'Benny? Benny? What's a Benny?'

Kai gave him a shrug, which was something. At least someone was listening to him.

Jude came pounding down the metal stairs, rushing to Crash's side.

'What happened?' she asked.

'She jumped in front…' Kai took a breath. 'She saved me.'

'The idiot king shot her,' said Bucky. 'And then our new engineer did some sort of magic, because apparently she's a witch as well as an engineer, and created a…a…Benny!' Bucky threw his hands up in the air as his sister stared blankly at him.

'A what?'

'Exactly!' Bucky cried, turning back to Cass. 'What the fuck is a Benny? What the hell just happened?'

Jude shook it off and stood.

'I need to get her into surgery, right now. Someone help me?'

Seph stepped forward and picked Crash up. For a small man, he was strong. Bucky had never questioned it.

'Nope,' Bucky said, as Cass stepped forward. 'Seph and Jude have this, you're staying right here and explaining to me what's going on.' Cass glanced at Kai. 'Yup, her too. She's got explaining to do too.'

'We need a pilot, Bucky,' Jude said as Seph carried Crash away. She followed, not waiting for a reply.

Bucky growled.

'Fine.' He pointed at Cassi 'But I want an explanation as soon as we're somewhere safe. And you.' He turned on Kai. 'You've got some explaining to do as well. Harley? Keep an eye on both of them. Take 'em to the mess, no one leaves.'

'Kai needs checking over,' Harley told him.

Bucky resisted the urge to roll his eyes and yell in frustration.

'Crash is more important. Kai can wait.' Bucky turned his back on all of them and huffed his way to the cockpit.

As he settled in Crash's chair, he relaxed a little. His muscles easing, his brow unfurrowing as he looked out at the valley beneath them. Taking a deep breath, putting his hands over the controls, Bucky hit the accelerator and felt the ship respond. He tried to keep it smooth, mindful of Jude operating on Crash, and for the first time it occurred to him that Crash had been shot. She'd been unresponsive. Yes, she was breathing but for how long?

Bucky chewed on his lip and then hit the intercom button for the mess.

'Harley?'

There was a pause, some static, and then, 'Captain?'

'Everything okay down there?'

'Sure. Everything okay up there?'

'Yup. No one followin', skies are clear. Erm, you hear anything from the med bay?'

'You told me not to leave Kai and Cassidy.'

'Yeah…' Bucky unwittingly left a silence as he navigated across a flight path, his mind filled with images of Crash on the operating table-come-dentist chair.

'Want me to check?' came Harley's voice.

Bucky did want him to check, but he didn't want Cassidy and Kai left to their own devices. Not that they could go anywhere. Not that Kai would do anything. Kai was probably fine. It was Cassidy he had issue with.

'Hang on.' Bucky put the ship back on auto-pilot. The way forward was clear, they should be okay. He leapt out of the cockpit and took the stairs two at a time, not stopping until he reached the med bay.

There was a large window along one wall of Jude's office, she usually had a curtain drawn for privacy but now it was open. Seph stood against it, arms crossed, peering inside.

'How's she doin'?' Bucky asked, almost too scared to look at the window to the two women beyond.

'Okay,' said Seph. 'I think.'

Bucky looked. Crash lay on her back with a mask over her face. Jude, thankfully, stood between them and the sight of Crash's wound. Jude's head was down, working furiously.

'She didn't want your help?'

Seph shook his head.

Gingerly, Bucky rapped his knuckles on the window.

Without flinching, Jude glanced over her shoulder and gave a nod. Another deep breath and Bucky opened the door to the med bay, sticking as little as possible of himself around it to talk to his sister.

'How's it going?' he murmured, as if a loud

noise would hurt Crash further.

'Good. Just sewing her up. She banged her head though, not sure how. That's why she's out. That and the blood loss. No major damage. She should, theoretically, wake up soon.'

'Theoretically?'

Jude went back to Crash.

'You never know, Buck. But this is Crash we're talking about. I'm surprised she's not awake right now.'

'Yeah…make sure she isn't.' Bucky pulled a face at the sharp instruments around Jude.

'You'll never guess where the wound is.'

'In her stomach?'

Jude glanced back to Bucky.

'Same place that Kai hurt herself when she had that bad dream.'

There was a pause as Bucky let that sink in.

'I need to talk to Cassidy about all this, want me to wait for you?' he asked.

'Might be good to have the whole crew there.'

'Right. Well, you let me know when.'

Jude nodded and went back to her work. Bucky slowly closed the door.

'Guess we just wait,' he said, rejoining Seph at the window. The mercenary nodded again.

'Want me to check on Harley?' he asked.

'No, it's okay. I'll go.' Reluctantly, Bucky turned away from Crash and Jude and made his way to the mess.

Kai was in the kitchenette. The sight sent a flush of warmth through Bucky. Cass sat at the table, tapping her fingernails against the wood. Harley, arms crossed against his broad chest, stood between them, leaning on the bar. They all looked up at him as he entered.

'How is she?' Kai asked, leaning across the worktop beside Harley.

'Don't know yet. Jude's workin' on her. She'll let us know when she's done.' He looked at Cass as he sat opposite her at the table. 'Guess I have to thank you. You ended all that pretty sharpish. Wouldn't have gotten in or out of there without you.'

Cass didn't respond, she stared down at the table and her fingernails. Bucky turned on Kai. 'Don't blame yourself. It was her own stupid fault for jumping in front of that bullet.'

Kai frowned and turned away, sniffing.

'Coffee?' she asked, a slight crack in her voice.

'Yeah. That might help, I guess. Don't suppose it's laced with whisky?'

'I-I can find some?'

'No. No, it's okay. I need to keep a straight head.' Bucky took the cup Kai offered him and took a sip. It was strong, just the way Crash liked it. He regarded it a moment and then offered it back to Kai. 'Needs some milk.'

She gave an apologetic smile.

'Wasn't anyone's fault,' said Harley in a low voice. Bucky studied him a moment. It made sense, he guessed, that the lawman should want to act as peacekeeper.

'S'pose not.' Bucky took the coffee with added milk from Kai. 'I'm not allowed to ask either of you questions until Jude, and maybe Crash, is back with us. But you both put my crew in danger.'

'You didn't have to come after me,' Kai said

quietly.

'You kiddin' me? I've seen you shoot and Crash has tasted your cake. 'Course we had to come get you. I mean, we would have come quicker if you were a navigator, or an engineer.' Bucky turned back to Cassidy. 'And while I appreciate your little toys getting us in and whatever the fuck a Benny is getting us out, and I appreciate that we all have our secrets aboard this ship, this isn't a place where you can keep secrets that big. Either of you. When Jude and Crash are ready, you're both telling us everythin' or you're off. Got it?'

Kai nodded a little too eagerly before sinking back. Cass gave a half-hearted shrug.

'Mind if I go to my cabin while we wait?' she asked.

'Yeah. I do mind.' Bucky took a swig of coffee. It was still too strong. He sat down at the table, ignoring Cass sulking. Kai turned back to the kitchenette and began moving things around. Bucky ignored her too.

'You did a good thing, Capt'n,' Harley rumbled, seating himself beside Bucky.

'Huh. Could've been the death of us. If we lose Crash…'

'Could we?'

'Jude says not. But I've seen bullets take those they shouldn't before.'

Harley took a breath.

'Crash did a good thing too.'

'She did a fuckin' reckless thing.' Bucky lifted his cup and watched it tremble before putting it back down without taking a sip.

Harley shook his head.

'You got your crew, Bucky,' Harley murmured. 'Don't mess it up.'

Bucky bristled and frowned.

'I got an engineer who could be a massive danger to my crew and a cook who can shoot, which I wasn't askin' for.' He looked at Harley. 'Not sure what's there to mess up.'

The communicator on his wrist beeped and the room turned to look at it. Bucky opened it.

'Yeah?'

'You want that meeting? Let's do it in here. Crash is stable. She might wake up sooner rather than later, especially if she can hear you shouting at us all.'

'I'm not gonna shout at you all,' Bucky told Jude. 'Just Kai and Cassidy. Be there in a moment.' He looked up at the women. Cass had perked up and he doubted it was because he had promised to shout. 'You heard. Everyone to the med bay, nice and calmly, don't wanna do more damage to Crash.'

They filed through the ship, Bucky led the way with Cass while Kai and Harley trailed behind. Kai was still in her wedding dress. Bucky had expected her to ask to change but it didn't appear to have crossed her mind.

He knew it wasn't her fault that this had happened, but that ball of rage in his stomach at seeing Crash so helpless just wouldn't forgive her right now. He gave Cass a sideways glance. She had helped them, they wouldn't have gotten through the castle without her, and then she'd saved them. She'd probably saved Crash's life. It was the lying Bucky couldn't handle, but had she lied? He'd never asked her about what she was bringing on board the ship, he'd never asked her what she'd be doing when she wasn't in The Magpie's engine room.

But then, he'd never asked any of his crew what they did in their spare time. He'd never cared much. Maybe it was time he started taking an interest.

Bucky knocked on the med bay door and it opened to reveal Jude sat next to the table where Crash lay, still asleep.

'Everything okay?' Bucky murmured, scared of waking his pilot when actually he wanted nothing more in that moment than to see her open her eyes.

Jude nodded.

'Just waiting for some of the pain meds to wear off, she should wake up then.' Jude's gaze flittered to Cassidy and Kai. 'So…what happened?'

Bucky opened his mouth to reply when there was a boom and the ship shook, violently lurching to one side.

Kai

Falling into the med bay door and standing on the hem of her stupid dress, Kai swore under her breath.

'What in the fuck was that?' Bucky roared, tearing past Harley and Kai, running to the cockpit. Harley put his hand on Kai's shoulder.

'Everyone all right?' he addressed the room. Kai flinched at the warmth of his hand through the lace against her bare skin and then missed it as he turned to follow Bucky. Cassidy stood over Crash, moving her over a little so she was central on the table. Jude was picking up instruments that had fallen to the floor.

'Will have to sterilise everything. Again,' she muttered.

'Can I do anything?' Kai asked.

Jude shook her head.

'You and Seph get upstairs. Bucky might need you. We'll stay with Crash.' Jude looked up at Kai and gave her a hurried smile. 'We're fine.'

Seph paused, waiting for Kai while she shared a moment of eye contact with Cass. The stranger gave her a nod. Kai sighed and followed Seph to the cockpit.

'How did you find that woman again?' she asked as they climbed the stairs.

'Crash found her,' came Seph's voice from ahead. 'While you were out getting supplies.'

'Oh. Right. The food.'

They reached the top floor and marched along the corridor to the cockpit. 'I'd bought good stuff, too,' Kai mumbled. All that food was probably still lying, wasted, on that little boat. Seph didn't respond, or he didn't hear. Kai sighed.

Reaching the cockpit, she peered over Seph's shoulder. Bucky was in Crash's seat, Harley was in the co-pilot's seat. Kai stood in the doorway beside Seph, staring out of the window. Nothing seemed out of the ordinary. There was blue sky, some clouds in front and above them, and below were trees, a town, a village. They were moving at speed.

'Someone shot at us,' Bucky grumbled. It seemed to Kai that he was purposefully not looking at her.

'Is it Bran?' she asked quietly.

Bucky looked at one of the screens.

'What type of ship would it be?'

Kai looked over his shoulder to the scan of what was behind them.

'Not that. I don't think. He wouldn't be following us. Losing me twice is an embarrassment.

He'll want to rebuild the castle first, if he does come after me.'

'You sure?' Bucky asked, still not looking at her. Kai screwed her eyes up at the screen, as if that would help make it clearer.

'Pretty sure. I didn't see that shape of ship on his landing pad. But, you know, it's hard to pay attention when you're running into the forest or you're tied up.' Bucky shifted in his seat. 'Capt'n?' Kai prodded. 'Couldn't it be someone else?'

'It could. While we were busy saving you, we should have been completing our job,' Bucky mumbled, glancing at Seph. 'There's a possibility it's them.'

Kai looked at Seph who stared out of the window. Harley caught her eye.

'Hold on!' shouted Bucky, too late, as the ship shook again. Kai landed on her hip, swearing loud at the pain and the hem of her dress ripped.

'Damn thing,' she muttered.

'Shit.'

Kai turned to Bucky as she found her feet.

'What?'

'Erm, we appear to be going down.'

'What?'

'Jude?' Bucky shouted into the intercom. 'Strap down. Strap Crash down. We're about to have a bumpy landing. Everyone hold on.'

Kai gripped onto the back of Bucky's chair. Black smoke filled the window and then they fell forward.

Kai smashed her head against the pilot's seat as her knees gave way, and there was darkness as she squeezed her eyes shut.

Head throbbing, she opened her eyes.

'All right, Capt'n?' came Seph's voice.

'Yeah. I'm alive. Harley?'

'Fine, Captain. Are you okay, Kai?'

'Alive too,' she croaked. 'You okay, Seph?'

'Nothing broken.'

There was a silence as they sat up, looking around. A beeping filled the cockpit, along with flashing lights. Leaves were pushed up against the window and Kai hoped they were on the ground and not in a tree.

'Bastards shot us down,' said Bucky.

No one replied. Kai bit her lip to stop her asking if she could go change out of her wedding dress.

Bucky stood as best he could and peered out of the window. Then, he tapped the intercom. 'Jude? Everyone okay?'

After a moment, Jude's voice came through.

'We're all okay.'

'Cassidy, probably need you in the engine room. Get me a damage report.'

They heard a soft, 'Cap't',' and then Jude's voice came back through.

'Crash has started stirring.'

'Good. Keep her there though and stay with her. Lock yourselves in, just to be on the safe side.'

Kai stared at Bucky.

'Why? Bucky, what's going on?' asked Jude.

Bucky glanced at Seph and then back to Kai.

'Err, probably nothing, but there's always a chance it's, err…'

'The people you shouldn't have taken the job from?' Jude offered.

'Maybe.'

Kai's stomach dipped, and after what they'd just been through, it sent a shot of bile up her throat. She swallowed it down, grimacing.

'Should I go change?' she murmured.

Bucky looked down at her dress and then back out of the window.

'Might not be time. Weapons first.' He gave Seph a nod. Seph pushed his way past Kai and out of the cockpit.

'You stay here, Harley. Don't want you gettin' involved in this and we might need someone at the helm.'

Harley didn't look happy about that but he didn't argue. 'Cassidy? How we doin'?' Bucky spoke into the intercom.

'Give me a chance, Capt'n,' came Cass' voice. Bucky pursed his lips.

'You still here?' He turned on Kai. 'Go get weapons. Earn your wage.'

'So, I'm still on the crew?'

'If you weren't on my crew, we wouldn't have gone after you. You think we're good Samaritans? Fuck that. You're one of the best shots I've ever seen. Now, go get a weapon or three. Loading bay. Now.'

Kai left the cockpit, hitching up her skirts and jogging through the corridor in her bare feet, down the steps towards the loading bay, a grin growing on her lips.

Seph had opened a large trunk filled with different types of guns.

'What do you want?' he asked, holding out a new silver semi-automatic pistol for her.

'That'll do. Two, if possible.'

Seph handed her another one and then a bag of ammo. Kai spotted a few rifles in the trunk, and an armful of grenades nestled between them.

'Why keep them this way? Can't be safe,' she murmured.

Seph shrugged.

'Capt'n's prerogative.'

Kai didn't have a response for that. She checked the guns and found them both empty. At least that was something. Sitting on a crate, she began to load them from the bag of bullets. Seph was doing the same with a revolver and a shotgun.

'Where'd you learn to shoot?' she asked. He glanced up at her, raising an eyebrow.

He was right, now wasn't really the time, but then conversational timing had never quite been Kai's thing.

'On the job,' he said after a moment of silence.

'You went into mercenary work without any experience?'

'Didn't say that,' said Seph, cracking his shotgun closed.

'What did you do before, then?'

Seph looked into her eyes again but this time he didn't answer. Kai waited, just in case, and then gave up. 'My aunt's first mate taught me to shoot,' she told him. 'My aunt didn't have much time. She protected me, kept me fed and watered and safe, but it was her crew who taught me most of the survival skills. I used to spend time with each one as much as I could, learning how to cook and how to shoot.'

'Shame you didn't learn maps,' Seph said.

'Or engines,' Kai agreed. 'I tried with engines,

but my brain doesn't work that way. And maps, well, I found them boring. Guns are more interesting than maps.'

Seph made an expression that could only mean that he agreed.

From outside, there came a boom and the ship shuddered.

'Ready?' Seph asked.

'Ready.' Kai looked around the loading bay. 'Shame we don't have time to create a barrier with these crates.'

'Most of these crates got weapons in 'em. Don't want 'em being shot at.'

Kai shrugged.

'Fair point.'

'Seph? Kai? You ready?' Bucky trotted down the stairs and caught the revolver that Seph threw him.

'Ready, Capt'n,' said Kai. Seph gave a nod.

Bucky looked down at Kai's dress and heaved a sigh.

'Try not to get killed and don't let anyone get past us. Last thing we need is someone getting to Jude and Crash.'

'How's the engine, Capt'n?' Kai asked as Bucky went to open the doors and let their attackers in.

'Cass's making repairs. She says there's not much wrong.'

'Well…that's good,' Kai murmured, aiming the gun in her right hand at the door.

Bucky peered out the window, gave a signal and opened the door, lowering the ramp.

Bright sunlight from the setting sun filled the loading bay, making Seph and Kai blink but she kept her concentration on the ramp as it touched down on the ground, in front of four men.

Cautiously, the men began walking up the ramp and as the front man caught sight of Kai and Seph's weapons, he pulled out a large handgun and aimed it at Bucky.

Kai kept her aim on the man, finger hovering over the trigger.

Out of the corner of her eye, she noticed the others do a double take at her.

Damn dress, she thought, keeping her focus on Bucky and the man approaching him.

'Captain Bucky Winters?' the man shouted. He'd stopped in the doorway of the ship, the other three waiting behind him.

'And you are?' Bucky called.

'Put up your weapons,' the man replied. 'I'm with Castell. I come with a message.'

'Pretty sure I can guess what it is,' said Bucky, not giving any signal for Kai or Seph to lower their guns.

The man smiled and gestured to those behind him. Each of the three men chose a target and aimed their weapons. Kai kept her focus and aim on the fourth man, still in front and bearing his teeth in a grin.

'You missed your rendezvous,' he told Bucky. The captain shrugged.

'Something came up. We were just on our way there now.'

'You're too late.'

'So I see.'

'Castell told you that if you were late, there would be consequences.'

'He did.'

Kai glanced at Bucky, her mouth dry. When had all this happened?

'And you were late.'

'Well, what can you do.'

The man cocked his head at Bucky and smiled.

'We have a procedure in place for such occasions.'

'Of course you do.'

Finally, the man looked at Kai and then Seph.

'Where's the rest of your crew, Captain? Hidden them away?'

'We encountered some trouble and then you blew us out of the sky. They're busy.'

'Bring them here.'

Bucky stiffened.

'No. We're enough. What's this procedure about?'

'Procedure dictates that you all be here, Captain. Bring them here.'

Kai pursed her lips. Who had Bucky signed up with? Some powerful, dangerous man who hired well-spoken educated mercenaries? Kai didn't know those types of mercs existed.

The man glanced at her again.

'Not interrupting a wedding, are we?'

'Sort of,' she said.

The man smiled and gave Seph a wink. Kai frowned, but wouldn't let him distract her. She kept her gun aimed, her trigger finger poised.

'I do apologise. I would say once we're done here, you can get back to getting married but alas, it's no longer meant to be.' The man turned back to Bucky, his expression falling. 'Get the others here.

Now.'

'Then what?'

'Castell will decide what to do with each of you, in turn.' The man glanced around the ship. 'Probably sell this piece of shit for scrap. If it'll even get back in the sky.'

As if in answer, The Magpie's engine fired up.

The man's eyes registered a hint of shock. He lifted his weapon and aimed it at Bucky's head.

'On your knees. You had your chance, Captain.'

With two weapons aimed at him, Bucky did the sensible thing and sank to his knees, placing his gun on the ground in front of him.

'Hands up.'

Bucky did as he was told, sneaking a quick glance at Kai. She allowed the corner of her mouth to lift ever so slightly in reply.

The man reached past Bucky to the intercom and rammed his fist on the button. His voice rang out through the ship, echoing behind them.

'Wherever you are, come to the loading bay right now. We've got your captain and his lackies. It's over. You got one minute. That's sixty seconds.'

A silence followed as no one moved.

The man looked down at Bucky.

'If they don't come, we'll go find them. Or they'll go with the ship for scrap.'

'There's worse things on this ship than two lackies,' Bucky told him with a quiet voice. The man raised an eyebrow. 'There's the man who'll slit your throat for the highest bidder, an infamous surgeon, a pilot who can thread this ship through the eye of a needle, a bounty hunter with lawman dreams, a sharpshooter and you don't want to know what's in the engine room.'

The man smiled.

'And what about you? Where do you fit into that?'

Bucky met his eyes.

'I'm the one who tells them who and when to shoot.'

There were three loud bangs, made worse by the echo of the loading bay, and the men behind went down, crumpling to the floor.

Their leader glanced behind him and flinched, aiming his weapon at Seph, then Kai, then back to Seph. Finally, it landed on Bucky.

'Which one do you think did the most damage? The little man or the girl in the wedding dress?' Bucky broke into a grin. 'Get off my ship. Go back to Castell, tell him I'll make the rendezvous, tomorrow morning. It'll be there. And my money better be there.'

The silence that followed was heavy, the gunshots still ringing in their ears. Kai shifted her weight, her two pistols easy in her hands, ready to be aimed at the man's head. Beside her, Seph hefted his own gun, catching the man's eye.

'He won't agree,' the man growled. 'You don't get second chances.'

Bucky laughed.

'My whole life has been based on second chances. He'll give it to me.'

'And why's that?'

'Because that's his only choice. Because every person he sends to bring me down, we'll kill. Much more cost effective for him to just let me do my job and for him to pay me.'

This time the man laughed.

'You're an idiot, Bucky Winters. But fine, I'll deliver your message. You deliver the goods. We'll see what happens.'

'Great. Feel free to take your friends with you.'

The man glared at Bucky who was still on his knees but with his arms down. He looked at Seph and then at Kai.

Kai stared back hard, her fingers twitching, ready to take aim. But the man turned away. He took a moment to look at his fallen colleagues before stepping over them and marching down the ramp and away.

Bucky exhaled loud, standing up and picking up his gun.

'Well, that was entertainin'.'

They all turned. At the top of the stairs, looking down over the loading bay, stood Cassidy, Harley, Jude and Crash, who was being held between Jude and Harley. Crash smiled. 'I think my favourite part was the pilot who can thread this ship through the eye of a needle.'

Jude

Jude kept a hand on Crash's shoulder as the crew settled around the dining table. Kai served them all coffee. Jude held up a hand to stop her pouring any for Crash.

'Oh,' Crash whined.

'No coffee. Not yet. And can't Kai go get changed?' Jude asked Bucky as her brother took his seat at the head of the table. He looked over at Kai, stood brandishing the coffee pot in her wedding dress.

'Oh, yeah, after this.' He waved them away.

Jude exchanged a look with Kai and then put her attention back onto Crash. Things weren't going well. The young woman was too…perky. She was being too…normal. Jude pursed her lips.

'So?' Bucky started as they all settled in their

seats, Kai leaning against the bar separating the dining area from the kitchenette, Harley leaning against the wall behind Bucky, his arms crossed. 'You've not got long to explain yourselves. I want to hear from Cassidy, and Kai, but first.' He looked from Jude to Crash. 'How're we doin'?'

'Right as rain, Capt'n.'

'Crash,' Jude said gently. 'Do you want me to talk to the crew? Do you want to maybe…go help Kai out of her dress or something?'

Crash laughed but said nothing and Jude felt something of a tremor beneath her hand that rested on Crash's shoulder. She squeezed.

'Just tell 'em. Let's get it over with,' Crash said quietly. So quietly that the crew leaned in to listen and then, on realising what they'd just done, exchanged worried glances.

'All right.' Jude moved to put an arm around Crash. 'She's alive and she can fly, those are the important things.'

Bucky glanced down at Crash.

'But?'

Jude took a deep breath.

'The bullet caught Crash's spine.'

Kai frowned.

'How? She jumped in front of me.'

'It went through and got lodged in the lumbar region,' Jude told her. 'It somehow grazed past anything vital but hit her spine. And, well, she can't move her legs.'

There was a silence. The longer it went on, the heavier it got until Jude cleared her throat, mostly just to make some noise.

Crash stared down at the table.

'You were standing on the stairs,' Bucky murmured.

'We were holding her up,' Jude told him. 'She can't stand on her own. She can't walk. Now,' she added quickly, feeling Crash tense beneath her. 'This might not always be the case. I've seen a number of supposed paraplegic patients regain the use of their lower limbs over time. Time is a healer, after all, and with the right exercises, the body can do amazing things. Sometimes.'

Bucky rubbed a hand over his face. Cass and Seph stared down at the table. With a small whimper, Kai put her hands over her mouth, her eyes becoming glassy with tears. Beneath Jude's arms, Crash shuddered.

'So, this might not be permanent?' Bucky asked, studying Crash.

'Maybe not. It might be that Crash regains the use of her legs in a few hours, or next week, or in a few months.'

'Or never,' came Crash's voice, almost unrecognisable in a low, husky tone. She didn't lift her face, unable to look at the crew.

'But we don't know,' Jude finished, giving Crash another squeeze.

'And you can still fly?' Bucky asked.

After a moment, Crash lifted her face and looked the captain in the eye. He remained steady, but there was pity in his eyes.

'Don't need my legs to fly, Capt'n. Just to run and walk and get about. So, I guess you can plonk me in the pilot's seat and have done with it. 'Cept who's gonna help me relieve myself, huh?' Crash's voice broke and she lowered her face again, rubbing at her eyes with her thumb. Jude produced some tissues from her pocket and handed them to her.

'We'll help,' Kai said gently. She looked from Crash to Bucky to Jude. 'Can't we? What can we do?'

They all turned to Jude.

'Well, there's no reason that Crash can't lead a completely normal life. Just like before.'

Crash scoffed. 'We'll just need to make a few changes,' Jude continued, giving Bucky a look. He bit on his lower lip and she knew what he was thinking. He was thinking of how much all of this was going to cost him. 'They don't all need to happen at once,' she added. 'Like I said, we don't know how long this will last. But the first thing we need is a way for Crash to get around without her needing our help all the time.'

'I can help with that,' came Cassidy's voice.

The crew looked at her and Bucky gave a nod.

'Good. Great. Jude will work with Crash, Cassidy will sort something out so Crash can get around and Crash will fly us. All right? All right.'

'We've got some exercises to try,' Jude told Crash, nodding to Bucky. 'If we keep at it, we could fix all of this.'

Crash gave a tired nod, folding her arms on the table and placing her head on the crook of her elbow.

'I'm bored of talkin' about me now,' she said, looking to Cass 'Everyone's been talkin' about some big white monster that I missed out on.'

'Ah, yes.' Bucky turned to Cassidy. The engineer sat back, her jaw tensing. 'Your turn. So?' Bucky glanced at Kai and did a double take. 'No!'

He held a hand up at Cassidy even though she hadn't moved. 'You first,' he told Kai. 'Let's save what could be the best 'til last. Anything else you need to tell us? Any more would-be grooms who happen to be kings comin' after you, Princess?'

Kai sighed and folded her arms.

'I'm not a princess and no, there's just the one king who wants to marry me, and no, I don't know if he's going to keep coming. I doubt it. At least, I hope he won't.'

Bucky raised an eyebrow.

'You're not a princess, Princess, but you are a Visionary.'

The entire crew, including Crash, turned to look at Kai. She wilted under their stare. With a sigh, she looked down at the floor.

'I'm the daughter of the High Priestess of Decima. Before I was born, I was betrothed to Prince Bran because the Visionaries foresaw that I would give him a son. I guess I was an easy choice. My mother died when I was a few days old and my father tried to raise me, but he was grieving. So, he gave me to his sister and she raised me, on her ship, to keep me away from Bran. I don't know what else I can tell you.'

'Did you inherit your mother's talents?' Bucky asked.

Kai met his eyes.

'Yes.'

Another heavy silence filled the room. 'But I'm not trained,' Kai continued when no one spoke. 'I see things, but I can't control them and I can't necessarily read them. They're not always obvious.' She looked at Cassidy. 'That night I woke you all up with my screaming, I dreamt I was lying on Bran's bed and he was on top of me, but I was saved by some huge white monster.'

Everyone turned to Cassidy except for Jude.

'So...that night, did you stab yourself?' Jude asked.

'Not as far as I'm aware. That's never happened before. I don't know how that happened.'

'Well, we might have a clue. The wound on your abdomen from that night matches Crash's bullet entry site.'

Kai faltered, her gaze flicking to Crash.

'So, you dreamed a big white monster saved you, and we're back on you,' Bucky said to Cassidy. 'What was that thing?'

Cass looked at each crew member in turn, ending on Crash.

'His name is Benny,' she murmured. 'He's a dragon.'

'Dragon? There's no such thing,' Bucky laughed.

'What did you think he was? When you saw him?' Cassidy asked, her eyes hard. Bucky shrugged.

'Okay, he's a dragon and his name is Benny. Makes sense.'

'Bucky has a point,' Jude murmured. 'Where did you find a dragon? They're a myth, a story we tell to children.'

'Dragons aren't from this world. They exist in a world that is lightyears from this planet.'

'Lightyears?' Bucky raised an eyebrow.

'Yes. There are many different types of dragon. They once came to this planet via a portal, but the portal closed and the dragons left behind were killed or died, so they became myth here.'

'So where did you find one?' Jude repeated. Cass looked at her.

'On his own planet.'

'You space travel?'

She turned back to Bucky.

'No.'

Bucky growled, slamming his hands down on the table, making Jude and Crash jump.

'I've had it. You've got one chance to tell me what the fuck you're talkin' about or you're off this ship.'

'She saved my life. So I'm told,' Crash argued.

Bucky looked into her eyes and took a deep breath.

'I nearly lost my crew today,' he said to the room. 'I don't say this often enough, but this ship is nothin' without you all. And while I appreciate that you saved Crash, that you saved all of us,' he told Cass. 'I'd appreciate some answers. Stop messin' around, stop being coy, and tell us what the hell is goin' on. Right now. Or you're off.'

They all turned to Cass, chewing on her lip.

She held her arm out in front of her and turned something on the device over her wrist. A small door opened on the copper brace and a bright light shone from it. As the light dimmed, a small, white dragon hovered in the air.

'This is Benny,' said Cassidy. 'I haven't lied to you, but I have withheld from you what I do. What I was doing when Crash met me. I was buying supplies, yes, but not for engines or to build things to sell. I'm a scientist and an engineer and…' Cass stopped, swallowed and studied Benny, as the dragon turned his head to look at her. 'I'm an explorer of other worlds. By other worlds, I mean worlds that exist beyond our own. When Crash found me, I was buying equipment because my last machine broke. I'm building a new one but it takes a lot of energy and a lot of experimenting because it doesn't always work the way it worked last time. Elements change, distances change, planets move, as does time. And I need to get back.'

'Back? To the dragon planet?' Jude asked, her eyes fixed on Benny. Crash had sat up and now she lifted her hand towards the dragon. Benny moved closer to her, touching his nose to her fingers. He was translucent and Jude could just make out the wall and Cass through him, but around him was that same bright shining light. Crash smiled as Benny's long tongue flicked out and curled around her finger.

'No. Not back to Benny's world. To another world. I have…unfinished business.'

'And this unfinished business, is it going to land us in any trouble?' Bucky asked, glancing at Kai.

'No. I don't see why it should. My purpose is personal but there's no one hunting me. Not really.'

'Not really?'

'I'm trying to make contact with someone. But they're not after me the way that man was after Kai. It'll bring no trouble.'

Bucky pondered this.

'Fine. All right. You keep our engine running, you fix any problems and you help Crash get movin' again, you can stay.'

'And I can build and run experiments in the

loading bay,' Cass added.

'You what?'

'I told her it'd be okay, Capt'n, to use the loading bay. So did you, you agreed,' croaked Crash.

Bucky glared at her.

'I can hardly say no now, can I? Not after all that.'

Crash grinned at him and for a moment, it was like it had always been.

'Fine. And what about this.' Bucky gestured at Benny. 'Wasn't he a lot bigger in that castle?'

'He's a spirit dragon,' Cass explained. 'He can change his size at will.'

'And he lives in your wrist?'

'We are bound together.' Cass shrugged. 'It's a long story.'

'Does it put us in danger?'

'No.'

'Then we don't need to hear it right now. Good. That everythin'? Good. That leaves me with you.' Bucky turned back to Kai. 'You're our cook and merc. I'll pay you, both of you,' he added to Cass. 'And in return you will keep us fed, keep the mess clean and you will shoot whoever I tell you to shoot. Am I clear?'

'Yes, Capt'n.'

'You wanna leave, you leave, and you take your troubles with you. And any more dreams that you think are those vision things, you tell me immediately. We'll see if we can't work them out together. Got it? No more secrets, Princess.'

'Will you stop callin' me Princess?'

'Nope. Deal?'

320

Kai nodded.

'Deal. And…thank you.' She glanced at Crash and Cassidy. 'Thank you. For coming after me. I owe all of you, with my life.'

'Yeah. You do. Right, everyone back to work. Crash, I want you back in the cockpit. We're gettin' the hell outta here and finishin' off this damn job. We're gettin' paid and then we'll find somewhere to lay low and lick our wounds. Any objections?'

No one replied.

'Good. What about you, Harley? You stayin' with us?'

Harley nodded, giving Kai a fleeting glance.

'Everyone back to work!' Bucky yelled, standing and moving to help Jude carry Crash to the cockpit.

Kai

The Magpie dipped to the right as it turned a corner and Kai placed her hand against the wall to steady herself. The familiar sight of the top of Crash's head, poking over the back of the pilot's chair, came into view. The same chopped blond hair that Kai had first seen of Crash all that time ago. Kai smiled. It had been weeks, despite feeling like months. She stood in the doorway of the cockpit.

'Capt'n?' she asked gently. Crash didn't move but Bucky, in the co-pilot's seat, jumped and turned to look up at her. 'Could I have a moment?' She gestured to Crash with her head.

'You know where we're goin', yeah?' Bucky asked.

'I always know where we're goin', Capt'n. 'Cept when I don't, 'cos we don't have a navigator.'

Bucky grinned and patted Crash on the shoulder.

'Don't start,' he muttered, pushing past Kai.

Kai dropped into his vacated chair and looked out of the window. Crash was flying almost leisurely.

'Are we not in a rush?' Kai asked.

'There's a speed limit round here,' Crash told her. 'And we're makin' good time. Don't you worry about that, Princess.'

'Shit. You're not going to call me that too, are you? What happened to New Girl?'

Crash grinned.

'You're not the new girl anymore. But I won't call you Princess. Not much, anyway. I reckon you owe me though.'

Kai watched the trees beneath them.

'I do owe you,' she murmured.

'It's not your fault, you know,' Crash told her.

'You wouldn't have been there if it wasn't for me. It's my fault.'

'Well, yeah, but it's not like you pulled me in front of you.'

Kai smiled, glancing at Crash. She wanted to see the old Crash, sat in her element, loudly joking and teasing the captain. That wasn't the Crash sat beside her. Her spark had dimmed and that caused Kai so much pain she could hardly breathe.

'I'm sorry.'

'You've said that. Loads of times. I believe you. It's fine. Apology accepted.' Crash kept her eyes on the sky. 'That why you came up here? To apologise for the billionth time?'

'I wish I could do somethin' to put it right,' Kai said. 'When I first came on board, you and Jude were both so kind to me. And I get that from Jude, she's a doctor, she's got to be kind and worried. That's her training, sort of. But you didn't have to be nice. You didn't have to tell me your story. And I wish I'd told you mine. I should have told you mine.'

'You did. Sort of.'

'But not enough. I didn't tell you about Bran. And I should have. I should have told you it was King Bran after me.'

Crash shook her head.

'You know what? I'm impressed you got away from the him the first time. How lax was his security then? How arrogant was that son of a bitch?'

'Arrogant.' Kai agreed. 'And naïve. It's a small kingdom and they don't really pay attention to the outside world.'

'No. I bet Benny the dragon scared the living shit outta them. I doubt they'll come after you now. And who brought Cass and Benny on board? That would be me. If anyone's a fuckin' princess on this ship, it's me.'

Kai grinned.

'It is you.'

'And hey, when you wanted to come on board, why didn't you tell the Capt'n you could shoot like that? Why say you could cook?'

'You don't think I can cook?'

'Oh you can cook, and you owe me another chocolate cake.'

'I owe you all the chocolate cake.'

'Yes, you do. But Capt'n would've brought you on if he'd seen you shoot.'

'He already had a merc.'

'Did you know Seph was a merc? Most people don't know that, not just by lookin' at him. It's why Capt'n likes him, and you. You're both a surprise to all the massive bastards most people hire as mercs.'

'I guess. I don't know why I didn't say. I was trying to protect myself. I was trying to keep a low profile.'

'Yeah, I guess.'

There was a pause as the women watched the clouds hitting the windows.

'Thank you,' Kai murmured.

Crash moaned.

'Yes, this again. You're sorry, you love me, I'm amazin'. I get it. You don't have to keep thankin' me. Well, no, you do, but thank me with cake. Remember?'

'Right.' Kai went to stand.

'Wait.' Crash shifted to look behind her then she turned to Kai. 'You get visions?'

'Yeah.' Kai shifted in her seat. She had never been entirely comfortable talking about her so-called gift, even with her family. She'd often had dreams on her aunt's ship, only to be pummelled with questions by the crew about what might be coming their way. She'd somehow learned to keep the dreams quiet after many years of trial and error, to ignore them to a certain extent. Kai placed a hand on her stomach, where the wound from her last vision was leaving a scar.

'Do you get them a lot?'

'Sometimes,' Kai admitted. 'They come and go. I don't have any control over them.'

'Is it just visions?' Crash studied her. 'Can you

do anything else?'

'Like what?'

'Could you heal me?'

Kai opened her mouth and then closed it. She looked out of the window.

'If I could heal you,' she said carefully, 'I would do. Right now. Without hesitation. But I can't. I'm sorry.'

Crash looked forward again.

'Worth askin',' she murmured. 'I had to ask.'

Kai nodded.

'Sure. And I wish I could.'

'I know.'

'Does it hurt?'

'No,' said Crash. 'I think that's one of the worst parts. It doesn't hurt and it should. It should hurt.'

Kai's eyes watered and she held her breath to hold back the tears. She wouldn't apologise again. She was pretty sure if she did, Crash would hit her.

'But you might see somethin'. Some day. Somethin' that could help. Maybe, you'll see me gettin' better?'

Kai turned back to Crash but the pilot was still watching the sky.

'If I see anythin', you'll be the first I tell.'

'Well, Capt'n'll be the first you tell, otherwise you'll be in a world of trouble.'

'Okay. You'll be the second I tell.'

Crash smiled.

'Okay. There was somethin' else I was wonderin' about.'

'Yeah?'

'You said that the night you woke us all up screamin' your head off, you'd dreamt that the idiot king was on top of you and then Benny appeared and saved you.'

'Yes.'

'But that's not what happened, is it? We got you out of that bedroom. We didn't see the idiot king until we were nearly out the door. And where were the rest of us in this dream of yours? You dreamt you were wounded but you came out of it without a scratch and I got shot. How do you explain that?'

Kai bit her lip. She didn't want to explain it, but what choice did she have? After all of the talk of not keeping secrets, of telling the crew everything she knew to keep them safe. After her promises to Bucky and what Crash had been through for her. Crash had nearly died and Bucky had compromised the crew and his ship, all for her.

How could she not tell Crash?

'There is a chance,' she started, trying to choose her words with care. 'That that dream wasn't about that particular…encounter. That's a chance that that dream told of something else.'

Crash barked a laugh and for a moment, Kai's heart lifted.

'You're tellin' me that one day the idiot king is gonna grab you again, try and have his way, stab you and Benny's goin' to save you? Again?'

Kai sighed.

'I hope not. But there's a chance, yes.'

'A chance?'

'Or maybe that's what would have happened if you'd arrived later, or not at all. Visions don't always happen the way you see them. They don't ever tell the whole story and they're open to interpretation. And the problem is that I haven't had the training. I can't read them the way I should. I might not even be dreaming them properly.'

Crash stared at her.

'Seriously? Then what's the point?'

Kai shrugged.

'There isn't much. It's probably best to just ignore them. But I've been sayin' that for years and no one's taken me seriously. So, I'll do what the Capt'n wants. I'll tell you what I see. They're near impossible to explain so I don't see what use they'll be. But,' Kai added, on seeing Crash's expression. 'I bake a mean chocolate cake and I can shoot.'

Crash grinned.

'Yeah, you can. So instead of wakin' us up screamin', how about you focus on making chocolate cakes and next time you see that idiot king, just shoot him between the eyes.'

Kai smiled.

'Sure thing. Today's chocolate cake is already cooling.'

Crash snapped round to her.

'You made a cake already?'

'Just need to cut it up.'

'Well, what are you waitin' for?'

Kai laughed.

'I'll go now, then.' She patted Crash on the shoulder.

'I'm glad you're stayin' on,' Crash murmured.

'Me too.'

'Finished your heart-to-heart?' Bucky appeared at the doorway and shooed Kai out of the way, dropping back into the co-pilot's chair. 'That chocolate cake on the side for all of us or just Crash?'

'It's mine,' said Crash.

Bucky rolled his eyes.

'I'll go cut it up and bring you a slice,' Kai murmured, turning to leave.

'Hey, Princess, you have a vision about a navigator, you let me know. We get one of them, we got a full crew. Dragon included. Unless you fancy learnin' maps?' asked Bucky.

Kai laughed and held up her hands.

'A lifetime of baking chocolate cakes and pointin' my gun wherever you ask is more than enough for me.'

Kai left the cockpit before Bucky could say any more on the subject. Wandering through the ship, towards the mess, she heard the clanking of Cassidy building something in the loading bay. She briefly wondered if it would be something for Crash or her world visiting machine before her thoughts strayed to Benny.

She passed the corridor leading to the med bay, where Jude was reading a book. Past the cabins, where she knew Seph was hiding, doing his own thing. Beside his cabin was hers, where her wedding dress was still stuffed into the corner.

Kai took a deep breath and smiled. It wasn't perfect, but it had potential. This had potential to be home. She turned the corner to the mess and walked straight into Harley's chest.

'Sorry,' she murmured, looking up into his soft blue eyes. He gave her a nod and went to move around her. 'You still lookin' for that man?' she asked. He frowned down at her and then seemed to catch up.

'Oh. Yeah.'

'I bet all of this has thrown you off his trail, huh?

I'm sorry about that.'

Harley cocked his head at her and gave a smile.

'Stop apologising,' he said. 'He has a head start, but it takes more than that to stop me.'

Kai returned the smile.

'Want some cake?'

'Thought that was for Crash.'

Kai shrugged.

'I'll bring you some.'

Harley nodded and continued along the corridor towards his cabin. Kai walked into the mess and surveyed the clean dining table and tidy kitchenette. The wonky, small cake stood on the side. Kai took another breath, relaxing.

This could definitely be home.

***

The crew of The Magpie will return.

If you enjoyed this book...